大学英语听力丛书

丛书主编　李道顺
丛书主审　余澄清

新感觉·大学英语听力教程（4）
College English
Listening Courses（4）

武汉科技大学中南分校
语言与语言教育研究所组织编写

主　审　余澄清
主　编　陆金燕　谢春林　李青云
副主编　鞠　丽　徐　慧　郑　青
编　者　齐　玲　贺华丽　黄红娟　胡　丽　胡丽娟
　　　　黄义强　王金平　邬　磊　孙沅媛　邵黎黎
　　　　唐月容　谭宗燕　李琳俐　张志英　刘　晶

武汉大学出版社

图书在版编目(CIP)数据

新感觉·大学英语听力教程.4/陆金燕,谢春林,李青云主编.—武
汉:武汉大学出版社,2008.12
大学英语听力丛书
ISBN 978-7-307-06656-4

Ⅰ.新… Ⅱ.①陆… ②谢… ③李… Ⅲ.英语—听说教学—高等
学校—教材 Ⅳ.H319.9

中国版本图书馆 CIP 数据核字(2008)第 167243 号

责任编辑:罗晓华 谢群英 责任校对:黄添生 版式设计:詹锦玲

出版发行:武汉大学出版社 (430072 武昌 珞珈山)
(电子邮件:cbs22@whu.edu.cn 网址:www.wdp.com.cn)
印刷:湖北省荆州市今印印务有限公司
开本:720×1000 1/16 印张:15.25 字数:276 千字
版次:2008 年 12 月第 1 版 2008 年 12 月第 1 次印刷
ISBN 978-7-307-06656-4/H·609 定价:26.00 元(含一张 MP3 光盘)

前　言

　　某厂有位员工，技术不错，就是组织纪律性差点，厂里出什么乱子时，总有他的参与。虽然经过几次劝导，他也是好一阵坏一阵。老板爱其才，不想轻易辞退他。经过观察，老板发现该员工特别喜爱足球，下班时爱和朋友们游戏一番，因此该员工被称为厂里第一脚。不久老板决定，成立厂里的足球队，由该员工担任主管，负责训练以及联系其他厂举行友谊赛。老板规定每次训练或比赛前必须先按质按量完成自己的工作。该员工觉得能够做自己感兴趣的事情，就爽快地答应了。由于有了动力，该员工不仅工作勤快认真，而且管理球队也是井井有条，工作纪律性和责任心有了很大的提高。

　　这则小故事说明，做任何事情，只要因材施教就能达到事半功倍的效果。就高校英语听力教学而言，我们也面临着这样一种形势：市场上现有的听力教材大多是按照普通一二批本科生的听力水平编写的，有的听力教材甚至超出目前中国高校学生的基本听力水平。这使许多独立院校、高职院校的学生在使用和学习这些教材的过程中非常困难，容易失去学习的信心。

　　针对学生的实际情况，我们组织了一批长期耕耘在教学第一线并长期从事教学研究的优秀教师编写了这套《新感觉·大学英语听力教程》（共有四册）。这套教材具有四个特点：

　　1. **专业素质与非专业素质并重，趣味性与技巧性同步，满足了成功素质教育教学的基本要求**。现在编写的教材过多强调专业知识的传授，而忽视了对学生整体素质的培养。成功素质教育是我国方兴未艾的素质教育的新突破，是大学人才培养模式的新创造，它是武汉科技大学中南分校率先提出的一种全新的大学教育理念。它是以让学生具备成功者所共有的特征即成功素质为培养目标，实行专业素质与非专业素质的有机结合，使学生在学校即具备成功素质，一跨出校门就能适应社会，并能在激烈的竞争中获得成功的一种教育理念和教育模式。成功素质教育教学观还要求教师应该让学生变被动学习为主动学习，变"要我学"为

"我要学"。在《新感觉·大学英语听力教程》这套书里，编者在基础阶段到提升阶段的编写内容上介绍了听力技巧和听力训练。这不仅便于学生自学和巩固所学的知识，而且还能激发学生主动学习英语的兴趣。

2. 教材体现了实用教学理念。 成功素质教育认为，教学最重要的原则是"管用、够用、会用"，即"三用"原则。"管用"即教学内容要管用，不管用的不教；"够用"即保证教学内容达到培养目标；"会用"就是保证教学内容为学生真正掌握。教学的主要目的不仅仅是传授知识，更应该是传授方法、训练思维、开启智慧。正是在这样一种教学理念的指导下我们编写了《新感觉·大学英语听力教程》系列教材。从教材每课题材的选择到每种题型的搭配，主编都一一把关，力求教材内容的编写符合"三用"原则的基本要求。

3. 教材的编写体现了因材施教理念。 成功素质教育认为，学生人人都可能成功，但同时又承认人的素质基础和素质特长的差异，因此主张因材施教。学校要根据学生基础和特长确定素质培养的目标和方法。前言开头的一个小故事正好说明了这一点。我们教材编写的整个过程也体现了这一基本理念。

4. 本教材的编写注重多元文化。 一直以来，英语教材都是一元文化。编写者只注意英、美文化而忽视了中国文化。本教材的编写坚持多元文化的原则，不仅注意英、美文化，同时也融入中国文化，因而促使中、西文化的融合与和谐发展。

这套大学英语听力丛书共由四个分册组成，每册 16 单元，每册后均附有测试题两套。每单元由 Listening Strategy 和 Listening Passages 两大部分组成。书后附有练习答案和录音材料，可供读者参考使用。本套教材可作为高等院校，尤其是独立院校、高职院校等类学生的大学英语听力教材，同时可供学有余力的英语爱好者及相关英语工作者作为扩大知识面、提高专业水平的英语听力学习材料。第四册以英语四级听力为主。第一部分为 13 套听力模拟试题；第二部分是历年四级全真试题。

新感觉·大学英语听力系列教材由武汉科技大学中南分校语言与语言教育研究所组织编写，丛书主编为李道顺教授，主审为余澄清教授。陆金燕、谢春林、李青云为第四册主编，余澄清主审。鞠丽、徐慧、郑青为副主编。齐玲、贺华丽、黄红娟、胡丽、胡丽娟、黄义强、王金平、邹磊、孙沅媛、邵黎黎、唐月容、谭宗燕、李琳俐、张志英、刘晶等参加编写。本系列教材在编写和出版过程中得到了武汉大学出版社领导和编辑人员的热忱关心和大力支持，在此表示感谢。

　　由于编者水平有限，加之时间仓促，书中错误之处在所难免。恳请广大同仁批评指正，也衷心希望广大读者能给我们提出宝贵的意见和建议，以便再版时修正。

编　者

2008 年 12 月于武昌

～ Contents ～

第一部分　听力模拟试题

Unit 1

Section A

Directions: In this section, you will hear 8 short conversations and 2 long conversations. At the end of each conversation, one or more questions will be asked about what was said. Both the conversations and the questions will be spoken only once. After each question there will be a pause. During the pause, you must read the four choices marked A, B, C and D, and decide which is the best answer.

1. A. The woman should have been more attentive.
   B. The woman needn't have attended the briefing.
   C. Mr. Robin's briefing was not relevant to the mission.
   D. Mr. Robin's briefing was unnecessarily long.

2. A. Repair a typewriter.
   B. Start a car.
   C. Play a tape recorder.
   D. Take a picture.

3. A. The couple's suitcase was stolen in the restaurant.
   B. An old lady took the couple's suitcase for her own.
   C. The man forgot to put the toys in their suitcase.
   D. The old lady sitting next to the couple likes toys very much.

4. A. She's going to say "goodbye" to Bill.
   B. She's leaving for Hong Kong with Bill.
   C. She is flying to Hong Kong.

D. She's going to buy an air ticket.

5. A. The two speakers are seniors at college.

B. The woman regrets spending her time idly.

C. The two speakers are at a loss about what to do.

D. The man is worried about his future.

6. A. She can recall the names of most characters in the novel.

B. She has learned a lot from the novel.

C. She usually has difficulty in remembering names.

D. She also found the plot difficult to follow.

7. A. She's also in need of a textbook.

B. She can help the man out.

C. She picked up the book from the bus floor.

D. She can find the right person to help the man.

8. A. They'd better change their mind.

B. The tennis game won't last long.

C. Weather forecasts are not reliable.

D. They shouldn't change their plan.

Conversation One

9. A. In a studio.

B. In a clothing store.

C. At a beach resort.

D. At a fashion show.

10. A. To live there permanently.

B. To stay there for half a year.

C. To find a better job to support herself .

D. To sell leather goods for a British company.

11. A. Designing fashion items for several companies.

B. Modeling for a world-famous Italian company.

C. Working as an employee for Ferragamo.

D. Serving as a sales agent for Burberry.

12. A. It has seen a steady decline in its profits.

B. It has become much more competitive.

C. It has lost many customers to foreign companies.

D. It has attracted a lot more designers from abroad.

Conversation Two

13. A. It helps her to attract more public attention.

    B. It improves her chance of getting promoted.

    C. It strengthens her relationship with students.

    D. It enables her to understand people better.

14. A. Passively.   B. Positively.

    C. Skeptically.   D. Sensitively.

15. A. It keeps haunting her day and night.

    B. Her teaching was somewhat affected by it.

    C. It vanishes the moment she steps into her role.

    D. Her mind goes blank once she gets on the stage.

Section B

Directions: In this section, you will hear 3 short passages. At the end of each passage, you will hear some questions. Both the passages and the questions will be spoken only once. After you hear a question, you must choose the best answer from the four choices marked A, B, C and D.

Passage One

16. A. A green Olympic Games.

    B. A great Olympic Games.

    C. A non-smoking Olympic Games.

    D. A nonstop Olympic Games.

17. A. By the end of 2006.

    B. By the end of 2007.

    C. In October, 2006.

    D. In October, 2007.

18. A. It is not very difficult for China to host a non-smoking Olympic Games.

    B. The ban would not apply to the public transport and offices.

    C. China is the world's largest producer and consumer of cigarettes with nearly

3

2 billion consumed a year.

    D. The World Health Organization estimates that smoking kills 1. 2 million people a year in China.

Passage Two

19. A. There can be no speedy recovery for mental patients.

    B. Approaches to healing patients are essentially the same.

    C. The mind and body should be taken as an integral whole.

    D. There is no clear division of labor in the medical profession.

20. A. A doctor's fame strengthened the patient's faith.

    B. Abuse of medicines was widespread in many urban hospitals.

    C. One third of the patients depended on harmless substances for cure.

    D. A patient's expectations of a drug had an effect on their recovery.

21. A. Expensive drugs might not prove the most effective.

    B. The workings of the mind might help patients recover.

    C. Doctors often exaggerated the effect of their remedies.

    D. Most illnesses could be cured without medication.

Passage Three

22. A. Germany.   B. Japan.

    C. The U. S. .   D. The U. K. .

23. A. By doing odd jobs at weekends.

    B. By working long hours every day.

    C. By putting in more hours each week.

    D. By taking shorter vacations each year.

24. A. To combat competition and raise productivity.

    B. To provide them with more job opportunities.

    C. To help them maintain their living standard.

    D. To prevent them from holding a second job.

25. A. Change their jobs.

    B. Earn more money.

    C. Reduce their working hours.

    D. Strengthen the government's role.

Section C

Directions: In this section, you will hear a passage three times. When the passage is read for the first time, you should listen carefully for its general idea. When the passage is read for the second time, you are required to fill in the blanks numbered from 26 to 33 with the exact words you have just heard. For blanks numbered from 34 to 36 you are required to fill in the missing information. For these blanks, you can either use the exact words you have just heard or write down the main points in your own words. Finally, when the passage is read for the third time, you should check what you have written.

If you are like most people, you've indulged in fake listening many times. You go to history class, sit in the 3rd row, and look (26) _____ at the instructor as she speaks. But your mind is far away, (27) _____ in the clouds of pleasant daydreams. (28) _____ you come back to earth. The instructor writes an important term on the chalkboard, and you (29) _____ copy it in your notebook. Every once in a while the instructor makes a (30) _____ remark, causing others in the class to laugh. You smile politely, pretending that you've heard the remark and found it mildly (31) _____. You have a vague sense of (32) _____ that you aren't paying close attention. But you tell yourself that any (33) _____ you miss can be picked up from a friend's notes. Besides, (34) _____ _____. So back you go into your private little world, only later do you realize you've missed important information for a test. Fake listening may be easily exposed, since many speakers are sensitive to facial cues and can tell if you're merely pretending to listen. (35) _____. Even if you are not exposed, there's another reason to avoid fakery. It's easy for this behavior to become a habit. For some people, the habit is so deeply rooted that (36) _____. As a result, they miss lots of valuable information.

Unit 2

Section A

Directions: In this section, you will hear 8 short conversations and 2 long conversations. At the end of each conversation, one or more questions will be asked about what was said. Both the conversations and the questions will be spoken only once. After each question there will be a pause. During the pause, you must read the four choices marked A, B, C and D, and decide which is the best answer.

1. A. Write a business letter.   B. Buy a table for his two sons.
   C. Have breakfast with someone.   D. Play table tennis with his friend.

2. A. Find a restaurant.   B. Attend a concert.
   C. Have a party.   D. Go to the cinema.

3. A. He is a teacher.   B. He is a governor.
   C. He is a football player.   D. He is a business manager.

4. A. Of good quality.   B. Of poor quality.
   C. Out of fashion.   D. Of modern design.

5. A. She has been ill.
   B. She has gone to see Miss Blake.
   C. The report is too difficult for her to write.
   D. She has had a lot of extra work to do.

6. A. Stayed at home.   B. Went to Hangzhou.
   C. Visited her brother.   D. Attended a meeting.

7. A. They should get some more paint.
   B. They should get someone to help them.
   C. They shouldn't delay any longer.
   D. They shouldn't paint the room again.

8. A. She will go out with the man.
   B. She will ask the man to post the letter.
   C. She will wait until the man comes back.
   D. She will write a letter after taking a walk with the man.

Conversation One

9. A. A new fuel for buses.

   B. The causes of air pollution.

   C. A way to improve fuel efficiency in buses.

   D. Careers in environmental engineering.

10. A. Her car is being repaired.

    B. She wants to help reduce pollution.

    C. Parking is difficult in the city.

    D. The cost of fuel has increased.

11. A. A fuel that burns cleanly.

    B. An oil additive that helps cool engines.

    C. A material from which filters are made.

    D. An insulating material sprayed on the engine.

Conversation Two

12. A. To see some relatives.

    B. To buy some toys.

    C. To sightsee.

    D. To go to the seashore.

13. A. The car was not moving fast enough.

    B. Their clothing was warm enough.

    C. The air outside was also hot.

    D. They were not feeling good.

14. A. The weather was so hot.

    B. He had done enough study.

    C. He did not want to stay in the library any longer.

    D. He wanted to have fun.

15. A. Waiting for Sue's parents to arrive.

    B. Waiting for the car to be repaired.

    C. Sight-seeing in Chicago.

    D. Visiting friends in Indiana.

Section B

Directions: In this section, you will hear 3 short passages. At the end of each passage, you will hear some questions. Both the passages and the questions will be spoken only once. After you hear a question, you must choose the best answer from the four choices marked A, B, C and D.

Passage One

16. A. Consult with her frequently.　　　B. Use the computer regularly.
　　C. Occupy the computer early.　　　D. Wait for one's turn patiently.
17. A. Computer classes.　　　B. Training sessions.
　　C. Laser printing.　　　D. Package borrowing.
18. A. Computer Aided Language Learning.　B. College library facilities.
　　C. The use of micro-computers.　　D. Printouts from the laser printer.

Passage Two

19. A. The possible origin of St. Valentine's Day.
　　B. The love story of a Christian named Valentine.
　　C. A story about valentines.
　　D. An unusual holiday.
20. A. He performed a lot of Christian marriages.
　　B. He fell in love with a Christian girl.
　　C. He refused to accept the Emperor's offer.
　　D. He sent a love letter to the daughter of a prison guard.
21. A. To celebrate the holiday.
　　B. To mark Valentine's birthday.
　　C. To express their admiration for each other.
　　D. To show their love and affection.

Passage Three

22. A. Because there are no signs to direct them.
　　B. Because no tour guides are available.
　　C. Because all the buildings in the city look alike.

D. Because the university is everywhere in the city.

23. A. They set their own exams.

    B. They select their own students.

    C. They award their own degrees.

    D. They organize their own laboratory work.

24. A. Most of them have a long history.

    B. Many of them are specialized libraries.

    C. They house more books than any other university library.

    D. They each have a copy of every book published in Britain.

25. A. Very few of them are engaged in research.

    B. They were not awarded degrees until 1948.

    C. They have outnumbered male students.

    D. They were not treated equally until 1881.

Section C

Directions: In this section, you will hear a passage three times. When the passage is read for the first time, you should listen carefully for its general idea. When the passage is read for the second time, you are required to fill in the blanks numbered from 26 to 33 with the exact words you have just heard. For blanks numbered from 34 to 36 you are required to fill in the missing information. For these blanks, you can either use the exact words you have just heard or write down the main points in your own words. Finally, when the passage is read for the third time, you should check what you have written.

   Some people like watching TV at home and others may love hiking. But I like being at a bookshop. Time spent in a bookshop can be most (26) _____, whether you are a book-lover or merely there to buy a book as a present. You may even have entered the shop to find (27) _____ from a sudden shower. Whatever the reason is, you can soon become totally (28) _____ of your surroundings. The opportunity to escape the (29) _____ of every day life is, I think, the main (30) _____ of a bookshop. Looking around, one might not be able to see many places where it is (31) _____ to do this. You can wander around such a place to your heart's (32) _____. If it is a good shop, no assistant will (33) _____ you with the inevitable greeting: "Can I help you, sir?" (34) _____

_____. Then, and only then, are his services necessary.

(35) _____. It is very easy to enter the shop looking for a book on, say, ancient coins and to come out carrying a copy of the latest best-selling novel. This sort of thing can be very dangerous.

(36) _____.

Unit 3

Section A

Directions: In this section, you will hear 8 short conversations and 2 long conversations. At the end of each conversation, one or more questions will be asked about what was said. Both the conversations and the questions will be spoken only once. After each question there will be a pause. During the pause, you must read the four choices marked A, B, C and D, and decide which is the best answer.

1. A. The fourth floor.　　　　　B. The fifth floor.
   C. The sixth floor.　　　　　D. The seventh floor.

2. A. John bought a cheap computer.
   B. John bought Morris a computer.
   C. Morris bought a computer from John.
   D. Morris bought a new computer.

3. A. Recognize Jane first.　　　B. Tell the woman why.
   C. Go on a diet.　　　　　　D. Feel at ease.

4. A. The white one.　　　　　B. The brick one.
   C. The prettier one.　　　　D. The better one.

5. A. The summer this year is terribly hot.　B. Last summer was even hotter.
   C. Hot weather helps lose weight.　　　D. Light was stronger this morning.

6. A. No one on the bus was injured.
   B. Everyone on the bus was injured.
   C. Only one student on the bus was injured.
   D. More than one student on the bus was injured.

7. A. Drawing some money.　　　B. Opening a deposit account.
   C. Saving much money.　　　　D. Putting money in the bank.

8. A. They have too little patience.
   B. They are not strict with students.
   C. They are very hard on students.
   D. They are more hardworking than before.

Conversation One

9. A. Two different types of bones in the human body.
   B. How bones help the body move.
   C. How bones continuously repair themselves.
   D. The chemical composition of human bones.
10. A. They defend the bone against viruses.
    B. They prevent oxygen from entering the bone.
    C. They break down bone tissue.
    D. They connect the bone to muscle tissue.
11. A. They have difficulty identifying these cells.
    B. They are not sure how these cells work.
    C. They have learned how to reproduce these cells.
    D. They have found similar cells in other species.
12. A. To learn how to prevent a bone disease.
    B. To understand differences between bone tissue and other tissue.
    C. To find out how specialized bone cells have evolved.
    D. To create artificial bone tissue.

Conversation Two

13. A. Walk the dog.   B. Clean the house.
    C. Go to the doctor.   D. Pick up her brother.
14. A. To the school.   B. To the doctor's.
    C. To the science museum.   D. To the supermarket.
15. A. At 12:00.   B. At 1:00 p. m. .
    C. At 2:00 p. m. .   D. At 4:30 p. m. .

Section B

Directions: In this section, you will hear 3 short passages. At the end of each passage, you will hear some questions. Both the passages and the questions will be spoken only once. After you hear a question, you must choose the best answer from the four choices marked A, B, C and D.

Passage One

16. A. From three to five months.   B. Three months.
    C. Five months.   D. Four months.
17. A. Watch traffic.   B. Obey commands.
    C. Cross streets safely.   D. Guard the door.
18. A. Three weeks.   B. Two weeks.
    C. Four weeks.   D. Five weeks.

Passage Two

19. A. Two to four times.   B. Four to six times.
    C. Four to eight times.   D. Six to ten times.
20. A. Sleeping pills made people go into REM sleep quickly.
    B. People had more dreams after they took sleeping pills.
    C. People became angry easily because they didn't take sleeping pills.
    D. Sleeping pills prevented people from going into REM sleep.
21. A. People dream so as to sleep better.
    B. People dream in order not to go into REM sleep.
    C. People dream because they may run into difficult problems in their dreams.
    D. People dream because in their dreams they may find the answers to their problems.

Passage Three

22. A. A sales representative.   B. A store manager.
    C. A committee chairperson.   D. A class monitor.
23. A. To determine who will graduate this year.
    B. To discuss the seating arrangement.
    C. To choose the chairperson of the ceremonies.
    D. To begin planning the graduation ceremonies.
24. A. Their names, phone numbers and job preference.
    B. The names and addresses of their guests.
    C. The names of the committee they worked on last year.

D. Their dormitory name, address and phone number.

25. A. In an hour.   B. Next week.

   C. In one month.   D. Next year.

Section C

Directions: In this section, you will hear a passage three times. When the passage is read for the first time, you should listen carefully for its general idea. When the passage is read for the second time, you are required to fill in the blanks numbered from 26 to 33 with the exact words you have just heard. For blanks numbered from 34 to 36 you are required to fill in the missing information. For these blanks, you can either use the exact words you have just heard or write down the main points in your own words. Finally, when the passage is read for the third time, you should check what you have written.

It's difficult to imagine the sea ever running out of fish. It's so vast, so deep, so (26) _____. Unfortunately, it's not bottomless. Over-fishing, (27) _____ with destructive fishing practices, is killing off the fish and (28) _____ their environment.

Destroy the fish, and you destroy the fishermen's means of living. At least 60 (29) _____ of the world's commercially important fish (30) _____ are already over-fished, or fished to the limit. As a result, governments have had to close down some areas of sea to (31) _____ fishing.

Big, high-tech fleets (32) _____ that everything in their path is pulled out of the water. Anything too small, or the wrong thing, is thrown back either dead or dying. That's an (33) _____ of more than 20 million metric tons every year.

(34) _____.

In some parts of the world, for every kilogram of prawns (对虾) caught, up to 15 kilograms of unsuspecting fish and other marine wildlife die, simply for being in the wrong place at the wrong time.

True, (35) _____, then catch them in a way that doesn't kill other innocent sea life.

(36) _____.

Unit 4

Section A

Directions: In this section, you will hear 8 short conversations and 2 long conversations. At the end of each conversation, one or more questions will be asked about what was said. Both the conversations and the questions will be spoken only once. After each question there will be a pause. During the pause, you must read the four choices marked A, B, C and D, and decide which is the best answer.

1. A. Because he works in the suburb.
   B. Because the expense in the city is higher.
   C. Because it is quieter in the suburb.
   D. Because his wife works in the suburb.

2. A. The sports meeting will be cancelled.
   B. The sports meeting will be postponed.
   C. There will be a sports meeting this Sunday.
   D. She would go out regardless of the weather.

3. A. Because he was usually absent.
   B. Because he was always late.
   C. Because he made a big mistake.
   D. Because he was not good at accounting.

4. A. Watch the match.
   B. Wait for 20 minutes.
   C. Carry the box downstairs.
   D. Tell the woman the result of the match.

5. A. Trying to lose weight.
   B. Keeping a diet.
   C. Working hard for the speech course.
   D. Preparing for the speech competition.

6. A. She watched the TV program.

    B. She slept over the program.

    C. She voted for the president.

    D. She had a snack.

7. A. Getting along with his roommates.

    B. Living with his troublesome roommates.

    C. Adjusting to living with other people.

    D. Leaving his roommates.

8. A. They haven't been returned.

    B. They have been returned by Michael.

    C. He will return them later.

    D. He will not return them.

Conversation One

9. A. 55: a mother, a father, and their 53 adopted children.

    B. 55: a mother, a father, and their 53 children.

    C. 20: a mother, a father, and their 18 children.

    D. 53: a mother, a father, and their children.

10. A. They are twins or triplets.

    B. They are living in Argentina.

    C. They are in their 30s and 40s.

    D. They are living with their parents.

11. A. Because they want to have as many children as possible.

    B. Because they know nothing about birth control.

    C. Because they like children.

    D. Because it is against their religion.

12. A. Because she is afraid other people won't take good care of them.

    B. Because she promised that she would always take care of their children herself.

    C. Because she has enough money to take care of them.

    D. Because no one wants to take care of them.

Conversation Two

13. A. Different types of wedding ceremonies.

    B. American wedding ceremonies.

    C. Religious wedding ceremonies.

    D. Civil wedding ceremonies.

14. A. It has a strong religious nature.

    B. Most people like this kind of wedding.

    C. The couple must be religious.

    D. Weddings of this kind are the same.

15. A. People can choose the ceremony they like in every country.

    B. In Germany civil ceremonies must take place in approved buildings.

    C. The civil ceremonies are much different from those in China.

    D. In France, the civil ceremony and the religious one are separate.

Section B

Directions: In this section, you will hear 3 short passages. At the end of each passage, you will hear some questions. Both the passages and the questions will be spoken only once. After you hear a question, you must choose the best answer from the four choices marked A, B, C and D.

Passage One

16. A. The meaning of DJ.

    B. The origin of DJ.

    C. The importance of radio station.

    D. The music played on radio station.

17. A. It meant radio men who talked and played music.

    B. It was used as a noun and a verb.

    C. It meant a professional horse rider.

    D. It meant to lead a horse into a good position.

18. A. Radio began to enter American homes in the 1940s.

    B. DJs could make a song popular.

    C. Whatever the DJs played was good.

D. Many people are not familiar with the DJs.

Passage Two

19. A. Because people like doing things themselves.
    B. Because they know how to repair cars.
    C. Because the labor costs are very high.
    D. Because they like the garages built by themselves.
20. A. The readers are the leading characters in the stories.
    B. It publishes children's books with the help of computers.
    C. There ware many pictures together with the stories.
    D. It has a special name.
21. A. Because they like to read stories.
    B. Because they like to see their names in print.
    C. Because the books help them learn how to read.
    D. Because the books are about pets.

Passage Three

22. A. The importance of using the exact words.
    B. The necessity of using imaginative words.
    C. The necessity of using humorous words.
    D. The importance of using the right words.
23. A. Use someone else's writing as your own.
    B. Use dictionaries.
    C. Research your topic by reading.
    D. Be careful about using colloquial language.
24. A. The little girl is really lovely.
    B. Adjectives and comparisons must be used when describing a person.
    C. Careful and imaginative words can leave a lasting impression.
    D. We should talk in a colorful and poetic manner.
25. A. Speeches can be enriched and made memorable.
    B. You must tell jokes when talking.
    C. Personal stories should be avoided.
    D. A long speech must be ended with a joke.

Section C

Directions: In this section, you will hear a passage three times. When the passage is read for the first time, you should listen carefully for its general idea. When the passage is read for the second time, you are required to fill in the blanks numbered from 26 to 33 with the exact words you have just heard. For blanks numbered from 34 to 36 you are required to fill in the missing information. For these blanks, you can either use the exact words you have just heard or write down the main points in your own words. Finally, when the passage is read for the third time, you should check what you have written.

In (26) _____ times the most important examinations were (27) _____, not written. In the schools of ancient Greece and Rome, testing usually consisted of saying poetry aloud or giving (28) _____. In the European universities of the Middle Ages, students who were working for (29) _____ degrees had to discuss questions in their field of study with people who had made a (30) _____ study of the subject. This custom exists today as part of the (31) _____ of testing candidates for the doctor's degree.

Generally, however, (32) _____ examinations are written. The written examination, where all students are tested on the same questions, was (33) _____ not known until the nineteenth century. (34) _____

_____.

A room full of candidates for a state examination, timed exactly by electric clocks and carefully watched over by managers, resembles a group of workers at an automobile factory. (35) _____

_____.

One type of test is sometimes called an objective test. It is intended to deal with facts, not personal opinions. (36) _____

_____.

Unit 5

Section A

Directions: In this section, you will hear 8 short conversations and 2 long conversations. At the end of each conversation, one or more questions will be asked about what was said. Both the conversations and the questions will be spoken only once. After each question there will be a pause. During the pause, you must read the four choices marked A, B, C and D, and decide which is the best answer.

1. A. She won't eat any dessert.
   B. She'll make the banana pie.
   C. She'll have some chocolate cake.
   D. She'll take a look at the menu.

2. A. They enjoyed the party better than the other guests.
   B. They thought the food and drinks were terrible.
   C. They knew none of the other guests at the party.
   D. They couldn't find the way to attend the party.

3. A. They should have gone to the cinema earlier.
   B. They should try to get to the cinema in time for the film.
   C. They could easily make it.
   D. They should see the film at 8:30.

4. A. Put the raincoat back to her room.
   B. Clear her room by noon.
   C. Wait for him until noon.
   D. Not to take the raincoat.

5. A. She has much work to do before going to the movies.
   B. She thinks the reading assignment is not important.
   C. She doesn't like going to the movies.
   D. She wants to see the movie first.

6. A. Lily likes her father better than her aunt.
   B. Lily agrees with her aunt.

C. Lily looks more like her father.

   D. Lily looks more like her aunt.

7. A. By bike.

   B. By car.

   C. By bus.

   D. On foot.

8. A. She wants to fix supper.

   B. She likes to go out to eat.

   C. She likes to eat at home.

   D. She wants to cook the meal.

Conversation One

9. A. Adam takes up two parking spaces in the parking lot.

   B. Adam's new roommate always makes noises when the woman studies.

   C. Adam's new roommate doesn't like to communicate with others.

   D. Adam hasn't been back to the apartment for two weeks.

10. A. She can't bear it.   B. She is interested in it.

    C. She enjoys it.   D. She doesn't mind it.

11. A. Dorathea is angry with Adam.

    B. Adam doesn't like his roommate.

    C. Adam will talk to his roommate.

    D. Dorathea will have a talk with Adam's roommate.

Conversation Two

12. A. They are not helpful to sports players at all.

    B. They don't live up to their fame.

    C. They may be comfortable but are too expensive.

    D. They are not good for all games.

13. A. Because he thinks it will cost him much money.

    B. Because he thinks his daughter doesn't run.

    C. Because he thinks Adidas is only for Chicago Bulls.

    D. Because he thinks Adidas is not so good for runners.

14. A. Because he also likes to wear Adidas.

B. Because he loves his daughter very much.

C. Because his daughter use an ad to convince him.

D. Because he thinks Adidas will help his daughter run better.

15. A. The father will buy a pair of Adidas for his daughter.

    B. The daughter will buy a pair of Adidas for herself.

    C. The father doesn't give his permission to his daughter.

    D. The father still thinks Adidas is too expensive.

Section B

Directions: In this section, you will hear 3 short passages. At the end of each passage, you will hear some questions. Both the passages and the questions will be spoken only once. After you hear a question, you must choose the best answer from the four choices marked A, B, C and D.

Passage One

16. A. Children make a lot of noise.

    B. Children carry their lanterns everywhere.

    C. People gather for a family reunion.

    D. People eat moon cakes and send them to friends and relatives.

17. A. The lovers.   B. The parents.

    C. The children.   D. The evil monsters.

18. A. Because they can enjoy themselves.

    B. Because they don't have to go to school.

    C. Because they like crying loudly.

    D. Because they want to drive the monster away.

19. A. Because it is rainy.

    B. Because it is cloudy.

    C. Because the evil monster eats up the moon.

    D. Because people can't see it.

Passage Two

20. A. The secret of becoming beautiful.

    B. The art of saying "thank you".

C. The importance of good manners.

  D. The complaints of bad manners.

21. A. They think "thank you" doesn't really matter.

  B. They think appearance is more important.

  C. They are too busy to do that.

  D. They don't want to behave kindly.

22. A. By wearing beautiful clothes.

  B. By wearing a little make-up.

  C. By being kind and generous.

  D. By decorating the home.

Passage Three

23. A. We can consult the experts.

  B. We can try our best to remember things.

  C. We can make a conscious effort of practice.

  D. We can force ourselves to remember things.

24. A. We can always find amusing stories caused by forgetfulness.

  B. We're tired of listening to new stories about professors.

  C. Absent-mindedness is sometimes troublesome.

  D. Memory sometimes may play tricks on us.

25. A. Forgetting things is serious and dangerous.

  B. Forgetfulness or absent-mindedness is funny and amusing.

  C. Absent-mindedness only happens to professors.

  D. Forgetfulness may happen to anyone.

Section C

Directions: In this section, you will hear a passage three times. When the passage is read for the first time, you should listen carefully for its general idea. When the passage is read for the second time, you are required to fill in the blanks numbered from 26 to 33 with the exact words you have just heard. For blanks numbered from 34 to 36 you are required to fill in the missing information. For these blanks, you can either use the exact words you have just heard or write down the main points in you own words. Finally, when the passage is read for the

third time, you should check what you have written.

A hobby can be almost anything a person likes to do in his spare time. Hobbyists (26) _____ pets, build model ships, weave baskets, or carve soap (27) _____. They watch birds, hunt animals, climb (28) _____, raise flowers, fish, ski, skate, and swim. Hobbyists also paint pictures, attend concerts and plays, and perform on musical (29) _____. They collect everything from books to (30) _____, and from shells to stamps.

People take up hobbies because these activities offer (31) _____, friendship, knowledge, and (32) _____. Sometimes they even yield financial (33) _____. Hobbies can help people relax after periods of hard work, and provide a balance between work and play. (34) _____. Anyone, poor or rich, old or young, sick or well, can follow a satisfying hobby, regardless of his age, position, or income.

(35) _____. Doctors have found that hobbies are valuable in helping patients recover from physical or mental illness. Hobbies give bedridden or wheel-chair bound patients something to do, and provide interests that keep them from thinking about themselves. (36) _____.

Unit 6

Section A

Directions: In this section, you will hear 8 short conversations and 2 long conversations. At the end of each conversation, one or more questions will be asked about what was said. Both the conversations and the questions will be spoken only once. After each question there will be a pause. During the pause, you must read the four choices marked A, B, C and D, and decide which is the best answer.

1. A. It is not sure that you will get wealthier.
   B. You will get a perfect job.
   C. You have to work overtime.
   D. It is better for your life.

2. A. Boss and employee.   B. Teacher and student.
   C. Doctor and patient.   D. Two friends.

3. A. She didn't feel very well.   B. She would like to ask for leave.
   C. Her son was seriously ill.   D. She had something wrong with her body.

4. A. She will check the bill again.
   B. She will go to take out the bill.
   C. She will be angry.
   D. She will take away the menu and bill.

5. A. He wants to know whether the woman will enroll in.
   B. He wants to know what the woman's savings account number is.
   C. He wants to know whether the woman's savings account is eligible.
   D. He wants to know whether the woman had a savings account at the bank here.

6. A. The test tomorrow is a little difficult.
   B. The test tomorrow is very easy to pass.
   C. The test tomorrow is very difficult to pass.
   D. I don't know who tells you that the tests are impossible to pass.

7. A. He will simplify some engineering concepts.

B. He don't know how to explain briefly and clearly some of the concepts for the high school students.

    C. He doesn't know some of the concepts about engineering.

    D. It is difficult to speak to a group of high school students.

8. A. It is not so hot this summer.

    B. It will be very hot later.

    C. It is so surprising that the man has turned on air-conditioner lately.

    D. It is so surprising that the man hasn't turned on air-conditioner in such hot days.

Conversation One

9. A. Because the part-time web designer did not complete the structure of BBS.

    B. Because the part-time web designer was not good enough.

    C. Because the part-time web designer was not qualified to build up a web.

    D. Because the part-time web designer wasn't frank.

10. A. She was not honest in the beginning.

    B. She was paid full fees although she was not frank.

    C. She couldn't do the BBS.

    D. She got the job half done.

11. A. He will fire the part-time web designer.

    B. He will pay her full fees.

    C. He will not pay her full fees.

    D. He will criticize the part-time web designer.

12. A. Asking the part-time web designer to finish her job.

    B. Asking their Part-time Job Center for help.

    C. Asking a professional for help.

    D. Teaching the part-time web designer how to deal with that.

Conversation Two

13. A. In the post office.   B. In the checking center.

    C. In the engineering company. D. In the mobile company.

14. A. He can't send short messages.

    B. He can't get the incoming call.

C. There is something wrong with his mobile phone.

D. His phone always gives others a busy signal.

15. A. The network is upgrading.

    B. The man's mobile phone cannot work.

    C. The man's telephone number is wrong.

    D. The man's warranty card is wrong.

Section B

Directions: In this section, you will hear 3 short passages. At the end of each passage, you will hear some questions. Both the passages and the questions will be spoken only once. After you hear a question, you must choose the best answer from the four choices marked A, B, C and D.

Passage One

16. A. Without stress, there could be no life.

    B. The right attitude towards stress.

    C. Stress is an unavoidable consequence of life.

    D. Distress can cause disease.

17. A. We need to find the proper level of stress that promotes optimal performance.

    B. No stress, no life.

    C. Increased stress results in increased productivity.

    D. Stress is some kind of new plague.

18. A. The speaker will discuss how to use stress to make you more productive.

    B. The speaker will discuss how to control stress.

    C. The speaker will discuss about taking part in the pursuit of learning.

    D. The speaker will discuss about explaining the relationship between mind and body.

Passage Two

19. A. Standing and lifting is easier on their backs than sitting.

    B. Sitting is easier on their backs than standing or lifting.

    C. People who sit for long periods of time suffer as much from back pain as those who lift all day long.

D. People who sit for long periods of time suffer as much from back pain as those who stand all day long.

20. A. Only four of every 10,000 people who experience back pain need surgery.

    B. The amount of pain has nothing to do with surgery.

    C. Only few patients benefit from surgery.

    D. If their back pain gets bad enough, they can always resort to surgery.

21. A. Because it is useless to cure back pain.

    B. Because it is not the norm now.

    C. Because their muscle strength will decline.

    D. Because it is not suitable for the starters.

Passage Three

22. A. The sweeping changes in agriculture by the mid-century.

    B. By late in the century, revolutionary advances in farm machinery had vastly increased production of specialized crops.

    C. In the 19th century the farmer's life was free and simple in the United States.

    D. The developing history of agriculture in 19th century's United States.

23. A. Farmers could get along just fine by relying on themselves, not on commercial ties with others.

    B. Farmers began to specialize in the raising of crops such as cotton, corn or wheat.

    C. Farm machinery had vastly increased production of specialized crops.

    D. Farmers could afford more and finer goods and achieve a much higher standard of living.

24. A. Farmers' lives were increasingly controlled by banks, which had power to grant or deny loans for new machinery.

    B. Farmers were no longer dependent.

    C. The airports set the rates for shipping their crops to market.

    D. Farmers' lives were not affected by weather any more.

25. A. An extensive network of railroads had linked farmers throughout the world.

    B. The agriculture had been influenced by world supply and demand.

    C. The price of wheat in Kansas had been strongly influenced by world market.

　　D. Farmers had to worry about national economic depressions.

Section C

Directions: In this section, you will hear a passage three times. When the passage is read for the first time, you should listen carefully for its general idea. When the passage is read for the second time, you are required to fill in the blanks numbered from 26 to 33 with the exact words you have just heard. For blanks numbered from 34 to 36 you are required to fill in the missing information. For these blanks, you can either use the exact words you have just heard or write down the main points in your own words. Finally, when the passage is read for the third time, you should check what you have written.

　　Psychologists have found that only about two percent of adults use their creativity, compared with ten percent of seven-year-old children. When five-year olds were tested, the results rose to ninety percent! (26) _____ and originality are daily occurrences for the small child, but somehow most of us lose the (27) _____ and flexibility of the child as we grow older. The need to "follow directions" and "do it right" plus the many social (28) _____ we put on ourselves (29) _____ us from using our creative potential.

　　It is never too late to tap our creative potential. Some of us, however, find it difficult to think in (30) _____ and flexible ways because of our set (31) _____ of approaching problems. When we are inflexible in our approach to situations, we close our minds to creative (32) _____.

　　Being creative doesn't necessarily mean being a (33) _____.
(34) _____.
Spontaneity is one of the key elements of creativity.

　　If you were to ask someone, "What's half of eight?" and received the answer "zero", you might laugh and say "That's wrong!" (35) _____

_____.

　　The ability to visualize our environment in new ways opens our perspective and allows us to make all kinds of discoveries. (36) _____

_____.

Unit 7

Section A

Directions: In this section, you will hear 8 short conversations and 2 long conversations. At the end of each conversation, one or more questions will be asked about what was said. Both the conversations and the questions will be spoken only once. After each question there will be a pause. During the pause, you must read the four choices marked A, B, C and D, and decide which is the best answer.

1. A. The man hates to lend his tools to other people.
   B. The man hasn't finished working on the bookshelf.
   C. The tools have already been returned to the woman.
   D. The tools the man borrowed from the woman are missing.

2. A. Save time by using a computer.
   B. Buy her own computer.
   C. Borrow Martha's computer.
   D. Stay home and complete her paper.

3. A. He has been to Seattle many times.
   B. He has chaired a lot of conferences.
   C. He holds a high position in his company.
   D. He lived in Seattle for many years.

4. A. Teacher and student.
   B. Doctor and patient.
   C. Manager and office worker.
   D. Travel agent and customer.

5. A. She knows the guy who will give the lecture.
   B. She thinks the lecture might be informative.
   C. She wants to add something to her lecture.
   D. She'll finish her report this weekend.

6. A. An art museum.
   B. A beautiful park.

C. A college campus.

D. An architectural exhibition.

7. A. The houses for sale are of poor quality.

B. The houses are worth the money.

C. The housing developers provide free trips for potential buyers.

D. The man is unwilling to take a look at the houses for sale.

8. A. Talking about sports.

B. Writing up local news.

C. Reading newspapers.

D. Putting up advertisements.

Conversation One

9. A. The benefits of strong business competition.

B. A proposal to lower the cost of production.

C. Complaints about the expense of modernization.

D. Suggestions concerning new business strategies.

10. A. It cost much more than its worth.

B. It should be brought up-to-date.

C. It calls for immediate repairs.

D. It can still be used for a long time.

11. A. The personnel manager should be fired for inefficiency.

B. A few engineers should be employed to modernize the factory.

C. The entire staff should be retrained.

D. Better-educated employees should be promoted.

12. A. Their competitors have long been advertising on TV.

B. TV commercials are less expensive.

C. Advertising in newspapers alone is not sufficient.

D. TV commercials attract more investments.

Conversation Two

13. A. Searching for reference material.

B. Watching a film of the 1930s'.

C. Writing a course book.

D. Looking for a job in a movie studio.

14. A. It's too broad to cope with.

    B. It's a bit outdated.

    C. It's controversial.

    D. It's of little practical value.

15. A. At the end of the online catalogue.

    B. At the Reference Desk.

    C. In *The New York Times*.

    D. In the *Reader's Guide to Periodical Literature*.

Section B

Directions: In this section, you will hear 3 short passages. At the end of each passage, you will hear some questions. Both the passages and the questions will be spoken only once. After you hear a question, you must choose the best answer from the four choices marked A, B, C and D.

Passage One

16. A. Electronic instruments and a regular tool.

    B. A human "guinea pig" and a regular tool.

    C. Electronic instruments and a human "guinea pig".

    D. Electronic instruments, a human "guinea pig" and a regular tool.

17. A. they are twisted and stretched

    B. they are in their normal positions

    C. they are tested with a human "guinea pig"

    D. they are tested with electronic instruments

18. A. improve efficiency   B. increase production

    C. reduce work load   D. improve comfort

Passage Two

19. A. most computer criminals who are caught blame their bad luck

    B. the rapid increase of computer crimes is a troublesome problem

    C. most computer criminals are smart enough to cover up their crimes

    D. many more computer crimes go undetected that are discovered

20. A. A strict law against computer crimes must be enforced.

    B. Companies usually hesitate to uncover computer crimes to protect their reputation.

    C. Companies will guard against computer crimes to protect their reputation.

    D. Companies need to impose restrictions on confidential information.

21. A. With a bad reputation they can hardly find another job.

    B. They may walk away and easily find another job.

    C. They will be denied access to confidential records.

    D. They must leave the country to go to jail.

22. A. Why computer criminals are often able to escape punishment.

    B. Why computer crimes are difficult to detect by systematic inspections.

    C. How computer criminals manage to get good recommendations from their former employers.

    D. Why computer crimes can't be eliminated.

Passage Three

23. A. They will be much bigger.

    B. They will have more seats.

    C. They will have three wheels.

    D. They will need intelligent drivers.

24. A. It doesn't need to be refueled.

    B. It will use solar energy as fuel.

    C. It will be driven by electrical power.

    D. It will be more suitable for long distance travel.

25. A. Choose the right route.

    B. Refuel the car regularly.

    C. Start the engine.

    D. Tell the computer where to go.

Section C

Directions: In this section, you will hear a passage three times. When the passage is read for the first time, you should listen carefully for its general idea. When the passage is read for the second time, you are required to fill in the blanks numbered from 26 to 33 with the exact words you have just heard. For blanks numbered from 34 to 36 you are required to fill in the missing information. For these blanks, you can either use the exact words you have just heard or write down the main points in your own words. Finally, when the passage is read for the third time, you should check what you have written.

Russia is the largest economic power that is not a member of the World Trade Organization. But that may change. Last Friday, the European Union said it would support Russia's (26) _____ to become a WTO member.

Representatives of the European Union met with Russian (27) _____ in Moscow. They signed a trade agreement that took six years to (28) _____.

Russia called the trade agreement (29) _____. It agreed to slowly increase fuel prices within the country. It also agreed to permit (30) _____ in its communications industry and to remove some barriers to trade.

In (31) _____ for European support to join the WTO, Russian President Putin said that Russia would speed up the (32) _____ to approve the Kyoto Protocol, an international (33) _____ agreement to reduce the production of harmful industrial gases. (34) _____.

Russia had signed the Kyoto Protocol, but has not yet approved it. The agreement takes effect when it has been approved by nations that produce at least 55 percent of the world's greenhouse gases. (35) _____.
Russia produces about 17 percent of the world's greenhouse gases. The United States, the world's biggest producer, withdrew from the Kyoto Protocol after President Bush took office in 2001. So, Russia's approval is required to put the Kyoto Protocol into effect.

(36) _____. Russia must still reach agreements with China, Japan, South Korea and the United States.

Unit 8

Section A

Directions: In this section, you will hear 8 short conversations and 2 long conversations. At the end of each conversation, one or more questions will be asked about what was said. Both the conversations and the questions will be spoken only once. After each question there will be a pause. During the pause, you must read the four choices marked A, B, C and D, and decide which is the best answer.

1. A. Twenty-five dollars.　　　　B. Twenty dollars.
　　C. Forty dollars.　　　　　　D. Fifty dollars.
2. A. To go to the French restaurant. B. To try a new restaurant.
　　C. To visit a friend.　　　　　D. To stay at home.
3. A. Easy-going and friendly.　　B. Very nervous.
　　C. Angry.　　　　　　　　　D. Not easy-going.
4. A. Peter plays jazz music.　　　B. Peter is a jazz fan.
　　C. Peter needs 300 jazz records. D. Peter likes classical music.
5. A. At a post office.　　　　　　B. At a bank.
　　C. At a restaurant.　　　　　　D. At an airport.
6. A. He was scared.　　　　　　　B. He was upset.
　　C. He hasn't got a car.　　　　D. He is glad to drive her there.
7. A. Lending money to a student.　B. Filling a form.
　　C. Reading a student's application.D. Asking for some financial aid.
8. A. 12:30.　　　　　　　　　　B. 11:30.
　　C. 12:00.　　　　　　　　　　D. 11:00.

Conversation One

9. A. To go sightseeing.　　　　　B. To have meetings.
　　C. To promote a new champagne. D. To join in a training program.
10. A. It can reduce the number of passenger complaints.
　　B. It can make air travel more entertaining.

    C. It can cut down the expenses for air travel.

    D. It can lessen the discomfort caused by air travel.

11. A. Took balanced meals with champagne.

    B. Ate vegetables and fruit only.

    C. Refrained from fish or meat.

    D. Avoided eating rich food.

12. A. Many of them found it difficult to exercise on a plane.

    B. Many of them were concerned with their well-being.

    C. Not many of them chose to do what she did.

    D. Not many of them understood the program.

Conversation Two

13. A. At a fair.   B. At a cafeteria.

    C. In a computer lab.   D. In a shopping mall.

14. A. The latest computer technology.

    B. The organizing of an exhibition.

    C. The purchasing of some equipment.

    D. The dramatic changes in the job market.

15. A. Data collection.

    B. Training consultancy.

    C. Corporate management.

    D. Information processing.

Section B

Directions: In this section, you will hear 3 short passages. At the end of each passage, you will hear some questions. Both the passages and the questions will be spoken only once. After you hear a question, you must choose the best answer from the four choices marked A, B, C and D.

Passage One

16. A. You have to buy a special electronic ticket.

    B. You have to travel a long way to visit the university.

    C. You need an expensive device designed especially for the museum.

D. You need a computer linked to a telephone.

17. A. To provide a place for computer artists to show their work.

B. To sell the art works more easily.

C. To save space of museums for other purposes.

D. To provide more fun for the artists.

18. A. It can help a computer artist to record his pictures electronically.

B. It can help a computer artist to send his pictures to others.

C. It can help a computer artist to print pictures on paper.

D. It can help a computer artist to connect his computer to the art museum.

Passage Two

19. A. 4 years.   B. 5 years.

C. 8 years.   D. at least 9 years.

20. A. Biology.   B. Chemistry.

C. Philosophy.   D. Medicine.

21. A. Each student must pass a national examination.

B. Students who do best in the studies have a greater chance.

C. They can seek to enter a number of medical schools.

D. There are many chances to gain the entrance.

Passage Three

22. A. Guarding the coasts of the United States.

B. Being part of the United States Navy.

C. Guiding people along the coast.

D. Protecting people from army attack.

23. A. Enforcing laws controlling navigation, shipping, immigration and fishing.

B. Enforcing laws affecting the privately-owned boats in the U. S. .

C. Searching for missing boats and rescuing people.

D. Training people to good swimmers along the beach.

24. A. 17, 000.   B. 1, 700.

C. 70, 000.   D. 7, 000.

25. A. Dangerous.   B. Hard.

C. Exciting.   D. Dull.

Section C

Directions: In this section, you will hear a passage three times. When the passage is read for the first time, you should listen carefully for its general idea. When the passage is read for the second time, you are required to fill in the blanks numbered from 26 to 33 with the exact words you have just heard. For blanks numbered from 34 to 36 you are required to fill in the missing information. For these blanks, you can either use the exact words you have just heard or write down the main points in your own words. Finally, when the passage is read for the third time, you should check what you have written.

Very high waves are destructive when they (26) _____ the land. Fortunately, this (27) _____ happens. One reason is that out at sea, waves moving in one direction almost always run into waves moving in a (28) _____ direction. The two (29) _____ of waves tend to cancel each other out. Another reason is that water is (30) _____ near the shore. As a wave gets closer to land, the shallow (31) _____ helps reduce its (32) _____ .

But the power of waves striking the (33) _____ can still be very great. During a winter gale, waves sometimes strike the shore with the force of 6,000 pounds for each square foot. That means a wave, 25 feet high and 500 feet along its face, (34) _____ .

Yet the waves, (35) _____ . During the most raging storms, (36) _____ .

Unit 9

Section A

Directions: In this section, you will hear 8 short conversations and 2 long conversations. At the end of each conversation, one or more questions will be asked about what was said. Both the conversations and the questions will be spoken only once. After each question there will be a pause. During the pause, you must read the four choices marked A, B, C and D, and decide which is the best answer.

1. A. His score in the driving test was 65.

   B. His score in the driving test was higher than 65.

   C. He wasn't the best in the driving test.

   D. He got less than 65 in the driving test.

2. A. Understanding.   B. Overjoyed.

   C. Annoyed.   D. Critical.

3. A. She hasn't finished the experiment.

   B. The experiment turned out well.

   C. The experiment will take her two days.

   D. She spent more time on the experiment than she had expected.

4. A. Because the tuition next term will be too much for her parents to afford.

   B. Because she has to pay her room and board herself.

   C. Because her parents can't help her financially.

   D. Because her parents want her to acquire more social experience.

5. A. An interview.

   B. The packing department.

   C. Job vacancy.

   D. Applicants for the job.

6. A. Reporter.   B. Weatherman.

   C. Mechanic.   D. Farmer.

7. A. He expresses no opinion.

   B. He thinks the punishment is too serious.

C. He feels sorry for the students.

D. He approves of the action.

8. A. Have a snack.

   B. Go to the library.

   C. Exchange information at the snack bar.

   D. Look for sources at the snack bar.

Conversation One

9. A. In the street.   B. In a hotel.

   C. In a travel agency.   D. In a restaurant.

10. A. The open-air market.   B. Tourist shops and cafes.

   C. The castle.   D. The city museum.

11. A. Because it has a long history.

   B. Because from the top of it people can have a beautiful view of the city.

   C. Because it overlooks the falls.

   D. Because people can buy souvenirs there.

12. A. The tourist shops and cafes. B. The castle.

   C. The restaurant.   D. All of the above.

Conversation Two

13. A. Because his motorbike has broken down.

   B. Because it is more convenient than a motorbike.

   C. Because he can't afford the fuel.

   D. Because he can afford a car now.

14. A. Because it's of excellent value for the price and it is very different from the Fiesta.

   B. Because it is a good-looking car.

   C. Because it is not expensive.

   D. Because it is only just arrived.

15. A. Yes. Because he has enough money.

   B. No. Because he can't afford it.

   C. Yes. Because he can pay it by monthly installments.

   D. No. Because he can't pay it by monthly installments.

Section B

Directions: In this section, you will hear 3 short passages. At the end of each passage, you will hear some questions. Both the passages and the questions will be spoken only once. After you hear a question, you must choose the best answer from the four choices marked A, B, C and D.

Passage One

16. A. Eyes.　　　　　　　　　B. Skin.
    C. Bones.　　　　　　　　　D. All of the above.
17. A. Vitamin B$_1$ helps people keep fit.
    B. Vitamin B$_2$ helps the eyes and teeth stay healthy.
    C. Vitamin B$_6$ helps the body use food better.
    D. Vitamin B$_{12}$ helps people build their body.
18. A. Vitamin A.　　　　　　　B. Vitamin B.
    C. Vitamin C.　　　　　　　D. Vitamin D.

Passage Two

19. A. The world's birth rate is higher than that of ten years ago.
    B. The world's birth rate has dropped rapidly during the past 10 years.
    C. Birth control has been carried out well all over the world.
    D. There is a serious shortage of workers all over the world.

20. A. More men and women are waiting longer to get married.
    B. More married people try to prevent or delay pregnancy.
    C. More women don't want to take care of children.
    D. More governments support family planning programs to reduce population growth.

21. A. Because they might have to help support the growing number of retired people.
    B. Because they will have higher living standards.
    C. Because they will earn more money.
    D. Because their government need some money to help education.

Passage Three

22. A. During the American Civil War.
    B. During the American Revolution.
    C. During World War I.
    D. During World War II.

23. A. One term.   B. Two terms.
    C. Three terms.   D. Four terms.

24. A. Washington attended many universities.
    B. Washington married twice.
    C. Washington had only one child.
    D. Washington was the first president of the United States.

25. A. His birthday is a federal holiday.
    B. His picture appears on postage stamps.
    C. Many counties, towns, cities, streets, bridges, lakes, parks, and schools have his name.
    D. He was buried in Washington D. C..

Section C

Directions: In this section, you will hear a passage three times. When the passage is read for the first time, you should listen carefully for its general idea. When the passage is read for the second time, you are required to fill in the blanks numbered from 26 to 33 with the exact words you have just heard. For blanks numbered from 34 to 36 you are required to fill in the missing information. For these blanks, you can either use the exact words you have just heard or write down the main points in your own words. Finally, when the passage is read for the third time, you should check what you have written.

The United States leads all industrial nations in the (26) _____ of its young men and women who receive higher education. Why is this? What (27) _____ a middle-income family with two children to take (28) _____ for up to $ 120,000 so that their son and daughter can (29) _____ private universities for four years? Why would both parents in a low-income family cost of $ 4,000? Why should a woman in her forties quit her job and use her savings to (30) _____ for the college education she didn't receive when she was younger?

Americans place a high personal value on higher education. This is an (31) _____ that goes back to the country's oldest political traditions. People in the United States have always believed that education is necessary for maintaining a (32) _____ government. They believe that it prepares the individual for informed, (33) _____, political participation, including voting.

(34) _____,
but the post-war period produced dozens of new questions for Americans. How should atomic power be used? Should scientists be allowed to experiment in splitting genes? Should money be spent on sending astronauts into space—or should it be used for aid to another nation? (35) _____.
But the representatives they elect do decide such issues. (36) _____
_____.

Unit 10

Section A

Directions: In this section, you will hear 8 short conversations and 2 long conversations. At the end of each conversation, one or more questions will be asked about what was said. Both the conversations and the questions will be spoken only once. After each question there will be a pause. During the pause, you must read the four choices marked A, B, C and D, and decide which is the best answer.

1. A. He is not very enthusiastic about his English lessons.
   B. He has made great progress in his English.
   C. He is a student of the music department.
   D. He is not very interested in English songs.

2. A. The woman didn't expect it to be so warm at noon.
   B. The woman is sensitive to weather changes.
   C. The weather forecast was unreliable.
   D. The weather turned cold all of a sudden.

3. A. At a clinic.   B. In a supermarket.
   C. At a restaurant.   D. In an ice cream shop.

4. A. The cost of a taxi is low.   B. The cost of a taxi is high.
   C. A coach is slow.   D. The cost of a coach is high.

5. A. The man's vacation will be expensive.
   B. She thought the man had already been to Paris.
   C. She could help the man budget his money.
   D. Summer is usually not a good time to go to Paris.

6. A. He doesn't spend enough time studying.
   B. He doesn't think the weather is nice.
   C. He'd prefer not to walk to class.
   D. He has little time for outdoor activities.

7. A. The man saw Mark on the street two months ago.
   B. The woman had forgotten Mark's phone number.

C. The woman made a phone call to Mark yesterday.

D. Mark and the woman had not been in touch for some time.

8. A. At 7:00.　　　　　　　B. At 7:30.

   C. At 9:30.　　　　　　　D. At 9:00.

Conversation One

9. A. He wants to become a cook.

   B. He hopes to go on to graduate school.

   C. He wants to travel around the world.

   D. He'd like to work at a hotel.

10. A. History.　　　　　　　B. French.

    C. Computer Science.　　　D. Hotel Management.

11. A. She has a part-time job.

    B. She received a scholarship.

    C. Her parents pay for it.

    D. She is working as a tourist guide.

12. A. At a bakery.　　　　　　B. In a library.

    C. At a restaurant.　　　　D. At a travel agency.

Conversation Two

13. A. Whether the man had experience as a security guard.

    B. Whether the man is a student.

    C. What the man is good at.

    D. Where the man lives.

14. A. He prefers to sleep late in the morning.

    B. He writes for the local paper in the morning.

    C. He has classes during the day.

    D. He wants a higher-paying evening job.

15. A. Complete an application form.

    B. Wait a few minutes.

    C. Go back home and wait for the information.

    D. Complete his resume as soon as possible.

Section B

Directions: In this section, you will hear 3 short passages. At the end of each passage, you will hear some questions. Both the passages and the questions will be spoken only once. After you hear a question, you must choose the best answer from the four choices marked A, B, C and D.

Passage One

16. A. Because of fun.
    B. Because they are forced to clean themselves.
    C. Because they're proud of their pretty feathers.
    D. Because they have an instinct for cleanliness.

17. A. Keeping it waterproof.
    B. Keeping its feather cool in summer.
    C. Communicating with other birds of the same species.
    D. Allowing it to fly.

18. A. Birds Use Their Beaks to Clean Their Feathers
    B. Feathers Are Very Important to Birds
    C. The Habits of Birds Are Interesting
    D. How Birds Clean Their Feathers

Passage Two

19. A. Because someone stopped the clock before it went off.
    B. Because she forgot to set the clock the night before.
    C. Because the clock was stolen.
    D. Because there was something wrong with it.

20. A. That she was late for class.
    B. That her clock didn't go off.
    C. That she had shoes of different colors on her feet.
    D. That she didn't dress herself properly.

21. A. Getting up late often makes a person feel embarrassed.
    B. Men are always more careless than women.
    C. Sara and Brown were embarrassed when they met again.

D. Carelessness can make people embarrassed.

Passage Three

22. A. About 45 million.　　　B. About 50 million.
    C. About 5. 4 million.　　　D. About 4. 5 million.
23. A. The actors and actresses are not paid for their performance.
    B. The actors and actresses only perform in their own community.
    C. They exist only in small communities.
    D. They only put on shows that are educational.
24. A. It provides them with the opportunity to watch performances for free.
    B. It provides them with the opportunity to make friends.
    C. It gives them the chance to do something creative.
    D. It gives them the chance to enjoy modern art.
25. A. Community Theatre　　　B. Profession Theatre Companies
    C. Modern Art　　　D. Free Contribution

Section C

Directions: In this section, you will hear a passage three times. When the passage is read for the first time, you should listen carefully for its general idea. When the passage is read for the second time, you are required to fill in the blanks numbered from 26 to 33 with the exact words you have just heard. For blanks numbered from 34 to 36 you are required to fill in the missing information. For these blanks, you can either use the exact words you have just heard or write down the main points in your own words. Finally, when the passage is read for the third time, you should check what you have written.

Children have their own rules in playing games. They seldom need a referee and rarely trouble to keep (26) _____. They don't care much about who wins or (27) _____, and it doesn't seem to worry them if the game is not finished. Yet, they like games that (28) _____ a lot on luck, so that their (29) _____ abilities cannot be directly (30) _____. They also enjoy games that move in stages, in which each stage, the choosing of leaders, the picking of sides, or the (31) _____ of which side shall start, is almost a game in itself.

Grown-ups can hardly find children's games exciting, and they often feel

(32) _____ at why there kids play such simple games again and again. However, it is found that a child plays games for very important (33) _____. He can be a good player without having to think whether he is a popular person, and (34) _____. He becomes a leader when it comes to his turn. He can be confident, too, in particular games, that (35) _____

_____.

It appears to us that when children play a game they imagine a situation under their control. Everyone knows the rules, and more importantly, everyone plays according to the rules. (36) _____

_____.

Unit 11

Section A

Directions: In this section, you will hear 8 short conversations and 2 long conversations. At the end of each conversation, one or more questions will be asked about what was said. Both the conversations and the questions will be spoken only once. After each question there will be a pause. During the pause, you must read the four choices marked A, B, C and D, and decide which is the best answer.

1. A. At a hairdresser's.   B. At a tailor's.
   C. At a butcher's.   D. At a photographer's.

2. A. Buy the pants the woman showed him.
   B. Wait until the pants are on sale.
   C. Look for the pants in a different color.
   D. Want the pants made of a different material.

3. A. Forget them until later.
   B. Go over them right away.
   C. Move them away from the coffee cup.
   D. Discuss them with Professor Johnson.

4. A. A journalist.   B. A maths student.
   C. An arithmetic teacher.   D. An accountant.

5. A. They shouldn't make too many requests.
   B. They should ask for three weeks to do the work.
   C. They shouldn't push the projector buttons.
   D. They should wish the professor good luck.

6. A. She thought the pay was too low.
   B. She didn't feel she was creative enough to work there.
   C. She didn't like her supervisor.
   D. She couldn't use her abilities.

7. A. In a supermarket.   B. In a drugstore.
   C. In a department store.   D. In a car repair shop.

49

8. A. A salary cut.
    B. A real estate bargain.
    C. A rent increase.
    D. A vacation trip.

Conversation One

9. A. Hurricanes.
    B. TV update.
    C. Names of hurricanes.
    D. Wind velocity.

10. A. A storm and a hurricane differ in the seasons it occurs.
    B. A storm and a hurricane differ in the speed wind travels.
    C. A hurricane is the least serious.
    D. A storm is less serious than a depression.

11. A. Those people discovered the hurricanes first.
    B. It's easy to tell hurricanes apart.
    C. Those people are pop stars.
    D. Those people are the weather forecasters.

12. A. Examine the map again.
    B. Turn on the radio.
    C. See the hurricane outdoors.
    D. Watch TV weather report.

Conversation Two

13. A. The place the woman has visited.
    B. A paper the woman is writing for a class.
    C. School activities they enjoy.
    D. The man's plans for the summer.

14. A. He has never been to Gettysburg.
    B. He took a political science course.
    C. His family still goes on vacation together.
    D. He's interested in the United States Civil War.

15. A. Why his parents wanted to go to Gettysburg.
    B. Why his family's vacation plans changed ten years ago.
    C. Where his family went for a vacation ten years ago.
    D. When his family went on their last vacation.

Section B

Directions: In this section, you will hear 3 short passages. At the end of each passage, you will hear some questions. Both the passages and the questions will be spoken only once. After you hear a question, you must choose the best answer from the four choices marked A, B, C and D.

Passage One

16. A. A housewife.   B. A singer.
    C. A teacher.   D. A musician.
17. A. A small violin.   B. A toy violin for children.
    C. A discounted violin. D. An expensive piano.
18. A. To live a more comfortable life. B. To give performances.
    C. To be a pupil of a famous violinist. D. To enter a famous university.

Passage Two

19. A. In the white pages.
    B. In the blue pages.
    C. In the yellow pages.
    D. In a special section.
20. A. On the first page of the telephone book.
    B. At the end of the telephone book.
    C. In the front of the white pages.
    D. Right after the white pages.
21. A. Check your number and call again.
    B. Tell the operator what has happened.
    C. Ask the operator to put you through.
    D. Ask the operator what has happened.

Passage Three

22. A. 10,000.   B. 35.
    C. 130.   D. 113.
23. A. Its specialization in transporting small packages.

   B. The low cost of its service.

   C. Being the first airline to send urgent letters.

   D. Its modern sorting facilities.

24. A. Because of its good airport facilities.

   B. Because of its location in the country.

   C. Because of its size.

   D. Because of its round-the-clock service.

25. A. Its full-time staff.

   B. The postmen who work in Memphis.

   C. Students who work in their spare time.

   D. The staff members of the International Airport.

Section C

Directions: In this section, you will hear a passage three times. When the passage is read for the first time, you should listen carefully for its general idea. When the passage is read for the second time, you are required to fill in the blanks numbered from 26 to 33 with the exact words you have just heard. For blanks numbered from 34 to 36 you are required to fill in the missing information. For these blanks, you can either use the exact words you have just heard or write down the main points in your own words. Finally, when the passage is read for the third time, you should check what you have written.

Cyber Café (网吧) computer centers are found in many cities around the world. Now, a few American high schools are (26) _____ these centers. All students can use the Cyber Café but school officials say it (27) _____ helps students who have no computer or cannot use the Internet at home.

The officials say thirteen percent of the students at the school are from poor families. Many students have (28) _____ in the United States from other countries only recently. Students in the school's (29) _____ for learning English speak twenty-three other languages. The idea for a Cyber Café began three years ago. At that time, officials were planning to (30) _____ the school building. Parents interested in technology (31) _____ a Cyber Café. They wanted this center even though schools in the area had suffered (32) _____ cuts. The community wanted to help. It wanted all students to have the best chances to learn.

Officials in the area (33) _____ the idea. (34) _____

_____.

Over two years, the foundation collected more than 170,000 dollars. (35) _____

_____.

In addition, they can send and receive electronic mail. (36) _____

_____.

The Cyber Café also serves a social purpose. Visitors can stop by for a drink of coffee, tea, or hot chocolate.

Unit 12

Section A

Directions: In this section, you will hear 8 short conversations and 2 long conversations. At the end of each conversation, one or more questions will be asked about what was said. Both the conversations and the questions will be spoken only once. After each question there will be a pause. During the pause, you must read the four choices marked A, B, C and D, and decide which is the best answer.

1. A. A race car coach.　　　　　B. A garage mechanic.
   C. A car dealer.　　　　　　　D. A policeman.

2. A. Mike is good at spelling.　　B. Mike is good at grammar.
   C. Mike is good at composition skills. D. None of the above is right.

3. A. The election is unfair.
   B. People should shout louder in the election.
   C. More people should come to the election.
   D. The other candidate is not qualified.

4. A. 7:05.　　　　　　　　　　B. 7:10.
   C. 7:15.　　　　　　　　　　D. 7:20.

5. A. In a bookstore.　　　　　　B. In a library.
   C. In an art gallery.　　　　　D. In a souvenir store.

6. A. To work at his office.　　　B. To work at home.
   C. To go out with the woman　　D. To go out with his colleague.

7. A. In a supermarket.　　　　　B. In a park.
   C. In an apartment　　　　　　D. In the street.

8. A. Student and teacher.　　　　B. Patient and doctor.
   C. Athlete and coach.　　　　　D. Client and lawyer.

Conversation One

9. A. The neighbors' son drives too fast.
   B. The radio of her neighbors' son often wakes up her children.

C. She hasn't met her neighbors.

D. Her neighbors' son was too noisy.

10. A. She doesn't want to make a bad first impression.

B. She is afraid that it will irritate the neighbors' son.

C. She is afraid that they won't listen.

D. She knows that they can't do anything about it.

11. A. She should call the neighbors to complain.

B. She should introduce her children to the neighbor.

C. She should go to visit the neighbor with a gift.

D. She should wait in order to be polite.

12. A. It is hard for Linda to get her children to go to sleep.

B. The son of Linda's neighbors always comes home very late.

C. Linda found it hard to complain to her new neighbors about their son.

D. Linda is annoyed by her neighbors' son blasting stereo all night.

Conversation Two

13. A. The women's husband.

B. The owner of the apartment.

C. The apartment manager.

D. The tenant who occupies the apartment now.

14. A. In a house. B. In a hotel.

C. In a two-bedroom apartment. D. In a three-bedroom apartment.

15. A. Because she thought the apartment was too small.

B. Because it was the first apartment she had seen.

C. Because her husband had not seen it.

D. Because the rent was too high.

Section B

Direction: In this section, you will hear 3 short passages. At the end of each passage, you will hear some questions. Both the passages and the questions will be spoken only once. After you hear a question, you must choose the best answer from the four choices marked A, B, C and D.

Passage One

16. A. An earthquake can happen under water.
    B. We are not aware of the occurrence of most earthquakes.
    C. Some major earthquakes can kill thousands of people and destroy complete towns and villages.
    D. All the major earthquakes last for some minutes.

17. A. $ 7 million.   B. $ 140 million.
    C. $ 137 million.   D. Beyond estimate.

18. A. To hold earthquake drills.
    B. To prevent earthquakes from happening.
    C. To teach volunteers how to put out fires and use essential equipment.
    D. To make preparations for the inevitable next big quake.

Passage Two

19. A. When the weather is hot and wet.
    B. When the weather is cold and dry.
    C. When the temperature is about 64 ℉.
    D. When people have high IQ scores.

20. A. Very hot weather.   B. Low air pressure.
    C. Violent windstorm.   D. Hurried activities.

21. A. About 65 ℉.
    B. About 64 ℉ with 65% humidity.
    C. About 65 ℉ with 64% humidity.
    D. About 65 ℉ with hurricanes.

Passage Three

22. A. Light darkens silver salt.
    B. Light darkens natural salt.
    C. Light darkens silver.
    D. Light darkens self-developing film.

23. A. By making use of special paper.
    B. By adding common salt to silver salt.

C. By using the temporary images.

D. By using a special piece of metal.

24. A. He was a soldier.

    B. He took war photographs.

    C. He painted portraits.

    D. He designed a portable camera.

25. A. A cheap process of developing film at home.

    B. A new kind of film.

    C. An automatic printer.

    D. The instant camera.

Section C

Directions: In this section, you will hear a passage three times. When the passage is read for the first time, you should listen carefully for its general idea. When the passage is read for the second time, you are required to fill in the blanks numbered from 26 to 33 with the exact words you have just heard. For blanks numbered from 34 to 36 you are required to fill in the missing information. For these blanks, you can either use the exact words you have just heard or write down the main points in your own words. Finally, when the passage is read for the third time, you should check what you have written.

Most of us grow up taking certain things for granted. We tend to assume that experts and (26) _____ leaders will tell us the truth. We tend to believe that things (27) _____ on television or in news papers can't be bad for us.

However, (28) _____ of critical thinking in students is one of the goals of most colleges and universities. Few professors (29) _____ students to share the professor's own (30) _____. In general, professors are more (31) _____ that students learn to question and critically (32) _____ the arguements of others. This does not mean that professors insist that you change your beliefs, either. It does mean, however, professors will usually ask you to support the views you (33) _____ in class or in your wiring.

(34) _____.

Most professors want you to recognize the premises of your argument, to examine whether you really accept them, and understand whether or not you draw logical conclusions. (35) _____.

On the other hand, if you intend to disagree with your professors in class, you should be prepared to offer a strong argument in support of your ideas. (36) _____

_____.

Many professors interpret it as rudeness.

Unit 13

Section A

Directions: In this section, you will hear 8 short conversations and 2 long conversations. At the end of each conversation, one or more questions will be asked about what was said. Both the conversations and questions will be spoken only once. After each question there will be a pause. During the pause, you must read the four choices marked A, B, C and D, and decide which is the best answer.

1. A. Two friends.
   B. A teacher and a student.
   C. Parents.
   D. A parent and a child.

2. A. He has been promoted by the board of directors.
   B. He is fired by the board of directors.
   C. He is willing to resign his position as president.
   D. He has solved the financial difficulties in the company.

3. A. $ 9.50.
   B. $ 15.00.
   C. $ 10.5.
   D. $ 6.00.

4. A. Go to work on foot.
   B. Repair her old car.
   C. Be a car dealer.
   D. Sell the old car and buy a new one.

5. A. The warm weather.
   B. Things to wear.
   C. A bright shirt.
   D. Best material for making clothes.

6. A. In the laboratory.
   B. In the woman's house.
   C. In the man's house.
   D. In the library.

7. A. Because he has been admitted by a university.
   B. Because he become a member of the university council.
   C. Because his scholarship has been approved.
   D. Because the woman has got a scholarship.

8. A. Sail a boat.
   B. Hang clothes.
   C. Catch a horse.
   D. Fish.

Conversation One

9. A. He hopes to get a job. B. He wants to attend summer school.

   C. He plans to baby-sit. D. He will travel to Europe.

10. A. Taking care of pets and a garden.

    B. Tending the house while the owner is away.

    C. Watching a family's kids in their house.

    D. Renting your house to students.

11. A. They look at the housemistress's grade.

    B. They interview the house-sitter's family.

    C. The make sure they know the house-sitter well.

    D. They ask the house-sitter for references.

12. A. Student-student. B. Student-professor.

    C. Clerk-client. D. Employee-employer.

Conversation Two

13. A. In a police station. B. In a hotel.

    C. In a restaurant. D. At a Lost Property Office.

14. A. One hour ago in his room.

    B. One hour ago in the gentlemen's toilet.

    C. 15 minutes ago in his room.

    D. 15 minutes ago in the gentlemen's toilet.

15. A. It is a digital watch.

    B. There is a second hand on the watch.

    C. There is a date indicator on the watch.

    D. There is a leather strap on the watch.

Section B

Direction: In this section, you will hear 3 short passages. At the end of each passage, you will hear some questions. Both the passages and the questions will be spoken only once. After you hear a question, you must choose the best answer from the four choices marked A, B, C and D.

Passage One

16. A. Synthetic fuel.   B. Solar energy.

    C. Alcohol.   D. Electricity.

17. A. Air traffic conditions.   B. Traffic jams on highways.

    C. Road conditions.   D. New traffic rules.

18. A. Go through a health check.   B. Take little luggage with them.

    C. Arrive early for boarding.   D. Undergo security checks.

Passage Two

19. A. In the early 17th century.   B. In the late 17th century.

    C. In the early 18th century.   D. In the late 18th century.

20. A. John Kersey.   B. Samuel Johnson.

    C. Daniel Webster.   D. Robert Cawdrey.

21. A. It showed the word histories.

    B. It was a complete list of difficult words.

    C. It was a twenty-volume work.

    D. It gave good meanings to each word.

Passage Three

22. A. Intellect.   B. Courteousness.

    C. Courage.   D. Pride.

23. A. A person who lets other people control him.

    B. A person who lets his instinct guide him.

    C. A person who has no will of his own.

    D. A person who has much imagination.

24. A. A sick man.

    B. A man whose nose has been hurt.

    C. A man who feels rejected and depressed.

    D. A man who wants to smell flowers.

25. A. A woman poet wished to have two noses.

    B. The nose is an important human organ for breathing and smelling.

    C. People are interested in Cleopatra's nose.

D. The human nose has provided us with various expressions.

Section C

Directions: In this section, you will hear a passage three times. When the passage is read for the first time, you should listen carefully for its general idea. When the passage is read for the second time, you are required to fill in the blanks numbered from 26 to 33 with the exact words you have just heard. For blanks numbered from 34 to 36 you are required to fill in the missing information. For these blanks, you can either use the exact words you have just heard or write down the main points in your own words. Finally, when the passage is read for the third time, you should check what you have written.

Nancy Jessie's sleeping difficulties began on (26) _____ a few summers ago. She (27) _____ the noisy motel room, but her sleeping did not improve at home. Instead of her usual six to seven hours a night, the 37-year-old teacher slept just three or four hours. "I'd toss and turn for hours, then get up and pace," she says.

Nancy tried going to bed earlier, but the (28) _____ noise, even her husband's (29) _____, disturbed her. She drank a glass of wine at bedtime and fell asleep immediately, but was (30) _____ two hours later. Her doctor (31) _____ a sleeping pill for two weeks. When she stopped taking the pills, though, she slept worse than ever.

Most of us have the (32) _____ short period of troubled sleep and then return to normal a few nights later. However, for one in six people insomnia is a (33) _____ problem.

Now the Johns Hopkins's Sleep Disorders Center in Baltimore (34) _____ _____ insomniacs cures themselves. It is based on the idea that by deliberately reducing time in bed and by modifying your waking activities (35) _____ .

Psychologist Richard Alien, co-director of the Johns Hopkins Center, considers insomnia a 24-hour disorder. Thus, his treatment, which draws on research done by Arthur Spielman of the Sleep Disorders Center of the City College of New York, (36) _____ .

第二部分　听力历年全真试题

2008年6月英语四级听力全真试题

Part III　　　　　　　　**Listening Comprehension**　　　　　　　**（35 minutes）**

Section A

Directions： In this section, you will hear 8 short conversations and 2 long conversations. At the end of each conversation, one or more questions will be asked about what was said. Both the conversations and the questions will be spoken only once. After each question there will be a pause. During the pause, you must read the four choices marked A, B, C and D, and decide which is the best answer. Then mark the corresponding letter on Answer Sheet 2 with a single line through the centre.

11. A. Treat his injury immediately.
    B. Continue his regular activities.
    C. Give his ankle a good rest.
    D. Be careful when climbing steps.

12. A. In a theater.　　　B. In a restaurant.
    C. On a plane.　　　D. On a train.

13. A. A sad occasion.
    B. A tragic accident.
    C. Smith's sleeping problem.
    D. Smith's unusual life story.

14. A. Compare notes with his classmates.
    B. Review the details of all her lessons.
    C. Talk with her about his learning problems.
    D. Focus on the main points of her lectures.

15. A. The man blamed the woman for being careless.

    B. The woman spilt coffee on the man's jacket.

    C. The man misunderstood the woman's apology.

    D. The woman offered to pay for the man's coffee.

16. A. Extremely tedious.

    B. Not worth seeing twice.

    C. Hard to understand.

    D. Lacking a good plot.

17. A. Reading very extensively.

    B. Attending every lecture.

    C. Doing lots of homework.

    D. Using test-taking strategies.

18. A. He thinks it unrealistic to have 500 channels.

    B. He is eager to see what the new system is like.

    C. The digital TV system will offer different programs.

    D. The new TV system may not provide anything better.

Questions 19 to 22 are based on the conversation you have just heard.

19. A. A notice by the electricity board.

    B. A new policy on pensioners' welfare.

    C. Ads promoting electric appliances.

    D. The description of a thief in disguise.

20. A. Showing them his ID.

    B. Speaking with a proper accent.

    C. Wearing an official uniform.

    D. Making friends with them.

21. A. To watch out for those from the electricity board.

    B. Not to let anyone in without an appointment.

    C. Not to leave senior citizens alone at home.

    D. To be on the alert when being followed.

22. A. She was robbed near the parking lot.

    B. All her money in the bank disappeared.

    C. She was knocked down in the post office.

    D. The pension she had just drawn was stolen.

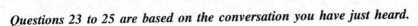

Questions 23 to 25 are based on the conversation you have just heard.

23. A. Luxury hotel management.

    B. Professional accountancy.

    C. Marketing consultancy.

    D. Business conference organization.

24. A. Being able to speak Japanese.

    B. Having been to the country before.

    C. Knowing some key people in tourism.

    D. Having a good knowledge of its customs.

25. A. It will give her more chances to visit Japan.

    B. It will involve lots of train travel.

    C. It will bring her potential into full play.

    D. It will enable her to improve her Chinese.

Section B

Directions: In this section, you will hear 3 short passages. At the end of each passage, you will hear some questions. Both the passages and the questions will be spoken only once. After you hear a question, you must choose the best answer from the four choices marked A, B, C and D. Then mark the corresponding letter on Answer Sheet 2 with a single line through the centre.

Passage One

Questions 26 to 28 are based on the passage you have just heard.

26. A. The quality of life.

    B. The lack of time.

    C. The pressure on working families.

    D. The frustrations at work.

27. A. They lived a hard life by hunting and gathering.

    B. They didn't complain as much as modern man.

    C. They saw the importance of collective efforts.

    D. They were just as busy as people of today.

28. A. To explore strategies for lowering production cost.

    B. To seek new approaches to dealing with complaints.

C. To find effective ways to give employees flexibility.

D. To look for creative ideas of awarding employees.

Passage Two

Questions 29 to 31 are based on the passage you have just heard.

29. A. The Great Depression.

B. Her father's disloyalty.

C. Family violence.

D. Her mother's bad temper.

30. A. His advanced age.

B. His improved financial condition.

C. His children's efforts.

D. His second wife's positive influence.

31. A. Love breeds love.

B. Love is blind.

C. Happiness is hard to find in blended families.

D. Divorce often has disastrous consequences.

Passage Three

Questions 32 to 35 are based on the passage you have just heard.

32. A. It went bankrupt all of a sudden.

B. It was located in a park.

C. Its owner died of heart attack.

D. Its potted plants were for lease only.

33. A. Helping a customer select some purchases.

B. Putting up a Going Out of Business sign.

C. Planting some trees in the greenhouse.

D. Writing a want ad to a local newspaper.

34. A. Building a big greenhouse of his own.

B. Keeping better relations with her company.

C. Opening an office in the new office park.

D. Developing fresh business opportunities.

35. A. Securing a job at the office park.

B. Cultivating more potted plants.

C. Owning the greenhouse one day.

D. Finding customers out of town.

Section C

Directions: In this section, you will hear a passage three times. When the passage is read for the first time, you should listen carefully for its general idea. When the passage is read for the second time, you are required to fill in the blanks numbered from 36 to 43 with the exact words you have just heard. For blanks numbered from 44 to 46 you are required to fill in the missing information. For these blanks, you can either use the exact words you have just heard or write down the main points in your own words. Finally, when the passage is read for the third time, you should check what you have written.

We're now witnessing the emergence of an advanced economy based on information and knowledge. Physical (36) _____, raw materials, and capital are no longer the key (37) _____ in the creation of wealth. Now the (38) _____ raw material in our economy is knowledge. Tomorrow's wealth depends on the development and exchange of knowledge. And (39) _____ entering the workforce offer their knowledge, not their muscles. Knowledge workers get paid for their education and their ability to learn. Knowledge workers (40) _____ in mind work. They deal with symbols: words, (41) _____, and data.

What does all this mean for you? As a future knowledge worker, you can expect to be (42) _____, processing, as well as exchanging information. (43) _____, three out of four jobs involve some form of mind work, and that number will increase sharply in the future. Management and employees alike (44) _____.

In the new world of work, you can look forward to being in constant training (45) _____. You can also expect to be taking greater control of your career. Gone are the nine-to-five jobs, lifetime security, predictable promotions, and even the conventional workplace, as you are familiar with. (46) _____.
And don't wait for someone to "empower" you. You have to empower yourself.

2007 年 12 月英语四级听力全真试题

Part Ⅲ　　　　　　　**Listening Comprehension**　　　　　　（**35 minutes**）
Section A

Directions：In this section，you will hear 8 short conversations and 2 long conversations. At the end of each conversation，one or more questions will be asked about what was said. Both the conversations and the questions will be spoken only once. After each question there will be a pause. During the pause，you must read the four choices marked A，B，C and D，and decide which is the best answer. Then mark the corresponding letter on the Answer Sheet 2 with a single line through the centre.

11. A. She used to be in poor health.
    B. She didn't do well at high school.
    C. She was popular among boys.
    D. She was somewhat overweight.

12. A. At the airport.
    B. At the hotel reception.
    C. In a restaurant.
    D. In a booking office.

13. A. Having confidence in her son.
    B. Telling her son not to worry.
    C. Teaching her son by herself.
    D. Asking the teacher for extra help.

14. A. Have a short break.
    B. Take two weeks off.
    C. Go on vacation with the man.
    D. Continue her work outdoors.

15. A. He is taking care of his twin brother.
    B. He worries about Rod's health.
    C. He has been in perfect condition.
    D. He has been feeling ill all week.

16. A. She bought a new set of furniture from Italy last month.

B. She sold all her furniture before she moved house.

C. She plans to put all her old furniture in the basement.

D. She still keeps some old furniture in her new house.

17. A. The woman forgot lending the book to the man.

B. The woman doesn't find the book useful any more.

C. The woman doesn't seem to know what the book is about.

D. The woman wondered why the man didn't return the book.

18. A. Most of the man's friends are athletes.

B. The man doesn't look like a sportsman.

C. Few people share the woman's opinion.

D. The woman doubts the man's athletic ability.

Questions 19 to 22 are based on the conversation you have just heard.

19. A. She is afraid that she has lost it.

B. She is going to get it at the airport.

C. She has packed it in one of her bags.

D. She has probably left it in a taxi.

20. A. It will cost her a lot.

B. It will last one week.

C. It ends in winter.

D. It depends on the weather.

21. A. There is a lot of stuff to pack.

B. There might be a traffic jam.

C. The plane is taking off soon.

D. The taxi is waiting for them.

22. A. At home.

B. In the man's car.

C. By the side of a taxi.

D. At the airport.

Questions 23 to 25 are based on the conversation you have just heard.

23. A. She is thirsty for promotion.

B. She is tired of her present work.

C. She wants a much higher salary.

D. She wants to save travel expenses.

24. A. Language instructor.
    B. Environmental engineer.
    C. Translator.
    D. Travel agent.
25. A. Devotion and work efficiency.
    B. Lively personality and inquiring mind.
    C. Communication skills and team spirit.
    D. Education and experience.

Section B

Directions: **In this section, you will hear 3 short passages. At the end of each passage, you will hear some questions. Both the passages and the questions will be spoken only once. After you hear a question, you must choose the best answer from the four choices marked A, B, C and D. Then mark the corresponding letter on the Answer Sheet 2 with a single line through the centre.**

Passage One

Questions 26 to 29 are based on the passage you have just heard.

26. A. They want children to keep them company.
    B. They want to enrich their life experience.
    C. They need looking after in their old age.
    D. They care a lot about children.
27. A. Their birth parents often try to conceal their birth information.
    B. They are usually adopted from distant places.
    C. Their birth information is usually kept secret.
    D. Their adoptive parents don't want them to know their birth parents.
28. A. They do not want to hurt the feelings of their adoptive parents.
    B. They have mixed feelings about finding their natural parents.
    C. They generally hold bad feelings towards their birth parents.
    D. They are fully aware of the expenses involved in the search.
29. A. Adoption has much to do with love.
    B. Understanding is the key to successful adoption.
    C. Most people prefer to adopt children from overseas.

D. Early adoption makes for closer parent-child relationship.

Passage Two

Questions 30 to 32 are based on the passage you have just heard.

   30. A. He suffered from mental illness.

       B. He bought the *Washington Post*.

       C. He was once a reporter for a major newspaper.

       D. He turned a failing newspaper into a success.

   31. A. She committed suicide because of her mental disorder.

       B. She got her first job as a teacher at the University of Chicago.

       C. She was the first woman to lead a big U. S. publishing company.

       D. She took over her father's position when he died.

   32. A. Catharine had exerted an important influence on the world.

       B. People came to see the role of women in the business world.

       C. American media would be quite different without Catharine.

       D. Catharine played a major part in reshaping Americans' mind.

Passage Three

Questions 33 to 35 are based on the passage you have just heard.

   33. A. It'll allow them to receive free medical treatment.

       B. It'll prevent the doctors from overcharging them.

       C. It'll enable them to enjoy the best medical care.

       D. It'll protect them from possible financial crises.

   34. A. They may not be able to receive timely medical treatment.

       B. They can only visit doctors who speak their native language.

       C. They have to go through very complicated application procedures.

       D. They can't immediately get back the money paid for their medical cost.

   35. A. They must send the receipts to the insurance company promptly.

       B. They have to pay a much higher price to get an insurance policy.

       C. They needn't pay the entire medical bill at once.

       D. They don't have to pay for the medical services.

Section C

Directions: In this section, you will hear a passage three times. When the passage is read for the first time, you should listen carefully for its general idea. When the passage is read for the second time, you are required to fill in the blanks numbered from 36 to 43 with the exact words you have just heard. For blanks numbered from 44 to 46 you are required to fill in the missing information. For these blanks, you can either use the exact words you have just heard or write down the main points in your own words. Finally, when the passage is read for the third time, you should check what you have written.

More and more of the world's population are living in towns or cities. The speed at which cities are growing in the less developed countries is (36) _____. Between 1920 and 1960, big cities in developed countries (37) _____ two and a half times in size, but in other parts of the world the growth was eight times their size.

The (38) _____ size of growth is bad enough, but there are now also very (39) _____ signs of trouble in the (40) _____ of percentages of people living in towns and percentages of people working in industry. During the 19th century, cities grew as a result of the growth of industry. In Europe the (41) _____ of people living in cities was always smaller than that of the (42) _____ working in factories. Now, however, the (43) _____ is almost always true in the newly industrialized world: (44) _____.

Without a base of people working in industry, these cities cannot pay for their growth. (45) _____.
There has been little opportunity to build water supplies or other facilities. (46) _____, a growth in the number of hopeless and despairing parents and starving children.

2007 年 6 月英语四级听力全真试题

Part Ⅲ　　　　　　　　**Listening Comprehension**　　　　　　（**35 minutes**）

Section A

Directions：**In this section, you will hear 8 short conversations and 2 long conversations. At the end of each conversation, one or more questions will be asked about what was said. Both the conversations and the questions will be spoken only once. After each question there will be a pause. During the pause, you must read the four choices marked A, B, C and D, and decide which is the best answer. Then mark the corresponding letter on the Answer Sheet 2 with a single line through the centre.**

11. A. It could help people of all ages to avoid cancer.

    B. It was mainly meant for cancer patients.

    C. It might appeal more to viewers over 40.

    D. It was frequently interrupted by commercials.

12. A. The man is fond of traveling.

    B. The woman is a photographer.

    C. The woman took a lot of pictures at the contest.

    D. The man admires the woman's talent in writing.

13. A. The man regrets being absent-minded.

    B. The woman saved the man some trouble.

    C. The man placed the reading list on a desk.

    D. The woman emptied the waste paper basket.

14. A. He quit teaching in June.

    B. He has left the army recently.

    C. He opened a restaurant near the school.

    D. He has taken over his brother's business.

15. A. She seldom reads books from cover to cover.

    B. She is interested in reading novels.

    C. She read only part of the book.

    D. She was eager to know what the book was about.

16. A. She was absent all week owing to sickness.

B. She was seriously injured in a car accident.

C. She called to say that her husband had been hospitalized.

D. She had to be away from school to take care of her husband.

17. A. The speakers want to rent the Smiths' old house.

B. The man lives two blocks away from the Smiths.

C. The woman is not sure if she is on the right street.

D. The Smiths' new house is not far from their old one.

18. A. The man had a hard time finding a parking space.

B. The woman found they had got to the wrong spot.

C. The woman was offended by the man's late arrival.

D. The man couldn't find his car in the parking lot.

Questions 19 to 22 are based on the conversation you have just heard.

19. A. The hotel clerk had put his reservation under another name.

B. The hotel clerk insisted that he didn't make any reservation.

C. The hotel clerk tried to take advantage of his inexperience.

D. The hotel clerk couldn't find his reservation for that night.

20. A. A grand wedding was being held in the hotel.

B. There was a conference going on in the city.

C. The hotel was undergoing major repairs.

D. It was a busy season for holiday-makers.

21. A. It was free of charge on weekends.

B. It had a 15% discount on weekdays.

C. It was offered to frequent guests only.

D. It was 10% cheaper than in other hotels.

22. A. Demand compensation from the hotel.

B. Ask for an additional discount.

C. Complain to the hotel manager.

D. Find a cheaper room in another hotel.

Questions 23 to 25 are based on the conversation you have just heard.

23. A. An employee in the city council at Birmingham.

B. Assistant Director of the Admissions Office.

C. Head of the Overseas Students Office.

D. Secretary of Birmingham Medical School.

24. A. Nearly fifty percent are foreigners.

    B. About fifteen percent are from Africa.

    C. A large majority are from Latin America.

    D. A small number are from the Far East.

25. A. She will have more contact with students.

    B. It will bring her capability into fuller play.

    C. She will be more involved in policy-making.

    D. It will be less demanding than her present job.

Section B

Directions: In this section, you will hear 3 short passages. At the end of each passage, you will hear some questions. Both the passages and the questions will be spoken only once. After you hear a question, you must choose the best answer from the four choices marked A, B, C and D. Then mark the corresponding letter on the Answer Sheet 2 with a single line through the centre.

Passage One

Questions 26 to 28 are based on the passage you have just heard.

26. A. Her parents thrived in the urban environment.

    B. Her parents left Chicago to work on a farm.

    C. Her parents immigrated to America.

    D. Her parents set up an ice-cream store.

27. A. He taught English in Chicago.

    B. He was crippled in a car accident.

    C. He worked to become an executive.

    D. He was born with a limp.

28. A. She was fond of living an isolated life.

    B. She was fascinated by American culture.

    C. She was very generous in offering help.

    D. She was highly devoted to her family.

Passage Two

Questions 29 to 32 are based on the passage you have just heard.

29. A. He suffered a nervous breakdown.

    B. He was wrongly diagnosed.

    C. He was seriously injured.

    D. He developed a strange disease.

30. A. He was able to talk again.

    B. He raced to the nursing home.

    C. He could tell red and blue apart.

    D. He could not recognize his wife.

31. A. Twenty-nine days.

    B. Two and half a month.

    C. Several minutes.

    D. Fourteen hours.

32. A. They welcomed the publicity in the media.

    B. The avoided appearing on television.

    C. They released a video of his progress.

    D. They declined to give details of his condition.

Passage Three

Questions 33 to 35 are based on the passage you have just heard.

33. A. For people to share ideas and show farm products.

    B. For officials to educate the farming community.

    C. For farmers to exchange their daily necessities.

    D. For farmers to celebrate their harvests.

34. A. By bringing an animal rarely seen on nearby farms.

    B. By bringing a bag of grain in exchange for a ticket.

    C. By offering to do a volunteer work at the fair.

    D. By performing a special skill at the entrance.

35. A. They contribute to the modernization of American farms.

    B. They help to increase the state governments' revenue.

    C. They provide a stage for people to give performances.

    D. They remind Americans of the importance of agriculture.

Section C

Directions: In this section, you will hear a passage three times. When the passage is read for the first time, you should listen carefully for its general idea. When the passage is read for the second time, you are required to fill in the blanks numbered from 36 to 43 with the exact words you have just heard. For blanks numbered from 44 to 46 you are required to fill in the missing information. For these blanks, you can either use the exact words you have just heard or write down the main points in your own words. Finally, when the passage is read for the third time, you should check what you have written.

Students' pressure sometimes comes from their parents. Most parents are well (36) _____, but some of them aren't very helpful with the problems their sons and daughters have in (37) _____ to college, and a few of them seem to go out of their way to add to their children's difficulties. For one thing, parents are often not (38) _____ of the kinds of problems their children face. They don't realize that the (39) _____ is keener, that the required (40) _____ of work are higher, and that their children may not be prepared for the change. (41) _____ to seeing A's and B's on high school report cards, they may be upset when their children's first (42) _____ college grades are below that level. At their kindest, they may gently (43) _____ why John or Mary isn't doing better, whether he or she is trying as hard as he or she should, and so on. (44) _____.
Sometimes parents regard their children as extensions of themselves and (45) _____. In their involvement and identification with their children, they forget that everyone is different and that each person must develop in his or her own way. They forget that their children, (46) _____.

2006 年 12 月英语四级听力全真试题

Part III   **Listening Comprehension**   **(35 minutes)**

Section A

Directions: In this section, you will hear 8 short conversations and 2 long conversations. At the end of each conversation, one or more questions will be asked about what was said. Both the conversations and the questions will be spoken only once. After each question there will be a pause. During the pause, you must read the four choices marked A, B, C and D, and decide which is the best answer. Then mark the corresponding letter on the Answer Sheet 2 with a single line through the centre.

11. A. Plan his budget carefully.

    B. Give her more information.

    C. Ask someone else for advice.

    D. Buy a gift for his girlfriend.

12. A. She'll have some chocolate cake.

    B. She'll take a look at the menu.

    C. She'll go without dessert.

    D. She'll prepare the dinner.

13. A. The man can speak a foreign language.

    B. The woman hopes to improve her English.

    C. The woman knows many different languages.

    D. The man wishes to visit many more countries.

14. A. Go to the library.

    B. Meet the woman.

    C. See Professor Smith.

    D. Have a drink in the bar.

15. A. She isn't sure when Professor Bloom will be back.

    B. The man shouldn't be late for his class.

    C. The man can come back sometime later.

    D. She can pass on the message to the man.

16. A. He has a strange personality.

    B. He's got emotional problems.

    C. His illness is beyond cure.

    D. His behavior is hard to explain.

17. A. The tickets are more expensive than expected.

    B. The tickets are sold in advance at half price.

    C. It's difficult to buy the tickets on the spot.

    D. It's better to buy the tickets beforehand.

18. A. He turned suddenly and ran into a tree.

    B. He was hit by a fallen box from a truck.

    C. He drove too fast and crashed into a truck.

    D. He was trying to overtake the truck ahead of him.

Questions 19 to 21 are based on the conversation you have just heard.

19. A. To go boating on the St. Lawrence River.

    B. To go sightseeing in Quebec Province.

    C. To call on a friend in Quebec City.

    D. To attend a wedding in Montreal.

20. A. Study the map of Quebec Province.

    B. Find more about Quebec City.

    C. Brush up on her French.

    D. Learn more about the local customs.

21. A. It's most beautiful in summer.

    B. It has many historical buildings.

    C. It was greatly expanded in the 18th century.

    D. It's the only French-speaking city in Canada.

Questions 22 to 25 are based on the conversation you have just heard.

22. A. It was about a little animal.

    B. It took her six years to write.

    C. It was adapted from a fairy tale.

    D. It was about a little girl and her pet.

23. A. She knows how to write best-selling novels.

    B. She can earn a lot of money by writing for adults.

    C. She is able to win enough support from publishers.

    D. She can make a living by doing what she likes.

24. A. The characters.

    B. The readers.

    C. Her ideas.

    D. Her life experiences.

25. A. She doesn't really know where they originated.

    B. She mainly drew on stories of ancient saints.

    C. They popped out of her childhood dreams.

    D. They grew out of her long hours of thinking.

Section B

Directions: In this section, you will hear 3 short passages. At the end of each passage, you will hear some questions. Both the passages and the questions will be spoken only once. After you hear a question, you must choose the best answer from the four choices marked A, B, C and D. Then mark the corresponding letter on the Answer Sheet 2 with a single line through the centre.

Passage One

Questions 26 to 28 are based on the passage you have just heard.

26. A. Monitor students' sleep patterns.

    B. Help students concentrate in class.

    C. Record students' weekly performance.

    D. Ask students to complete a sleep report.

27. A. Declining health.   B. Lack of attention.

    C. Loss of motivation.   D. Improper behavior.

28. A. They should make sure their children are always punctual for school.

    B. They should ensure their children grow up in a healthy environment.

    C. They should help their children accomplish high-quality work.

    D. They should see to it that their children have an adequate sleep.

Passage Two

Questions 29 to 32 are based on the passage you have just heard.

29. A. She stopped being a homemaker.

    B. She became a famous educator.

C. She became a public figure.

      D. She quit driving altogether.

30. A. A motorist's speeding.

      B. Her running a stop sign.

      C. Her lack of driving experience.

      D. A motorist's failure to concentrate.

31. A. Nervous and unsure of herself.

      B. Calm and confident of herself.

      C. Courageous and forceful.

      D. Distracted and reluctant.

32. A. More strict training of women drivers.

      B. Restrictions on cell phone use while driving.

      C. Improved traffic conditions in cities.

      D. New regulations to ensure children's safety.

Passage Three

Questions 33 to 35 are based on the passage you have just heard.

33. A. They haven't devoted as much energy to medicine as to space travel.

      B. There are too many kinds of cold viruses for them to identify.

      C. It is not economical to find a cure for each type of cold.

      D. They believe people can recover without treatment.

34. A. They reveal the seriousness of the problem.

      B. They indicate how fast the virus spreads.

      C. They tell us what kind of medicine to take.

      D. They show our body is fighting the virus.

35. A. It actually does more harm than good.

      B. It causes damage to some organs of our body.

      C. It works better when combined with other remedies.

      D. It helps us to recover much sooner.

Section C

Directions: In this section, you will hear a passage three times. When the passage is read for the first time, you should listen carefully for its general idea. When

the passage is read for the second time, you are required to fill in the blanks numbered from 36 to 43 with the exact words you have just heard. For blanks numbered from 44 to 46 you are required to fill in the missing information. For these blanks, you can either use the exact words you have just heard or write down the main points in your own words. Finally, when the passage is read for the third time, you should check what you have written.

You probably have noticed that people express similar ideas in different ways, depending on the situation they are in. This is very (36) _____. All languages have two general levels of (37) _____: a formal level and an informal level. English is no (38) _____. The difference in these two levels is the situation in which you use a (39) _____ level. Formal language is the kind of language you find in textbooks, (40) _____ books, and in business letters. You would also use formal English in compositions and (41) _____ that you write in school. Informal language is used in conversation with (42) _____, family members and friends, and when we write (43) _____ notes or letters to close friends.

Formal language is different from informal language in several ways. First, formal language tends to be more polite. (44) _____.
For example, I might say to a friend or family member "Close the door, please," (45) _____
Another difference between formal and informal language is some of the vocabulary. (46) _____. Let's say that I really like soccer. If I am talking to my friend I might say "I am just crazy about soccer!", but if I were talking to my boss, I would probably say "I really enjoy soccer."

2006 年 6 月英语四级听力全真试题

Part I   Listening Comprehension   (20 minutes)

Section A

Directions: In this section, you will hear 10 short conversations. At the end of each conversation, a question will be asked about what was said. Both the conversations and the questions will be spoken only once. After each question there will be a pause. During the pause, you must read the four choices marked A, B, C and D, and decide which is the best answer. Then mark the corresponding letter on the Answer Sheet with a single line through the center.

1. A. They went a long way to attend the party.
   B. They didn't think much of the food and drinks.
   C. They knew none of other guests at the party.
   D. They enjoyed the party better than other guests.

2. A. To the bookstore.
   B. To the dentist's.
   C. To the market.
   D. To the post office.

3. A. Dr. Andrews has been promoted for his thoroughness.
   B. She disagrees with Dr. Andrews on many occasions.
   C. Dr. Andrews used to keep his patients waiting.
   D. She dislikes Dr. Andrews as much as the new physician.

4. A. Tom is usually talkative.
   B. Tom has a very bad temper.
   C. Tom has dozens of things to attend to.
   D. Tom is disliked by his colleagues.

5. A. To pick up the woman from the library.
   B. To make a copy of the schedule for his friend.
   C. To find out more about the topic for the seminar.
   D. To get the seminar schedule for the woman.

6. A. The woman has to get the textbooks in other ways.
   B. The woman has sold her used textbooks to the bookstore.

C. The man is going to buy his textbooks from a bookstore.

    D. The man doesn't want to sell his textbooks to the woman.

7. A. Attend a conference.

    B. Give a speech.

    C. Meet his lawyer.

    D. Make a business trip.

8. A. Jessie always says what she thinks.

    B. Jessie seems to have a lot on her mind.

    C. Jessie is wrong to find fault with her boss.

    D. Jessie should know the marketing director better.

9. A. Helen is talkative.

    B. Helen is active.

    C. Helen is sociable.

    D. Helen is quiet.

10. A. Jimmy will regret marrying a Frenchwoman.

    B. Jimmy is not serious in making decisions.

    C. Jimmy is rich enough to buy a big house.

    D. Jimmy's words are often not reliable.

Section B

Directions: In this section, you will hear 3 short passages. At the end of each passage, you will hear some questions. Both the passages and the questions will be spoken only once. After you hear a question, you must choose the best answer from the four choices marked A, B, C and D. Then mark the corresponding letter on the Answer Sheet with a single line through the centre.

Passage One

Questions 11 to 13 are based on the passage you have just heard.

11. A. It can be used by farmers to protect large buildings.

    B. It was brought to the northern USA by Asian farmers.

    C. It has done more harm than good in the southern USA.

    D. It was introduced into the USA to kill harmful weeds.

12. A. People will have to rely on Kudzu for a living.

B. They will soon be overgrown with Kudzu.

　　　C. They will become too hard to plough.

　　　D. People will find it hard to protect the soil.

　13. A. The farmers there have brought it under control.

　　　B. The factories there have found a good use for it.

　　　C. The climate there is unfavorable to its growth.

　　　D. The soil there is not so suitable for the plant.

Passage Two

Questions 14 to 16 are based on the passage you have just heard.

　14. A. A business corporation.

　　　B. The universe as a whole.

　　　C. A society of legal professionals.

　　　D. An association of teachers and scholars.

　15. A. Its largest expansion took place during that period.

　　　B. Its role in society went through a dramatic change.

　　　C. Small universities combined to form bigger ones.

　　　D. Provincial colleges were taken over by larger universities.

　16. A. Private donations.

　　　B. Government funding.

　　　C. Grants from corporations.

　　　D. Fees paid by students.

Passage Three

Questions 17 to 20 are based on the passage you have just heard.

　17. A. He was wounded in the Spanish Civil War.

　　　B. He was interested in the study of wild animals.

　　　C. He started the organization Heifer International.

　　　D. He sold his cows to many countries in the world.

　18. A. To help starving families to become self-supporting.

　　　B. To make plans for the development of poor communities.

　　　C. To teach people how to use new skills to raise animals.

　　　D. To distribute food to the poor around the world.

19. A. They should help other families in the way they have been helped.
    B. They should offer all baby animals to their poor neighbors.
    C. They should submit a report of their needs and goals.
    D. They should provide food for the local communities.

20. A. It has improved animal breeding skills all over the world.
    B. It has helped relieve hunger in some developing countries.
    C. It has promoted international exchange of farming technology.
    D. It has bridged the gap between the rich and the poor in America.

2005 年 12 月英语四级听力全真试题

Part Ⅰ   Listening Comprehension   （20 minutes）

Section A

Directions：In this section, you will hear 10 short conversations. At the end of each conversation, a question will be asked about what was said. Both the conversations and the questions will be spoken only once. After each question there will be a pause. During the pause, you must read the four choices marked A, B, C and D, and decide which is the best answer. Then mark the corresponding letter on the Answer Sheet with a single line through the center.

1. A. See a doctor.

   B. Stay in bed for a few days.

   C. Get treatment in a better hospital.

   D. Make a phone call to the doctor.

2. A. The 2:00 train will arrive earlier.

   B. The 2:30 train has a dining car.

   C. The woman prefers to take the 2:30 train.

   D. They are gong to have some fast food on the train.

3. A. She has been longing to attend Harvard University.

   B. She'll consider the man's suggestion carefully.

   C. She has finished her project with Dr. Garcia's help.

   D. She'll consult Dr. Garcia about entering graduate school.

4. A. Alice didn't seem to be nervous during her speech.

   B. Alice needs more training in making public speeches.

   C. The man can hardly understand Alice's presentation.

   D. The man didn't think highly of Alice's presentation.

5. A. It's worse than 30 years ago.

   B. It remains almost the same as before.

   C. There are more extremes in the weather.

   D. There has been a significant rise in temperature.

6. A. At a publishing house.   B. At a bookstore.

   C. In a reading room.   D. In Prof. Jordan's office.

7. A. The man can stay in her brother's apartment.

   B. Her brother can help the man find a cheaper hotel.

   C. Her brother can find an apartment for the man.

   D. The man should have booked a less expensive hotel.

8. A. Priority should be given to listening.

   B. It's most helpful to read English newspapers every day.

   C. It's more effective to combine listening with reading.

   D. Reading should come before listening.

9. A. It can help solve complex problems.

   B. It will most likely prove ineffective.

   C. It is a new weapon against terrorists.

   D. It will help detect all kinds of liars.

10. A. Help the company recruit graduate students.

    B. Visit the electronics company next week.

    C. Get a part-time job on campus before graduation.

    D. Apply for a job in the electronics company.

Section B

Directions: In this section, you will hear 3 short passages. At the end of each passage, you will hear some questions. Both the passages and the questions will be spoken only once. After you hear a question, you must choose the best answer from the four Choices marked A, B, C and D. Then mark the corresponding letter on the Answer sheet with a single line through the center.

Passage One

Questions 11 to 13 are based on the passage you have just heard.

11. A. It has been proven to be the best pain-killer.

    B. It is a possible cure for heart disease.

    C. It can help lower high body temperature effectively.

    D. It reduces the chance of death for heart surgery patients.

12. A. It keeps blood vessels from being blocked.

    B. It speeds up their recovery after surgery.

    C. It increases the blood flow to the heart.

D. It adjusts their blood pressure.

13. A. It is harmful to heart surgery patients with stomach bleeding.

    B. It should not be taken by heart surgery patients before the operation.

    C. It will have considerable side effects if taken in large doses.

    D. It should not be given to patients immediately after the operation.

Passage Two

Questions 14 to 16 are based on the passage you have just heard.

14. A. They strongly believe in family rules.

    B. They are very likely to succeed in life.

    C. They tend to take responsibility for themselves.

    D. They are in the habit of obeying their parents.

15. A. They grow up to be funny and charming.

    B. They often have a poor sense of direction.

    C. They get less attention from their parents.

    D. They tend to be smart and strong-willed.

16. A. They usually don't follow family rules.

    B. They don't like to take chances in their lives.

    C. They are less likely to be successful in life.

    D. They tend to believe in their parent's ideas.

Passage Three

Questions 17 to 20 are based on the passage you have just heard.

17. A. They wanted to follow his example.

    B. They fully supported his undertaking.

    C. They were puzzled by his decision.

    D. They were afraid he wasn't fully prepared.

18. A. It is more exciting than space travel.

    B. It is much cheaper than space travel.

    C. It is much safer than space travel.

    D. It is less time-consuming than space travel.

19. A. They both attract scientists' attention.

    B. They can both be quite challenging.

C. They are both thought-provoking.

       D. They may both lead to surprising findings.

20. A. To show how simple the mechanical aids for diving can be.

       B. To provide an excuse for his changeable character.

       C. To explore the philosophical issues of space travel.

       D. To explain why he took up underwater exploration.

2005 年 6 月英语四级听力全真试题

Part I   Listening Comprehension   (20 minutes)

Section A

Directions: In this section, you will hear 10 short conversations. At the end of each conversation, a question will be asked about what was said. Both the conversations and the questions will be spoken only once. After each question there will be a pause. During the pause, you must read the four choices marked A, B, C and D, and decide which is the best answer. Then mark the corresponding letter on the Answer Sheet with a single line through the center.

1. A. The man hates to lend his tools to other people.
   B. The man hasn't finished working on the bookshelf.
   C. The tools have already been returned to the woman.
   D. The tools the man borrowed from the woman are missing.

2. A. Give the ring to a policeman.
   B. Wait for the owner of the ring in the rest room.
   C. Hand in the ring to the security office.
   D. Take the ring to the administration building.

3. A. Save time by using a computer.
   B. Buy her own computer.
   C. Borrow Martha's computer.
   D. Stay home and complete her paper.

4. A. The man doesn't have money for his daughter's graduate studies.
   B. The man doesn't think his daughter will get a business degree.
   C. The man insists that his daughter should pursue her studies in science.
   D. The man advises his daughter to think carefully before making her decision.

5. A. The cinema is some distance away from where they are.
   B. He would like to read the film review in the newspaper.
   C. They should wait to see the movie at a later time.
   D. He'll find his way to the cinema.

6. A. He's been to Seattle many times.
   B. He has chaired a lot of conferences.

91

C. He has a high position in his company.

    D. He lived in Seattle for many years.

7. A. Teacher and student.

    B. Doctor and patient.

    C. Manager and office worker.

    D. Travel agent and customer.

8. A. She knows the guy who will give the lecture.

    B. She thinks the lecture might be informative.

    C. She wants to add something to her lecture.

    D. She'll finish her report this weekend.

9. A. An art museum.

    B. A beautiful park.

    C. A college campus.

    D. An architectural exhibition.

10. A. The houses for sale are of poor quality.

    B. The houses are too expensive for the couple to buy.

    C. The housing developers provide free trips for potential buyers.

    D. The man is unwilling to take a look at the houses for sale.

Section B

Directions: In this section, you will hear 3 short passages. At the end of each passage, you will hear some questions. Both the passages and the questions will be spoken only once. After you hear a question, you must choose the best answer from the four choices marked A, B, C and D. Then mark the corresponding letter on the Answer Sheet with a single line through the centre.

Passage One

Questions 11 to 13 are based on the passage you have just heard.

11. A. Synthetic fuel.   B. Solar energy.

    C. Alcohol.   D. Electricity.

12. A. Air traffic conditions.   B. Traffic jams on highways.

    C. Road conditions.   D. New traffic rules.

13. A. Go through a health check.   B. Carry little luggage.

C. Arrive early for boarding.　　　D. Undergo security checks.

Passage Two

Questions 14 to 17 are based on the passage you have just heard.

14. A. In a fast-food restaurant.　　B. At a shopping center.
    C. At a county fair.　　　　　　D. In a bakery.
15. A. Avoid eating any food.　　　 B. Prepare the right type of pie to eat.
    C. Wash his hands thoroughly.　 D. Practise eating a pie quickly.
16. A. On the table.　　　　　　　　B. Behind his back.
    C. Under his bottom.　　　　　　D. On his lap.
17. A. Looking sideways to see how fast your neighbor eats.
    B. Eating from the outside toward the middle.
    C. Swallowing the pie with water.
    D. Holding the pie in the right position.

Passage Three

Questions 18 to 20 are based on the passage you have just heard.

18. A. Beauty.　　　　　　　　　　 B. Loyalty.
    C. Luck.　　　　　　　　　　　　D. Durability.
19. A. He wanted to follow the tradition of his country.
    B. He believed that it symbolized an everlasting marriage.
    C. It was thought a blood vessel in that finger led directly to the heart.
    D. It was supposed that the diamond on that finger would bring a good luck.
20. A. The two people can learn about each other's likes and dislikes.
    B. The two people can have time to decide if it is a good match.
    C. The two people can have time to shop for their new home.
    D. The two people can earn enough money for their wedding.

第三部分 听力模拟试题答案

Unit 1

1. A 2. C 3. B 4. C 5. A 6. D 7. B 8. D 9. A 10. B
11. A 12. B 13. D 14. B 15. C 16. C 17. B 18. D 19. C
20. D 21. B 22. B 23. D 24. A 25. C

26. squarely 27. floating 28. Occasionally 29. dutifully 30. witty

31. humorous 32. guilt 33. material

34. the instructor talks about road construction in ancient Rome, and nothing could be more boring

35. Your blank expression, and the faraway look in your eyes are the cues that betray your inattentiveness

36. they automatically start daydreaming when a speaker begins talking on something complex or uninteresting

Unit 2

1. C 2. A 3. D 4. C 5. D 6. A 7. C 8. A 9. C 10. B
11. D 12. C 13. C 14. A 15. B 16. B 17. C 18. B 19. A
20. C 21. D 22. D 23. B 24. B 25. B

26. enjoyable 27. shelter 28. unaware 29. realities 30. attraction

31. possible 32. content 33. approach

34. In a bookshop, an assistant should remain in the background until you have finished browsing

35. You have to be careful not to be attracted by the variety of books in a bookshop

36. Apart from running up a huge amount, you can waste a great deal of time

wandering from section to section

Unit 3

1. B　2. A　3. C　4. B　5. A　6. B　7. D　8. B　9. C　10. C
11. B　12. A　13. B　14. B　15. C　16. A　17. D　18. C　19. B
20. D　21. D　22. C　23. D　24. A　25. B
26. mysterious　27. coupled　28. ruining　29. percent　30. species
31. commercial　32. ensure　33. average
34. When you consider that equals a quarter of the world catch, you begin to see the size of the problem
35. some countries are beginning to deal with this problem, but it's vital that we find a rational way of fishing
36. Before every ocean becomes a dead sea, it would make sense to give the fish enough time to recover, grow to full size and reproduce

Unit 4

1. B　2. C　3. C　4. A　5. D　6. B　7. C　8. B　9. B　10. A
11. D　12. B　13. A　14. B　15. D　16. B　17. A　18. B　19. C
20. A　21. B　22. D　23. A　24. C　25. A
26. ancient　27. spoken　28. speeches　29. advanced　30. special
31. process　32. modern　33. probably
34. Perhaps it came into existence with the great increase in population and the development of modern industry
35. Certainly, during examinations, teachers and students are expected to act as machines
36. To make up an objective test, the teacher writes a series of questions, each of which has only one correct answer

Unit 5

1. A　2. C　3. B　4. D　5. A　6. C　7. D　8. B　9. B　10. A

11. C　12. C　13. A　14. C　15. B　16. D　17. C　18. D　19. C
20. C　21. A　22. C　23. C　24. B　25. D
26. raise　27. figures　28. mountains　29. instruments　30. butterflies
31. enjoyment　32. relaxation　33. profit
34. Hobbies also offer interesting activities for persons who have retired
35. Hobbies can help a person's mental and physical health
36. Many hospitals treat patients by having them take up interesting hobbies or pastimes

Unit 6

1. C　2. C　3. B　4. A　5. D　6. B　7. B　8. D　9. A　10. C
11. C　12. B　13. D　14. C　15. A　16. B　17. A　18. A　19. B
20. A　21. C　22. D　23. B　24. A　25. B
26. Curiosity　27. freedom　28. constraints　29. prevent　30. imaginative
31. pattern　32. possibilities　33. genius
34. It means looking at situations in a new way or putting something together in a new form that makes sense
35. But the figure 8 can be visualized as two zeros, one on top of the other, or it can also be seen as two 3s standing face to face
36. If each of us asked the question "why" more often and investigated "other" alternatives to problem solving, our lives would be more interesting and exciting

Unit 7

1. D　2. B　3. A　4. C　5. B　6. C　7. D　8. C　9. D　10. B
11. B　12. C　13. A　14. A　15. D　16. D　17. B　18. D　19. C
20. B　21. B　22. D　23. C　24. C　25. D
26. effort　27. officials　28. negotiate　29. balanced　30. competition
31. exchange　32. process　33. environmental
34. These "greenhouse gases" trap heat in the atmosphere and are blamed for changing the world's climate
35. But currently, nations producing only 44 percent have approved the Protocol
36. To join the WTO, a country must reach trade agreements with major trading

countries that are also WTO members

Unit 8

1. A 2. D 3. D 4. B 5. A 6. D 7. D 8. C 9. B 10. D
11. D 12. C 13. A 14. C 15. B 16. D 17. A 18. C 19. D
20. C 21. D 22. A 23. D 24. D 25. D
26. strike 27. seldom 28. different 29. sets 30. shallower
31. bottom 32. strength 33. shore
34. may strike the shore with a force of 75 million pounds
35. no matter how big or how violent, affect only the surface of the sea
36. the water a hundred fathoms (600 feet) beneath the surface is just as calm as on the day without a breath of wind

Unit 9

1. B 2. C 3. D 4. B 5. C 6. D 7. D 8. C 9. B 10. D
11. B 12. B 13. B 14. A 15. C 16. D 17. C 18. D 19. B
20. C 21. A 22. B 23. B 24. D 25. D
26. proportion 27. motivates 28. loans 29. attend 30. enroll
31. attitude 32. democratic 33. intelligent
34. Before World War II, a high school education seemed adequate for satisfying most people's needs
35. Americans rarely express a direct vote on such complex matters
36. In recent years, as a result, many Americans have begun to regard a college education as necessary to becoming an informed American voter

Unit 10

1. A 2. D 3. C 4. B 5. A 6. D 7. D 8. C 9. D 10. C
11. B 12. C 13. A 14. C 15. A 16. D 17. A 18. B 19. B
20. C 21. D 22. D 23. A 24. C 25. A
26. scores 27. loses 28. depend 29. personal 30. compared

31. determining 32. puzzled 33. reasons
34. he can find himself being a useful partner to someone of whom he is ordinarily afraid
35. it is his place to give order, to pretend to be dead, to throw a ball actually at someone, or to kiss someone he had caught
36. Those rules may be childish, but they make sure that every child has a chance to win

Unit 11

1. A 2. D 3. B 4. D 5. A 6. D 7. B 8. C 9. A 10. B
11. B 12. D 13. D 14. A 15. B 16. D 17. A 18. C 19. B
20. C 21. B 22. C 23. A 24. B 25. C
26. opening 27. especially 28. arrived 29. program 30. restore
31. proposed 32. budget 33. supported
34. So did parents, teachers, former students, and business community and some organizations
35. Students use the Internet to complete research, writing homework and required papers on the computers
36. That is especially helpful for the many students who have family members in other nations

Unit 12

1. B 2. D 3. C 4. D 5. B 6. C 7. C 8. C 9. D 10. A
11. C 12. D 13. C 14. B 15. C 16. D 17. B 18. D 19. A
20. C 21. B 22. A 23. D 24. B 25. D
26. religious 27. advertised 28. encouragement 29. require 30. beliefs
31. concerned 32. examine 33. express
34. If your arguments are not logical, professors personally point out the false reasoning in your arguments
35. Put it this way: professors don't tell you what to think, they try to teach you how to think
36. Arguing just for the sake of arguing usually does not promote a critical examination

of ideas

Unit 13

1. D 2. B 3. C 4. D 5. B 6. D 7. C 8. D 9. A 10. B

11. D 12. A 13. B 14. D 15. A 16. D 17. A 18. B 19. A

20. B 21. A 22. D 23. B 24. C 25. D

26. vacation 27. blamed 28. slightest 29. breathing 30. awaked

31. prescribed 32. occasional 33. continual

34. has developed a nine-step treatment to help

35. you will be able to sleep more soundly

36. includes advice on daytime as well as bedtime behavior.

第四部分 听力历年全真试题答案

2008 年 6 月英语四级听力答案

11. C 12. A 13. A 14. D 15. B 16. C 17. B 18. D 19. D
20. A 21. B 22. D 23. C 24. A 25. B 26. B 27. D 28. C
29. A 30. D 31. A 32. C 33. B 34. D 35. C

36. labor 37. ingredients 38. vital 39. individuals 40. engage 41. figures
42. generating 43. Currently

44. will be making decisions in such areas as product development, quality control and customer satisfaction

45. to acquire new skills that will help you keep up with improved technologies and procedures

46. Don't expect the companies will provide you with a clearly defined career path

2007 年 12 月英语四级听力答案

11. D 12. B 13. A 14. A 15. C 16. D 17. A 18. B 19. C
20. B 21. D 22. A 23. B 24. C 25. D 26. D 27. C 28. B
29. A 30. B 31. C 32. A 33. D 34. D 35. C

36. alarming 37. increased 38. sheer 39. disturbing 40. comparison
41. proportion 42. workforce 43. reverse

44. The percentage of people living in cities is much higher than the percentage working in industry

45. There is not enough money to build adequate houses for the people that live there, let alone the new arrivals

46. So the figure for the growth of towns and cities represent proportional growth of unemployment and underemployment

2007 年 6 月英语四级听力答案

11. C　12. D　13. B　14. A　15. C　16. D　17. D　18. A　19. D
20. B　21. A　22. C　23. B　24. A　25. C　26. C　27. B　28. D
29. C　30. A　31. B　32. D　33. A　34. B　35. D
36. meaning　37. adjusting　38. aware　39. competition　40. standards
41. Accustomed　42. semester　43. inquire
44. At their worst, they may threaten to take their children out of college, or cut off funds
45. think it only right and natural that they determine what their children do with their lives
46. who are now young adults, must be the ones responsible for what they do and what they are

2006 年 12 月英语四级听力答案

11. B　12. C　13. A　14. C　15. D　16. B　17. D　18. A　19. D
20. C　21. B　22. A　23. D　24. C　25. A　26. C　27. B　28. D
29. C　30. D　31. A　32. B　33. B　34. D　35. A
36. natural　37. usage　38. exception　39. particular　40. reference
41. essays　42. colleagues　43. personal
44. What we may find interesting is that it usually takes more words to be polite
45. But to a stranger, I probably would say, "Would you mind closing the door?"
46. There are bound to be some words and phrases that belong in formal language and others that are informal

2006 年 6 月英语四级听力答案

1. C　2. B　3. C　4. A　5. D　6. A　7. B　8. A　9. D　10. D　11. C
12. B　13. C　14. D　15. A　16. B　17. C　18. A　19. A　20. B

2005 年 12 月英语四级听力答案

1. A 2. C 3. D 4. A 5. C 6. B 7. A 8. C 9. B 10. D 11. D
12. A 13. A 14. B 15. C 16. A 17. C 18. B 19. B 20. D

2005 年 6 月英语四级听力答案

1. D 2. C 3. B 4. D 5. A 6. A 7. C 8. B 9. C 10. D 11. D
12. A 13. B 14. C 15. A 16. B 17. B 18. A 19. C 20. B

第五部分　听力模拟试题
录音原稿

Unit 1

Section A

Directions： In this section, you will hear 8 short conversations and 2 long conversations. At the end of each conversation, one or more questions will be asked about what was said. Both the conversations and the questions will be spoken only once. After each question there will be a pause. During the pause, you must read the four choices marked A, B, C and D, and decide which is the best answer.

1. W：Mr. Robin's briefing seems to go on forever. I was barely able to stay awake.

   M：How could you sleep through that? It was very important for the mission we are going to carry out.

   Q：What does the man imply?

2. M：Did you check the power plug and press the "play" button?

   W：Yes, the power indicator was on, and it was running, but somehow the sound didn't come through.

   Q：What was the woman probably trying to do?

3. W：What are these things in our suitcase? There aren't any toys at all. Where have you put them?

   M：Oh no. This is not our suitcase. The old lady must have taken ours by mistake. She was sitting next to us at the restaurant.

   Q：What can be inferred from the conversation?

4. M：Are you really leaving for Hongkong tomorrow morning?

W: Yeah, I guess so. I've got my air ticket, and just can't wait to see Bill there.

Q: What's the woman going to do?

5. W: I just can't believe this is our last year. College is going by fast.

M: Yeah. We'll have to face the real world soon. So have you figured out what you're going to do after graduation?

Q: What do we learn from the conversation?

6. M: I had a hard time getting through this novel.

W: I share your feeling. Who can remember the names of 35 different characters?

Q: What does the woman imply?

7. M: Can I borrow your math textbook? I lost mine on the bus.

W: You've asked the right person. I happen to have an extra copy.

Q: What does the woman mean?

8. W: If the weather is this hot tomorrow, we may as well give up the idea of playing tennis in the afternoon.

M: Oh, I don't think it will last long. The weather forecast says it will cloud over by mid-afternoon.

Q: What does the man mean?

Now you will hear two long conversations.

Conversation One

M: Hello, and welcome to our program— "Working Abroad". Our guest this evening is a Londoner, who lives and works in Italy. Her name's Jane Hill. Jane, welcome to the program. You live in Florence, how long have you been living there?

W: Since 1982. But when I went there in 1982, I planned to stay for only 6 months.

M: Why did you change your mind?

W: Well, I'm a designer, I design leather goods, mainly shoes and handbags. Soon after I arrived in Florence, I got a job with one of Italy's top fashion houses— Ferragamo. So, I decided to stay.

M: How lucky! Do you still work for Ferragamo?

W: No, I've been a freelance designer for quite a long time now. Since 1988, in fact.

M: So does that mean you design for several different companies now?

W: Yes, that's right. I design many fashion items for a number of Italian companies, and during last four years, I've also been designing for the British company—Burberry.

M: What have you been designing for them?

W: Mostly handbags, and small leather goods.

M: How's the fashion industry in Italy changed since 1982?

W: Oh, yes. It's become a lot more competitive because the quality of products from other countries has improved a lot. But its high quality and design is still world-famous.

M: And do you ever think of returning to live in England?

W: No, not really. Working in Italy is more interesting. I also love the Mediterranean sun and the Italian life style.

M: Well, thank you for talking to us, Jane.

W: It was a pleasure.

Questions 9 to 12 are based on the conversation you have just heard.

9. Where does this conversation most probably take place?

10. What was the woman's original plan when she went to Florence?

11. What has the woman been doing for a living since 1988?

12. What do we learn about the change in Italy's fashion industry?

Conversation Two

M: So, Susan, you're into drama!

W: Yes, I have a master's degree in drama and theatre. At the moment, I'm hoping to get onto a Ph. D program.

M: What excite you about drama?

W: Well, I find it's a communicative way to study people and you learn how to read people in drama. So usually I can understand what people are saying even though they might be lying.

M: That would be useful.

W: Yeah, it's very useful for me as well. I'm in English lecture, so use a lot of drama in my classes such as role plays. And I ask my students to create mini-dramas. They really respond well. At the moment, I'm hoping to get onto a Ph. D course. I'd like to concentrate on Asian drama and try to bring Asian theatre to the world's attention. I don't know how successful I would be, but, here's hoping.

M: Oh, I'm sure you'll be successful. Now, Susan, what do you do for stage fright?

W: Ah, stage fright! Well, many actors have that problem. I get stage fright every time I'm going to teach a new class. The night before, I usually can't sleep.

M: What? For teaching?

W: Yes. I get really bad stage fright. But the minute I step into the classroom or get onto the stage, it just all falls into place. Then I just feel like: Yeah, this is what I mean to do. And I'm fine.

M: Wow, that's cool!

Questions 13 to 15 are based on the conversation you have just heard.

    13. Why does the woman find study in drama and theatre useful?

    14. How did the woman's students respond to her way of teaching English?

    15. What does the woman say about her stage fright?

Section B

Directions: In this section, you will hear 3 short passages. At the end of each passage, you will hear some questions. Both the passages and the questions will be spoken only once. After you hear a question, you must choose the best answer from the four choices marked A, B, C and D.

Passage One

    China vowed on Monday to organize a "non-smoking" Olympic Games, but health officials admitted that changing the habits of 350 million smokers would be difficult.

    China would enforce a ban on smoking in public places. Zhangbin, a health ministry official, held a news conference on Monday, with those places that offer services to children a top concern. "Smoking will be banned at all Olympic-designated hospitals by the end of 2007," Xinhua News Agency quoted Zhang as saying. The ban would also apply to public transport and offices, Zhang said, acknowledging that changing habits would be hard, "China faces many obstacles to overcome in hosting a non-smoking Olympics," he said.

    The ministry's vow came as Beijing passed the 10th anniversary of its ban on smoking in public places. In practice, many of the capital's millions of smokers habitually ignore the bans given that they run only a slight risk of punishment or complaint from bystanders.

China is the world's largest producer and consumer of cigarettes with nearly 2 trillion consumed a year. The World Health Organization estimates that smoking kills 1. 2 million people a year in China.

Questions 16 to 18 are based on the passage you have just heard.

16. According to the passage, what kind of Olympic Games did China vow on Monday to hold?

17. When will smoking be banned at all Olympic-designated hospitals?

18. Which of the following statements is true according to the passage?

Passage Two

Western doctors are beginning to understand what traditional healers have always known——the body and the mind are inseparable. Until recently, modern urban physicians heal the body, psychiatrists the mind, and priests the soul. However, the medical world is now paying more attention to holistic medicine which is an approach based on the belief that people's state of mind can make them sick or speed up their recovery from sickness. Several studies show that the effectiveness of a certain drug often depends on the patient's expectations of it. For example, in one recent study, psychiatrists and a major hospital tried to see how patients could be made calm. They divided them into two groups. One group was given a drug while the other group received a harmless substance instead of medicine without their knowledge. Surprisingly, more patients in the second group showed the desired effect than those in the first group. In the study, there's a positive reaction in almost one-third of the patients taking harmless substances. How was this possible? How could such a substance have an effect on the body? Evidence from a 1997 study at the University of California showed that several patients who received such substances were able to produce their own natural drug, that was, as they took the substance their brains released natural chemicals that acted like a drug. Scientists theorized that the amount of these chemicals released by a person's brain quite possibly indicated how much faith the person had in his or her doctor.

Questions 19 to 21 are based on the passage you have just heard.

19. According to the speaker, what are western doctors beginning to understand?

20. What did the recent study at a major hospital seem to prove?

21. What did the evidence from a 1997 study at the University of California show?

Passage Three

Americans suffer from an overdose of work. Regardless of who they are or what they do, Americans have spent more time at work than on anything else since World War II. In 1950, the U.S. had fewer working hours than any other industrialized country. Today it exceeds any country but Japan, where industrial employees log 2,155 hours a year, compared with 1,951 in the U.S., and 1,603 in the former West Germany. Between 1969 and 1989 employed Americans added an average of 138 hours to their yearly work schedules. The work week has remained at about 40 hours, but people are working more weeks each year. Specifically, paid time off, holidays, vacations, sick leave shrank by 50 % in the 1980's. As corporations experienced stiff competition and slower growth productivity, they pressed employees to work longer. Cost cutting lay-offs in the 1980's reduced the professional and managerial ranks leaving fewer people to get the job done. In lower paid occupations, when wages are reduced, workers add hours in overtime or extra jobs to preserve their living standards. The government estimates that more than 7 million people hold a second job. For the first time, large numbers of people say they want to cut back on working hours even if it means earning less money. But most employers are unwilling to let them do so. The government, which has stepped back from its traditional role as a regulator of work time should take steps to make shorter hours possible.

Questions 22 to 25 are based on the passage you have just heard.

22. In which country do the employees work the longest hours?
23. How do employed Americans manage to work more hours?
24. Why do corporations press the employees to work longer hours according to the speaker?
25. What do many Americans prefer to do according to the speaker?

Section C

Directions: In this section, you will hear a passage three times. When the passage is read for the first time, you should listen carefully for its general idea. When the passage is read for the second time, you are required to fill in the blanks numbered from 26 to 33 with the exact words you have just heard. For blanks numbered from 34 to 36 you are required to fill in the missing

information. For these blanks, you can either use the exact words you have just heard or write down the main points in your own words. Finally, when the passage is read for the third time, you should check what you have written.

If you are like most people, you've indulged in fake listening many times. You go to history class, sit in the 3rd row, and look (26) squarely at the instructor as she speaks. But your mind is far away, (27) floating in the clouds of pleasant daydreams. (28) Occasionally you come back to earth. The instructor writes an important term on the chalkboard, and you (29) dutifully copy it in your notebook. Every once in a while the instructor makes a (30) witty remark, causing others in the class to laugh. You smile politely, pretending that you've heard the remark and found it mildly (31) humorous. You have a vague sense of (32) guilt that you aren't paying close attention. But you tell yourself that any (33) material you miss can be picked up from a friend's notes. Besides, (34) the instructor talks about road construction in ancient Rome, and nothing could be more boring. So back you go into your private little world, only later do you realize you've missed important information for a test. Fake listening may be easily exposed, since many speakers are sensitive to facial cues and can tell if you're merely pretending to listen. (35) Your blank expression, and the faraway look in your eyes are the cues that betray your inattentiveness. Even if you are not exposed, there's another reason to avoid fakery. It's easy for this behavior to become a habit. For some people, the habit is so deeply rooted that (36) they automatically start daydreaming when a speaker begins talking on something complex or uninteresting. As a result, they miss lots of valuable information.

Unit 2

Section A

Directions: In this section, you will hear 8 short conversations and 2 long conversations. At the end of each conversation, one or more questions will be asked about what was said. Both the conversations and the questions will be spoken only once. After each question there will be a pause. During the pause, you must read the four choices marked A, B, C and D, and decide which is the best answer.

1. M: Good morning. Do you have a table for two, please?

   W: Certainly. Where would you like to sit? By the window or further back?

   Q: What is the man going to do?

2. W: Well, do you mind if I don't join you for lunch? I have something rather urgent to attend to.

   M: What could be more urgent than having lunch since it's 12:00 already?

   Q: What are the speakers likely to do then?

3. W: Do you ever meet the customers by yourself?

   M: Oh, yes. Quite often. The important customers, such as the Government, always deal directly with me.

   Q: What does the man do?

4. W: I think what we need is a new product. The products we are selling now are becoming old-fashioned.

   M: But we haven't got the money to pay for a new design.

   Q: What does the woman think about the products they are selling?

5. M: Alice. You haven't finished your report yet?

   W: It's like this, you see. I've had all Miss Blake's work to do because she's been ill this week.

   Q: Why hasn't the woman finished her report?

6. M: I thought you were going to see your brother last weekend.

   W: I intended to, but at the last minute he called and said that he would be in Hangzhou for a meeting at the weekend, so I stayed home altogether!

   Q: What did the woman do last weekend?

7. W: I really don't want to paint the room this weekend, Tom.

   M: Neither do I. But I think we should get it over.

   Q: What does the man suggest?

8. M: It's a lovely day. Why don't we go for a walk?

   W: Can you wait a few minutes? I have to finish this letter.

   Q: What do you think the woman will do?

Now you will hear two long conversations.

Conversation One

M: Hi, Claire, mind if I sit down?

W: Not at all, Jason. How have you been?

M: Good. But I'm surprised to see you on the city bus. Your car in the shop?

W: No. I've just been thinking a lot about the environment lately. So I decided the air would be a lot cleaner if we all used public transportation when we could.

M: I'm sure you are right. The diesel bus isn't exactly pollution free.

W: True. They'll be running a lot cleaner soon. We were just talking about that in my environmental engineering class.

M: What could the city do? Install pollution filters in all their buses?

W: They could, but those filters make the engines work harder and really cut down on the fuel efficiency. Instead they found a way to make their engines more efficient.

M: How?

W: Well, there is a material that's a really good insulator. And a thin coat of it gets sprayed on the certain part of the engine.

M: An insulator?

W: Yeah. What it does is reflecting back the heat of burning fuel. So the fuel will burn much hotter and burn up more completely.

M: So a lot less unburned fuel comes out to pollute the air.

W: And the bus will need less fuel, so with the saving on fuel cost, they say this will all pay for itself in just six months.

M: Sounds like people should all go out and get some of this stuff to spray their car engines.

W: Well, it's not really that easy. You see, normally, the materials are fine powder. To melt it so you can spray a coat of it on the engine parts, you first have to heat it over 10,000 degrees and then, well, you get the idea. It's not something you or I will be able to do ourselves.

Questions 9 to 11 are based on the conversation you have just heard.

    9. What is the conversation mainly about?

    10. Why did the woman decide to take the city bus?

    11. What is the new material?

Conversation Two

M: How was your weekend?

W: It was awful.

M: Awful? Really? But I thought you planned to be going on a trip. Did you cancel it?

W: No. Unfortunately. I would have been better off if we had canceled it.

M: What do you mean?

W: Well. Five of us were supposed to go to Chicago in Tina's car...

M: Yeah?

W: And we were going to stay at Sue's parents' house which is in Chicago...

M: Right?

W: So it's about a four-hour trip, and we were going to get there on Friday evening, and spend Saturday sight-seeing, and come back last night so we could go to classes this morning.

M: OK. That sounds like a good plan. So what went wrong?

W: What didn't go wrong? First of all, we were all crammed into Tina's tiny car with all our bags.

M: Sounds pretty uncomfortable.

W: Hold on. I'm just getting started. Remember how hot it was this weekend?

M: Yeah, it was so bad that I had to get out of the library. I ended up going to the beach both days.

W: Well, we were stuck in Tina's car Friday afternoon and the air conditioning wasn't working.

M: Why didn't you open the windows?

W: We did, but the breezes blowing in were also hot.

M: I think you were glad to get to Chicago.

W: That's the worst part. We never made it. The car broke down and we were waiting for the car to be repaired the whole Saturday in some small town near the Indiana border.

M: Couldn't Sue's parents come to pick you up?

W: They were out of town.

Questions 12 to 15 are based on the conversation you have just heard.

12. What's the purpose of their trip to Chicago?

13. Why didn't opening the car's windows make them comfortable?

14. Why did the man go to the beach during the weekend?

15. How did the woman probably spend most of the past weekend?

Section B

Directions: In this section, you will hear 3 short passages. At the end of each passage, you will hear some questions. Both the passages and the questions will be spoken only once. After you hear a question, you must choose the best answer from the four choices marked A, B, C and D.

Passage One

Right, everybody. Welcome to Central College Library Services. My name's Kathy Jenkins. I'll give you a brief introduction to the library. We have a well-stocked bank of resources which are in three main locations: the library itself, with books and periodicals; the self-access language centre with audio and video material; and the micro-computer lab. I'll start with the micro-computer lab, or micro-lab as we call it. It is fitted with 24 personal computers.

If you are a member of the library, you may borrow CALL discs in French, German, Italian, Spanish and Russian as well as English. By the way, CALL stands for computer aided language learning: C A double L, "CALL", for short. You may also borrow a range of word processing and desktop publishing packages. All disks are, of course, strictly for use in the micro-lab only. If you wish to print anything, you should use one of the five machines around the outside of the room. Four are connected to the dot matrix printers, one is connected to the laser printer. If you want a top quality printout from the laser printer, come and see myself or any of the library staff. Dot-matrix printouts are free but there is a charge for using the laser printer.

There is always a queue to get to the terminals towards the end of term. Come in and get to know how to use the computers early in the term and use them regularly, rather than just before exams and essay deadlines, in order to avoid delay or disappointment. Training sessions are held on a regular basis, on the first and third Thursday of each month, and are free to full-time students of the college. See you there. Now, any questions?

Questions 16 to 18 are based on the passage you have just heard.

16. What does the speaker suggest that the students should do during the term?
17. What service must be paid for?
18. What is the passage mainly about?

Passage Two

St. Valentine's Day

On February 14th many people in the world celebrate an unusual holiday—St. Valentine's Day, a special day for lovers. Valentine cards usually are red and shaped like hearts with messages of love written on them. Lovers send these cards to each other on that day, often without signing their names.

The origin of this holiday is uncertain but according to one story it gets its name from a Christian named Valentine who lived in Rome during the 3rd century A. D. . His job was to perform marriages for Christian couples. Unfortunately the Emperor of Rome didn't allow Christian marriages. So they had to be performed in secret. Finally Valentine was arrested and put into prison. While he was in prison he fell in love with the daughter of the prison guard. After one year the Emperor offered to release Valentine if he would stop performing Christian marriages. Valentine refused and so he was killed in February, 270 A. D. . Before he was killed, Valentine sent a love letter to the daughter of the prison guard. He signed the letter "from your Valentine". That was the valentine.

Today tens of millions of people send and receive valentines on St. Valentine's Day. Whether it is an expensive heart-shaped box of chocolates from a secret admirer or a simple hand-made card from a child, a valentine is a very special message of love.

Questions 19 to 21 are based on the passage you have just heard.

19. What is the passage mainly about?
20. Why was Valentine killed?
21. Why do people send valentines to each other nowadays?

Passage Three

"Where is the university" is a question many visitors to Cambridge ask, but no one could point them in any one direction because there is no campus. The university consists of thirty-one self-governing colleges. It has lecture halls, libraries, laboratories, museums and offices throughout the city.

Individual colleges choose their own students, who have to meet the minimum entrance requirements set by the university. Undergraduates usually live and study in their colleges, where they are taught in very small groups. Lectures, and laboratory and practical work are organized by the university and held in university buildings.

The university has a huge number of buildings for teaching and research. It has more than sixty specialist subject libraries, as well as the University Library, which, as a copyright library, is entitled to a copy of every book published in Britain.

Examinations are set and degrees are awarded by the university. It allowed women to take the university exams in 1881, but it was not until 1948 that they were awarded degrees.

Questions 22 to 25 are based on the passage you have just heard.

22. Why is it difficult for visitors to locate Cambridge University?
23. What does the passage tell us about the colleges of Cambridge University?
24. What can be learned from the passage about the libraries in Cambridge University?
25. What does the passage tell us about women students in Cambridge University?

Section C

Directions: In this section, you will hear a passage three times. When the passage is read for the first time, you should listen carefully for its general idea. When the passage is read for the second time, you are required to fill in the blanks numbered from 26 to 33 with the exact words you have just heard. For blanks numbered from 34 to 36 you are required to fill in the missing information. For these blanks, you can either use the exact words you have just heard or write down the main points in your own words. Finally, when the passage is read for the third time, you should check what you have written.

Some people like watching TV at home and others may love hiking. But I like being at a bookshop. Time spent in a bookshop can be most (26) <u>enjoyable</u>, whether you are a book-lover or merely there to buy a book as a present. You may even have entered the shop to find (27) <u>shelter</u> from a sudden shower. Whatever the reason is, you can soon become totally (28) <u>unaware</u> of your surroundings. The opportunity to escape the (29) <u>realities</u> of every day life is, I think, the main (30) <u>attraction</u> of a bookshop. Looking around, one might not be able to see many places where it is (31) <u>possible</u> to do this. You can wander around such a place to your heart's (32) <u>content</u>. If it is a good shop, no assistant will (33) <u>approach</u> you with the inevitable greeting: "Can I help you, sir?" (34) <u>In a bookshop, an assistant should remain in the background until you have finished browsing</u>. Then, and only then, are his services necessary.

(35) <u>You have to be careful not to be attracted by the variety of books in a bookshop</u>. It is very easy to enter the shop looking for a book on, say, ancient coins and to come out carrying a copy of the latest best-selling novel. This sort of thing can be very dangerous. (36) <u>Apart from running up a huge amount, you can waste a great deal of time wandering from section to section</u>.

Unit 3

Section A

Directions: In this section, you will hear 8 short conversations and 2 long conversations. At the end of each conversation, one or more questions will be asked about what was said. Both the conversations and the questions will be spoken only once. After each question there will be a pause. During the pause, you must read the four choices marked A, B, C and D, and decide which is the best answer.

1. M: Excuse me, could you tell me where Dr. Brown's office is?

   W: The doctor's office is on the fifth floor, but the elevator can only go to the fourth. So you'll have to use the stairs to reach there. It's the seventh room on the left.

   Q: On which floor is the doctor's office?

2. M: Did you hear about the computer that John bought from Morris?

   W: He got a bargain, didn't he?

   Q: What do we learn from the conversation?

3. W: Your sister Jane didn't recognize me at first.

   M: I'm not surprised. Why on earth don't you lose some weight?

   Q: What does the man suggest the woman do?

4. M: Between the two houses we saw yesterday, which one do you prefer?

   W: I think the white one is prettier, but the brick one has a bigger yard, so I like it better.

   Q: Which house does the woman prefer?

5. M: It sure is hot today. This must be the hottest summer in years.

   W: Well, it's certainly hotter than last summer. I was out in the sun today, and I think I'm five pounds lighter than I was this morning.

   Q: What does the woman mean?

6. M: I heard the student bus was overturned in a traffic accident.

   W: Yes, and what's more, no one on the bus was not injured.

   Q: What do we learn from the conversation?

7. W: Hello, Robert. What are you doing here? Drawing money?

M: No. I only want to put some money in my deposit account. Not very much, but I'm trying to save.

Q: What is the man doing?

8. M: Oh, no, I am not lazy. You should have seen my school report! They said I was reliable, industrious and conscientious.

W: Well, teachers nowadays expect too little.

Q: What does the woman think of teachers nowadays?

Now you will hear two long conversations.

Conversation One

W: OK, last night you were supposed to read an article about human bones. Are there any comments about it?

M: Well, to begin with, I was surprised to find out there was so much going on in bones. I always assumed they were pretty lifeless.

W: Well, that's an assumption many people make. But the fact is bones are made of dynamic living tissue that requires continuous maintenance and repair.

M: Right. That's one of the things I found so fascinating about the article the way the bones repair themselves.

W: OK. So can you tell us how the bones repair themselves?

M: Sure. See, there are two groups of different types of specialized cells in the bone that work together to do it. The first group goes to an area of the bone that needs repair. This group of cells produces the chemical that actually breaks down the bone tissue, and leaves a hole in it. After that the second group of specialized cells comes and produces the new tissue that fills in the hole that was made by the first group.

W: Very good. This is a very complex process. In fact, the scientists who study human bones don't completely understand it yet. They are still trying to find out how it all actually works. Specifically, because sometimes after the first group of cells leaves a hole in the bone tissue, for some reason, the second group doesn't completely fill in the hole. And this can cause real problems. It can actually lead to a disease in which the bone becomes weak and is easily broken.

M: OK, I get it. So if the scientists can figure out what makes the specialized cells work, maybe they can find a way to make sure the second group of cells completely

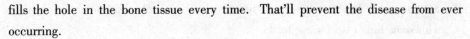

fills the hole in the bone tissue every time. That'll prevent the disease from ever occurring.

Questions 9 to 12 are based on the conversation you have just heard.

9. What is the conversation mainly about?

10. What is the function of the first group of specialized cells discussed in the conversation?

11. What does the woman say about scientists who study the specialized cells in human bones?

12. According to the man, what is one of the important purposes of studying specialized cells in human bones?

Conversation Two

M: So, Lisa, do you have anything planned for this Saturday?

W: Uh, I'm kind of busy. Why do you ask?

M: Oh, I was wondering if you'd like to get together and do something, like watching a movie or taking a walk down the lake.

W: I'd love to, but I'm really going to be busy all day on Saturday.

M: What are you going to do on that day?

W: First, my mom asked me to help clean the house in the morning, and then I have a doctor's appointment at 12:30. I can't miss that because I've canceled twice before.

M: Well, what about after that?

W: Well, I'm going to be running around all day. After the doctor's appointment, I need to meet Julie at 2:00 p. m. to help her with her science project that's due on Monday morning at school.

M: Okay, but are you free after that?

W: Hardly. Then I have to pick up my brother from soccer practice at 4:30 p. m., and my mom asked me to cook dinner for the family at 5:30 p. m. . I feel like a slave sometimes. Then, I have to clean the dishes and finish doing my history assignment. Who knows how long that will take.

M: Wow, sounds like you're going to have a full day. Hey, listen, why don't I come over later in the evening, and we can make some popcorn and watch a video.

W: Oh, that'd be great, but our video machine is broken.

M: Huh. Well, let's just play a game or something else.

W: Sounds good, but give me a call before you come. My mom might try to come up with something else for me to do.

Questions 13 to 15 are based on the conversation you have just heard.

13. What does Lisa have to do on Saturday morning?
14. Where does Lisa have to go at 12:30?
15. When is Lisa meeting Julie?

Section B

Directions: In this section, you will hear 3 short passages. At the end of each passage, you will hear some questions. Both the passages and the questions will be spoken only once. After you hear a question, you must choose the best answer from the four choices marked A, B, C and D.

Passage One

A guide dog is a dog especially trained to guide a blind person. Dogs chosen for such training must show good intelligence, physical fitness, and responsibility.

At the age of about fourteen months, a guide dog begins an intensive course that lasts from three to five months. It becomes accustomed to the leather harness and stiff leather handle it will wear when guiding its blind owner. The dog learns to watch traffic and to cross streets safely.

The most important part of the training course is a four-week program in which the guide dog and its future owner learn to work together. However, many blind people are unsuited by personality to work dogs. Only about a tenth of the blind find a guide dog useful.

Questions 16 to 18 are based on the passage you have just heard.

16. How long does the intensive course last?
17. Which of the following is NOT a necessary skill guide dogs have to learn?
18. How long does the most important part of the training course last?

Passage Two

People dream four to six times a night. They dream while they are in the REM stage of sleep, which means rapid eye movement stage in one's sleep. Sleepers go into the REM stage about every 90 minutes. The first dream of the night may last about ten minutes. Each dream gets a little longer. The last dream of the night may be an hour long.

People need their dreams. Younger children spend more time dreaming. Babies spend almost half of their sleep in the REM stage.

One experiment showed that everyone needs to dream. Doctors gave some people sleeping pills. These sleeping pills didn't let them go to REM sleep. After a few nights without dreams, they began to feel bad. They became angry easily, they worried a lot, and they wanted to fight with everyone. Then they stopped taking the sleeping pills. They all began to dream all night for a few nights to catch up.

Why do people dream? Dreams give them time to find the answers to some of their problems. If they think they will have difficult problems the next day, they may spend more time on REM sleep the night before. In their dreams, they may find an answer to their problems.

Questions 19 to 21 are based on the passage you have just heard.

19. How often does a person dream each night?

20. Which of the following statements is true according to the passage?

21. Why do people dream?

Passage Three

OK, everybody. Can we start the meeting now? I'm Jeff Milton, the chairperson of the Graduation Committee for this year. You've all been selected as representatives to plan the graduation ceremonies. I'm sending around the sheet of paper for you to fill in your name and telephone number. Also, please write down what part of the ceremonies you would like to work on. Remember, as a representative, you will have a lot of responsibilities. So only sign up if you feel you have the time to participate. When everyone has finished writing down the information, please return the paper to me. At our next meeting one week from today, we'll start to discuss the details of the ceremonies.

Questions 22 to 25 are based on the passage you have just heard.

22. Who is the speaker?

23. What is the purpose of the meeting?

24. What should the students write on the paper?

25. When is the next meeting?

Section C

Directions: In this section, you will hear a passage three times. When the passage is read for the first time, you should listen carefully for its general idea. When the passage is read for the second time, you are required to fill in the blanks numbered from 26 to 33 with the exact words you have just heard. For blanks numbered from 34 to 36 you are required to fill in the missing information. For these blanks, you can either use the exact words you have just heard or write down the main points in your own words. Finally, when the passage is read for the third time, you should check what you have written.

It's difficult to imagine the sea ever running out of fish. It's so vast, so deep, so (26) mysterious. Unfortunately, it's not bottomless. Over-fishing, (27) coupled with destructive fishing practices, is killing off the fish and (28) ruining their environment.

Destroy the fish, and you destroy the fishermen's means of living. At least 60 (29) percent of the world's commercially important fish (30) species are already over-fished, or fished to the limit. As a result, governments have had to close down some areas of sea to (31) commercial fishing.

Big, high-tech fleets (32) ensure that everything in their path is pulled out of the water. Anything too small, or the wrong thing, is thrown back either dead or dying. That's an (33) average of more than 20 million metric tons every year.

(34) When you consider that equals a quarter of the world catch, you begin to see the size of the problem.

In some parts of the world, for every kilogram of prawns (对虾) caught, up to 15 kilograms of unsuspecting fish and other marine wildlife die, simply for being in the wrong place at the wrong time.

True, (35) some countries are beginning to deal with this problem, but it's vital that we find a rational way of fishing, then catch them in a way that doesn't kill other innocent sea life.

(36) Before every ocean becomes a dead sea, it would make sense to give the fish enough time to recover, grow to full size and reproduce.

Unit 4

Section A

Directions: In this section, you will hear 8 short conversations and 2 long conversations. At the end of each conversation, one or more questions will be asked about what was said. Both the conversations and the questions will be spoken only once. After each question there will be a pause. During the pause, you must read the four choices marked A, B, C and D, and decide which is the best answer.

1. M: Where are you going to live after you leave here?

   W: I would like to live in the city for the sake of my job, but my husband prefers to have a house in the suburb to save on expenses.

   Q: Why does the husband want to live in the suburb?

2. M: If it rains this Sunday, the sports meeting will be postponed.

   W: It doesn't matter. It will be held regardless of the weather.

   Q: What does the woman mean?

3. M: I am sorry to hear that John has been fired, although he was absent a lot and always late for work.

   W: Oh, no. John made a big mistake in accounting last week.

   Q: Why was John fired?

4. W: Can you do me a favor to carry this box upstairs?

   M: Wait a moment. The football match will have a result in 20 minutes.

   Q: What will the man do?

5. M: Jane seems to have lost a lot of weight recently.

   W: Yes. She has been working hard for the speech contest.

   Q: What has Jane been doing?

6. M: Did you see last night's presidential election on TV?

   W: Well. I intended to watch it, but I slept through it.

   Q: What did the woman do last night?

7. W: How do you feel about your roommates?

   M: Well. They are quite nice, although I'm having trouble getting used to living with so many people.

Q: What's the man's problem?

8. W: Have you returned your books to the library?

      M: No. I got Michael do it.

      Q: What does the man say about his books?

Now you will hear two long conversations.

Conversation One

M: How many people are there in your family?

W: Well. There are 7. I think it is really a large one.

M: Really? The largest family in the world has 53 children.

W: Oh, my god! I can't believe it.

M: Mr. and Mrs. Albina don't know where all their grown-up children are living now. Some of them, they know, are in Argentina, but they aren't sure where in Argentina. They aren't sure how old all their children are, either.

W: How is it possible? How can one woman give birth to so many children in her lifetime?

M: Every time Mrs. Albina gave birth, she had twins or triplets.

W: It is so funny. How can they make a living with so many children?

M: Life is really hard for them. The family lives in a two-room hut in Colina, Chile. At times there is very little food in the Albinas' small house. The couple always makes sure the youngest children do not go hungry.

W: Obviously, the Albinas do not have enough money for their big family. Why, then, do they continue to have children?

M: The Albinas do not use birth control because it is against their religion.

W: But they could let other people take care of their children.

M: Mrs. Albina will not allow it.

W: Why?

M: When her two brothers and herself were babies, their mother left them and never returned. Later her two brothers were adopted and she was left behind. So she promised that she would never give her children away.

W: How is the family now?

M: The oldest Albina children are in their 30s and 40s. They are on their own now, but 18 of the Albina children still live with their parents.

W: Will there be more children?

M: Mr. Albina is 77 years old, and Mrs. Albina is 59. She says if God sends her more children, there will be more.

Questions 9 to 12 are based on the conversation you have just heard.

    9. How many people are there in the world's largest family?

   10. Which of the following statements is true about the children?

   11. Why don't the Albinas use birth control?

   12. Why doesn't Mrs. Albina have their children adopted?

Conversation Two

M: What are you going to do this weekend?

W: Well. This Saturday I am going to attend a wedding ceremony in a church.

M: So romantic and sweet! Here in China most wedding ceremonies are held in the hotel.

W: In the United States one can get married in either a civil or religious ceremony.

M: What is a religious ceremony?

W: It is a kind of "all-in-one" event. The couple is bound before the law according to their religious tradition.

M: The majority of Americans have some religious background, so most weddings in the U. S. are of this sort, I think.

W: Yes. And because of the attraction of "walking down the aisle" in a beautiful church ceremony, together with flowers and music, even many couples who aren't religious choose to get married in this traditional way.

M: That is to say their wedding might be held in a church, but not have any strong religious nature to it.

W: Yeah. And, to make it more personal, the couples decide on many things together— from the colour of the flowers, to the dresses and the vows.

M: What about the civil ceremony?

W: It is not much different from those held in China. It takes place usually in the office of a judge.

M: But in most parts of Europe, though, regulations limit one's choices.

W: Yes. In England civil ceremonies must take place in approved buildings.

M: And in France and Germany, the civil wedding and the religious one are completely

125

separate.

W: And I'd like to choose a religious one when I get married.

Questions 13 to 15 are based on the conversation you have just heard.

13. What are they talking about?

14. Which can be inferred about the religious ceremony?

15. Which of the following statements is true according to the conversation?

Section B

Directions: In this section, you will hear 3 short passages. At the end of each passage, you will hear some questions. Both the passages and the questions will be spoken only once. After you hear a question, you must choose the best answer from the four choices marked A, B, C and D.

Passage One

Fifty years ago, in America, "jockey" was used as a noun — a professional horse rider— and as a verb, "to jockey", meaning to lead and steer a horse or something else into a good position.

In the 1920s, radio began to enter American homes. Communication improved and many new words were added to the language. Then, in the 1940s, television appeared. Radio took a back seat. But radio stations still had to entertain. It was then that "jockey" took on a new meaning.

Across the country, thousands of radio stations began to play recorded songs. The records were also known as "discs". Men who knew music, and who could talk and entertain, got jobs on the big city radio stations.

In time, a name was invented for these radio men who talked and played music. They were called "disc jockeys" or DJs probably because they had an influence in making a song popular. They jockeyed (influenced) public taste in music, for many believed that whatever the disc jockeys played was good.

Today, in America, "jockey" can be used for any person who leads or guides something or even himself into a better position or place, often at the expense of others. But it is the DJ with whom we are most familiar. He is the one we hear when we turn on the radio. He plays music for us and brightens up our day with little jokes and old sayings.

Questions 16 to 18 are based on the passage you have just heard.

16. What is the passage mainly about?

17. Which of the following is NOT true about "jockey" 50 years ago?

18. Which of the following statements is true according to the passage?

Passage Two

In America, where labor costs are so high, "do it yourself" is a way of life. Many people repair their own cars, build their own garages, and even rebuild their own houses. Soon many of them will also be writing their own books. In Hollywood there is a company that publishes children's books with the help of computers. Although other book companies also publish that way, this company is not like the others. It allows the reader to become the leading character in the stories with the help of computers. Here is how they do it. Let us suppose the child is named Henry. He lives in New York, and has a dog named Jody. The computer uses this information to make up a story with pictures. The story is then printed up. A child who receives such a book might say, "This book is about me." So the company calls itself the "Me-Books Publishing Company".

Children like the Me-Books because they like to see in print their own names and the names of their friends and their pets. But more important, in this way, readers are much more interested in reading the stories. Me-Books are helping a child to learn to read.

Questions 19 to 21 are based on the passage you have just heard.

19. Why is "do it yourself" a way of life in America?

20. What's the difference between the "Me-Books Publishing Company" and others?

21. Why do children like the Me-Books?

Passage Three

In normal speech we often search for the correct words to convey our exact meaning. The beauty of speech writing is that you can take time to find the correct words. You can use dictionaries. You can also research your topic by reading, which will give you ideas about suitable vocabulary. Do not, however, use someone else's writing as your own as this is stealing. Be careful about using colloquial language, especially when speaking to an international audience. Remember you have to be understood, so ensure that your choice of words is suitable for your listeners.

A careful and imaginative choice of vocabulary can create images in your listeners' minds that will leave a lasting impression. For example, "I saw a little girl" is easily forgotten. What is easier to picture and remember would be: "I saw a delicate child with soft curly blond hair and sparkling blue eyes. She was wearing a simple pale blue dress that brought out her small frame and complimented the delicacy of her milky white complexion."

The use of adjectives and comparisons brings alive a speech, allowing you to convey your message in a memorable way. However, be careful to use language appropriate to your topic and audience. An audience of busy businessmen will not thank you for wasting their time by talking at length in a colourful and poetic manner about a new computer system. What they are interested in is how much it will cost, what will be the savings, what it will do and whether it is reliable.

It is true to say that almost all speeches are enriched and made more memorable by the use of humour. This does not necessarily mean the telling of jokes, although if you know one related to your topic, it may be useful. An occasional joke, humorous comparison or funny personal story that is related to your topic is often a good way to start or end a long speech. If you hear laughter, you will at least know that your audience is still awake!

Questions 22 to 25 are based on the passage you have just heard.

22. What is the the passage mainly about?
23. Which of the following should NOT be done to find the correct words?
24. What does the example show?
25. Which of the following statements is true about using humor?

Section C

Directions: In this section, you will hear a passage three times. When the passage is read for the first time, you should listen carefully for its general idea. When the passage is read for the second time, you are required to fill in the blanks numbered from 26 to 33 with the exact words you have just heard. For blanks numbered from 34 to 36 you are required to fill in the missing information. For these blanks, you can either use the exact words you have just

heard or write down the main points in your own words. Finally, when the passage is read for the third time, you should check what you have written.

In (26) <u>ancient</u> times the most important examinations were (27) <u>spoken</u>, not written. In the schools of ancient Greece and Rome, testing usually consisted of saying poetry aloud or giving (28) <u>speeches</u>. In the European universities of the Middle Ages, students who were working for (29) <u>advanced</u> degrees had to discuss questions in their field of study with people who had made a (30) <u>special</u> study of the subject. This custom exists today as part of the (31) <u>process</u> of testing candidates for the doctor's degree.

Generally, however, (32) <u>modern</u> examinations are written. The written examination, where all students are tested on the same questions, was (33) <u>probably</u> not known until the nineteenth century. (34) <u>Perhaps it came into existence with the great increase in population and the development of modern industry.</u> A room full of candidates for a state examination, timed exactly by electric clocks and carefully watched over by managers, resembles a group of workers at an automobile factory. (35) <u>Certainly, during examinations, teachers and students are expected to act as machines.</u>

One type of test is sometimes called an objective test. It is intended to deal with facts, not personal opinions. (36) <u>To make up an objective test, the teacher writes a series of questions, each of which has only one correct answer.</u>

Unit 5

Section A

Directions: In this section, you will hear 8 short conversations and 2 long conversations. At the end of each conversation, one or more questions will be asked about what was said. Both the conversations and the questions will be spoken only once. After each question there will be a pause. During the pause, you must read the four choices marked A, B, C and D, and decide which is the best answer.

1. M: What would you like for dessert? I think I'll have banana pie and ice cream.

   W: The chocolate cake looks great, but I have to watch my weight. You go ahead and get yours.

   Q: What will the woman most probably do?

2. M: I think the hostess really went out of her way to make the party a success.

   W: Yes, the food and drinks were great, but if only we had known a few of the other guests.

   Q: What did the two speakers think of the party?

3. M: The film starts at 8:30. It's already 8:15.

   W: Let's try to make it.

   Q: What does the woman suggest?

4. W: I left my raincoat in my room. Wait while I go back to get it.

   M: Don't bother, the weather report said it would clear up by noon.

   Q: What does the man advise the woman to do?

5. M: Are you going to the movies tonight?

   W: Only if I finish all my reading assignment first.

   Q: What does the woman's reply suggest?

6. M: Most people agree that Lily looks exactly like her aunt Rose.

   W: Don't you think she takes more after her father?

   Q: What does the woman mean?

7. W: I hardly ever go shopping by car now. The shopping centre is within walking distance.

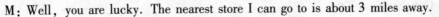

M: Well, you are lucky. The nearest store I can go to is about 3 miles away.

Q: How does the woman go shopping?

8. M: Would you rather eat at home or go out tonight?

W: I'd rather go out, but I don't mind fixing supper at home if you'd rather not go.

Q: What does the woman want to do?

Now you will hear two long conversations.

Conversation One

W: Hi, Adam, do you have a minute to spare?

M: Yes, Dorothea, how can I help you?

W: Well, I have been getting music noises coming from your apartment and it seems like it is always during 9 p.m. to 12 a.m. when I am trying to study. Is it possible to tune down and contain the noise to your apartment then?

M: Oh, I'm so sorry about that. I hadn't been back to my apartment for two weeks and in fact, I just got back today. It must be my new roommate then.

W: I realize that. Could you have a word with him and get him to lower the volume because it is disturbing during the night. It's just, how it is around this time of the year with midterms and everything.

M: Oh, no problem, and I tell you what I won't even mention that it was you who complained.

W: Well, Adam, I appreciate it but I'm afraid that this is not the only issue I want to bring up. Your new roommate is also taking up two parking spaces in the parking lot.

M: Really? I didn't know that! That's selfish of him. Well, Dorothea, not to worry. You bet I will give him a piece of my mind tonight.

W: All right, I hope you can settle all of this soon. Sorry to give you all this bad news now.

M: Oh, don't worry, Dorothea, this will be all settled without a hitch.

Questions 9 to 11 are based on the conversation you have just heard.

9. What does the woman want to complain?

10. What does the woman think of the new roommate's music?

11. What can be concluded from the conversation?

Conversation Two

W: Dad!

M: Yes? What's the matter, Doris?

W: I'm wondering if I should buy a pair of tennis shoes. I'm going to join the tennis club in school.

M: Why not? It's good that you finally play sports.

W: But I'd like to have Adidas.

M: Adidas? It's expensive. It's for the Chicago Bulls!

W: No. All the guys in the school tennis team are wearing Adidas, boys, as well as girls...

M: But none of us has ever had Adidas and we used to play quite OK.

W: Here, Dad, is an ad about Adidas. Can I read it to you?

M: Go ahead.

W: "Over forty years ago, Adidas gave birth to a new idea in sports shoes. And the people who wear our shoes have been running and winning ever since. In fact, Adidas has helped them set over 400 world records in track and field alone."

M: Nonsense! The players have to go through a lot of hard training and practice. It's nothing to do with the shoes. They may be comfortable, but...

W: You're right, Dad. The ad goes on to say "You are born to run. And we were born to HELP YOU DO IT BETTER".

M: Hmm. It may be good for running, but you don't run.

W: Listen, "... Maybe that's why more and more football, soccer, basketball and tennis", see? "TENNIS players are turning to Adidas. They know that, whatever their game is, they can rely on Adidas workmanship and quality in every product we make."

M: OK, OK, dear, I know Adidas is good. But how much is a pair of your size?

W: You don't have to worry about that, Dad. I've saved some money since last Christmas. I just want to hear your opinion.

M: That's good. I have been wanting to have a pair of Adidas sneakers myself.

Questions 12 to 15 are based on the conversation you have just heard.

    12. What does the father think about Adidas shoes?

    13. Why is the father against Doris's idea of buying Adidas?

    14. Why does the father finally agree?

15. What can be inferred from the conversation?

Section B

Directions: In this section, you will hear 3 short passages. At the end of each passage, you will hear some questions. Both the passages and the questions will be spoken only once. After you hear a question, you must choose the best answer from the four choices marked A, B, C and D.

Passage One

The Mooncake Festival or the Mid-Autumn Festival is celebrated by Chinese all over the world every year. It is on the fifteenth day of the eighth month of the Chinese calendar. At this time of the year, the moon appears to be at its brightest and closest to the earth.

On this day families gather for a reunion dinner at home. Delicious dishes are prepared and served. Most important of all, moon cakes are eaten and also sent to friends and relatives as gifts.

In the evening, the children enjoy themselves the most. They light up their lanterns and carry them proudly and happily.

If clouds hide the moon, the children make a lot of noise. Old stories say that the evil monster wants to eat up the moon. The noise will drive the monster away.

Questions 16 to 19 are based on the passage you have just heard.

16. What is the most important thing to do on Mid-Autumn Festival?
17. Who enjoy themselves most in the evening?
18. Why do children make a lot of noise?
19. Why doesn't the moon come out, according to old stories?

Passage Two

Do you remember a time when people were a little nicer and gentler with each other? I certainly do. And I feel that much of the world has somehow gotten away from that. Too often I see people rushing into elevators without giving those inside a chance to get off first, or never saying "thank you" when others hold a door open for them. We get lazy and in our laziness we think that something like a simple "thank you" doesn't really matter. But it can matter very much.

The fact is that no matter how nicely we dress or how beautifully we decorate our homes, we can't be truly elegant without good manners, because elegance and good manners always go hand in hand. In fact, I think of good manners as a sort of hidden beauty secret. Haven't you noticed that the kindest, most generous people seem to keep getting prettier? It's funny how that happens. But it does. Take the long-lost art of saying "thank you". Like wearing a little make-up or making sure your hair is neat, getting into the habit of saying "thank you" can make you feel better about yourself. Good manners add to your image, while an angry face makes the best dressed person look ugly.

Questions 20 to 22 are based on the passage you have just heard.

 20. What is the passage mainly about?

 21. Why don't people say "thank you" now?

 22. According to the speaker, how can we improve our image?

Passage Three

 Memory, they say, is a matter of practice and exercise. If you have the wish and really make a conscious effort, then you can quite easily improve your ability to remember things. But even if you are successful, there are times when your memory seems to play tricks on you.

 Sometimes you remember things that really did not happen. One morning last week, for example, I got up and found that I had left the front door unlocked all night, yet I clearly remember locking it carefully the night before. Memory "tricks" work the other way as well. Once in a while you remember not doing something and then find out that you did. One day last month, for example, I was sitting in a barber shop waiting for my turn to get a haircut, and suddenly I realized that I got a haircut two days before at the barber shop across the street from my office.

 We always seem to find something funny and amusing in incidents caused by people's forgetfulness or absent-mindedness. Stories about absent-minded professors have been told for years, and we never get tired of hearing new ones. Unfortunately, however, absent-mindedness is not always funny. There are times when "tricks" of our memory can cause us great trouble.

Questions 23 to 25 are based on the passage you have just heard.

 23. According to the speaker, what can we do to improve our ability to memorize?

 24. Which of the following statements is NOT true according to the passage?

25. What can be inferred from the passage?

Section C

Directions: In this section, you will hear a passage three times. When the passage is read for the first time, you should listen carefully for its general idea. When the passage is read for the second time, you are required to fill in the blanks numbered from 26 to 33 with the exact words you have just heard. For blanks numbered from 34 to 36 you are required to fill in the missing information. For these blanks, you can either use the exact words you have just heard or write down the main points in you own words. Finally, when the passage is read for the third time, you should check what you have written.

A hobby can be almost anything a person likes to do in his spare time. Hobbyists (26) <u>raise</u> pets, build model ships, weave baskets, or carve soap (27) <u>figures</u>. They watch birds, hunt animals, climb (28) <u>mountains</u>, raise flowers, fish, ski, skate, and swim. Hobbyists also paint pictures, attend concerts and plays, and perform on musical (29) <u>instruments</u>. They collect everything from books to (30) <u>butterflies</u>, and from shells to stamps.

People take up hobbies because these activities offer (31) <u>enjoyment</u>, friendship, knowledge, and (32) <u>relaxation</u>. Sometimes they even yield financial (33) <u>profit</u>. Hobbies can help people relax after periods of hard work, and provide a balance between work and play. (34) <u>Hobbies also offer interesting activities for persons who have retired.</u> Anyone, poor or rich, old or young, sick or well, can follow a satisfying hobby, regardless of his age, position, or income.

(35) <u>Hobbies can help a person's mental and physical health.</u> Doctors have found that hobbies are valuable in helping patients recover from physical or mental illness. Hobbies give bedridden or wheel-chair bound patients something to do, and provide interests that keep them from thinking about themselves. (36) <u>Many hospitals treat patients by having them take up interesting hobbies or pastimes.</u>

Unit 6

Section A

Directions: In this section, you will hear 8 short conversations and 2 long conversations. At the end of each conversation, one or more questions will be asked about what was said. Both the conversations and the questions will be spoken only once. After each question there will be a pause. During the pause, you must read the four choices marked A, B, C and D, and decide which is the best answer.

1. M: One good thing about it is the higher salary. It's perfect for me.

   W: I'm sure you will be better off, but I guess you might have to work longer hours.

   Q: What does the woman mean?

2. M: Well, Mrs. White, I've completed my examination and I'm happy to say that there's nothing serious.

   W: Don't you think I should have X-rays?

   Q: What's the probable relationship between the two speakers?

3. M: Is anything wrong? You look pale.

   W: My son is in the hospital. I must ask for a leave to take care of him.

   Q: What happened to the woman?

4. M: What's my share of the bill? $ 18.50? That can't be right! I only had a salad for dinner.

   W: Don't get excited. Let me check it out.

   Q: What will the woman probably do next?

5. W: I'd like to enroll in the free seminar you advertised in the newspaper. I mean the one on managing your personal finances.

   M: Okay. Now the ad did say that you have to have a savings account at our bank to be eligible. Do you have one here?

   Q: What does the man want to know?

6. W: Tomorrow we are having our first test in my history class. I'm really worried about it. You've taken one of Dr. Parker's tests, haven't you? I hear they're impossible to pass.

M: I don't know who you've been talking to. My experience was just the opposite.

Q: What does the man imply?

7. W: What's the problem, Paul? You really look worried.

M: I am speaking to a group of high school students about engineering this afternoon, but I have no idea how I am going to simplify some of the concepts for them.

Q: What is the man's problem?

8. M: I haven't turned on my air-conditioner at all this summer.

W: That's surprising, considering how hot it's been lately.

Q: What does the woman find surprising?

Now you will hear two long conversations.

Conversation One

M: Hi Kathy, please come in and take a seat.

W: Well, you would like to check the progress of the website design, right?

M: Yes, but it seems that we've got some problems with the BBS. The part-time web designer was not as good as what we had thought before. She informed us just now that she could not complete this task.

W: Well, didn't you talk with her about what she should do at the beginning?

M: Not really. She was recommended by James and from what he told me, she sounded to be pretty qualified to do the job. I'm not asking for a terrific web design but to build up a structure with all the basic elements of web design.

W: Did you ask her why she wasn't frank with you in the beginning if she couldn't do the BBS?

M: I did. But she said it was a communication problem.

W: So now what do you plan to do since she got the job half done?

M: On one side, I will not pay her full fees since she wasn't honest with me in the beginning. On the other side, I have to search around for another guy to complete the job.

W: Agreed. That should also teach her a lesson. For us, I think we had better turn to our Part-time Job Center for help. There, we can get a professional to work at it.

Questions 9 to 12 are based on the conversation you have just heard.

    9. Why hasn't the website been completed?

    10. What was the website designer NOT honest about?

    11. How did the man deal with the dishonest website designer?

    12. What does the woman suggest about the following steps to be taken?

Conversation Two

W: Good morning. This is Delia speaking. What can I do for you?

M: Hi, I am calling to complain about the mobile phone I bought from you. The problem is that I cannot send any short messages to my friends. Sometimes I cannot even receive the incoming call and it always gives others a busy signal. Do you know what the problem could be?

W: Could you please tell me how long this has been happening?

M: How long? Is that the point?

W: Sir, I ask that because it will likely tell me whether the problem is with your equipment or reception.

M: OK, I get it. Just three days ago. Initially I thought it could be the mobile's problem but then I realized it was probably caused by the signal.

W: Could you please give the serial number of your mobile phone, so I can check whether there is any problem with the mobile phone itself?

M: Sure, where is it?

W: The number is on the warranty card and 08381 begins the sequence.

M: Just a minute. Let me see.... Aha, it is 08381823923.

W: Thank you. Please hold and I will get back to you in a minute.

W: Sorry to keep you waiting, Sir. I have checked your mobile's status and everything is fine. It is said by our engineer that it could be due to our network upgrading and your number could be affected. Our apologies for any inconvenience brought to you.

M: Then how long do I have to wait till the signal returns to normal?

W: Well, a couple more days. I tell you that, I will give your feedback to our support center and if the problem still exists after two days, please give us a call and we will help you to solve it.

M: OK, thanks for your help and I really hope I won't need to call you again for that.

Questions 13 to 15 are based on the conversation you have just heard.

    13. Where did the conversation most probably take place?

    14. What is the man's problem?

    15. According to the woman, what could be the problem?

Section B

Directions: In this section, you will hear 3 short passages. At the end of each passage, you will hear some questions. Both the passages and the questions will be spoken only once. After you hear a question, you must choose the best answer from the four choices marked A, B, C and D.

Passage One

    Stress comes in all shapes and sizes and it's hard to get through a day without hearing or reading something about stress. Some doctors refer to stress as some kind of new plague. However, numerous surveys confirm that the problem has been progressively serious since the 1980s. Stress is an unavoidable consequence of life. Without stress, there could be no life. However, just as distress can cause disease, there are good stresses that offset this, and promote wellness. Increased stress results in increased productivity—up to a point. However, this level differs for each of us. We all need to find the proper level of stress that promotes optimal performance. Good health is more than just the absence of illness. Rather, it is a very robust state of physical and emotional well being that acknowledges the importance and inseparability of mind and body relationships. Later, in the next program, I hope you will join me in the pursuit of learning how to harness stress, so that it can work for you and make you more productive.

Questions 16 to 18 are based on the passage you have just heard.

    16. What is the passage mainly about?

    17. How can we deal with stress according to the speaker?

    18. What will the speaker discuss in the next program?

Passage Two

    Many people think that sitting is easier on their backs than standing or lifting. Not true. People whose jobs require them to sit for long periods of time suffer as much from back pain as people who lift all day long. Many world-class researchers believe that the huge increase in back pain over the past couple of decades—and it is huge—has a lot to do with the fact that more and more of us are spending our work days in chairs. A lot of people have the notion that, if their back pain gets bad enough, they can always resort to surgery. Nothing could be further from the truth. The amount of pain someone has has very little to do with whether or not he or she would benefit from surgery. One British researcher has estimated that for every 10,000 people who experience back pain, only four need surgery. Not very many years ago, back pain patients were routinely put to bed, sometimes for weeks or months. No longer. Two or three days of bed-rest is now the norm. After that, people are advised to return to their normal activities, gradually if necessary. The reasons for the 180° shift are interesting. For starters, if you stay in bed, your muscle strength can decline by as much as 30% a day.

Questions 19 to 21 are based on the passage you have just heard.

    19. What misunderstanding about back pain do people hold in the beginning?

    20. What role does surgery play in curing back pain?

    21. Why aren't back pain patients put to bed for more than two or three days?

Passage Three

    One of the most popular myths about the United States in the 19th century was that of the free and simple life of the farmer. It was said that farmers worked hard on their own land to produce whatever their families needed. They might sometimes trade with their neighbors, but in general they could get along just fine by relying on themselves, not on commercial ties with others. This is how Thomas Jefferson idealized the farmer at the beginning of the 19th century. And at that time, this might have been close to the truth, especially on the frontier.

    But by the mid-century, sweeping changes in agriculture were well under way as farmers began to specialize in the raising of crops such as cotton, corn or wheat. By late in the century, revolutionary advances in farm machinery had vastly increased production of specialized crops and an extensive network of railroads had linked farmers throughout the country to markets in the east and even overseas. By raising and selling specialized crops, farmers could afford more and finer goods and achieve a much higher standard of living—but at a price.

    Now farmers were no longer dependent just on the weather and on their own efforts.

Their lives were increasingly controlled by banks, which had power to grant or deny loans for new machinery, and by the railroads which set the rates for shipping their crops to market. As businessmen, farmers now had to worry about national economic depressions and the influence of world supply and demand, for example, the price of wheat in Kansas. And so by the end of the 19th century, the era of Jefferson's independent farmer had come to a close.

Questions 22 to 25 are based on the passage you have just heard.

22. What is the passage mainly about?

23. According to the passage, what was the major change in agriculture during the 19th century?

24. What was one result of the increased use of machinery on farms in the United States?

25. According to the passage, why was the world market important for United States agriculture?

Section C

Directions: In this section, you will hear a passage three times. When the passage is read for the first time, you should listen carefully for its general idea. When the passage is read for the second time, you are required to fill in the blanks numbered from 26 to 33 with the exact words you have just heard. For blanks numbered from 34 to 36 you are required to fill in the missing information. For these blanks, you can either use the exact words you have just heard or write down the main points in your own words. Finally, when the passage is read for the third time, you should check what you have written.

Psychologists have found that only about two percent of adults use their creativity, compared with ten percent of seven-year-old children. When five-year olds were tested, the results rose to ninety percent! (26) Curiosity and originality are daily occurrences for the small child, but somehow most of us lose the (27) freedom and flexibility of the child as we grow older. The need to "follow directions" and "do it right" plus the many social (28) constraints we put on ourselves (29) prevent us from using our creative potential.

It is never too late to tap our creative potential. Some of us, however, find it difficult to think in (30) imaginative and flexible ways because of our set (31) pattern of approaching problems. When we are inflexible in our approach to situations, we close our minds to creative (32) possibilities.

Being creative doesn't necessarily mean being a (33) genius. (34) It means looking at situations in a new way or putting something together in a new form that makes sense. Spontaneity is one of the key elements of creativity.

If you were to ask someone, "What's half of eight?" and received the answer "zero", you might laugh and say "That's wrong!" (35) But the figure 8 can be visualized as two zeros, one on top of the other, or it can also be seen as two 3s standing face to face.

The ability to visualize our environment in new ways opens our perspective and allows us to make all kinds of discoveries. (36) If each of us asked the question "why" more often and investigated "other" alternatives to problem solving, our lives would be more interesting and exciting.

Unit 7

Section A

Directions: In this section, you will hear 8 short conversations and 2 long conversations. At the end of each conversation, one or more questions will be asked about what was said. Both the conversations and the questions will be spoken only once. After each question there will be a pause. During the pause, you must read the four choices marked A, B, C and D, and decide which is the best answer.

1. W: Simon, could you return the tools I lent you for building the bookshelf last month?

   M: Uh, well, I hate to tell you this... but I can't seem to find them.

   Q: What do we learn from the conversation?

2. W: I'm going to Martha's house. I have a paper to complete, and I need to use her computer.

   M: Why don't you buy one yourself? Think how much time you could save.

   Q: What does the man suggest the woman do?

3. W: Bob said that Seattle is a great place for conferences.

   M: He's certainly in a position to make that comment. He's been there so often.

   Q: What does the man say about Bob?

4. W: Mr. Watson, I wonder whether it's possible for me to take a vacation early next month.

   M: Did you fill out a request form?

   Q: What is the probable relationship between the two speakers?

5. M: Do you want to go to the lecture this weekend? I hear the guy who's going to deliver the lecture spent a year living in the rain forest.

   W: Great! I'm doing a report on the rain forest. Maybe I can get some new information and add to it.

   Q: What does the woman mean?

6. W: Wow! I do like this campus: all the big trees, the green lawns, and the old buildings with tall columns. It's really beautiful.

M: It sure is. The architecture of these buildings is in the Greek style. It was popular in the eighteenth century here.

Q: What are the speakers talking about?

7. M: This article is nothing but advertising for housing developers. I don't think the houses for sale are half that good.

W: Come on, David. Why so negative? We're thinking of buying a home, aren't we? Just a trip to look at the place won't cost us much.

Q: What can be inferred from the conversation?

8. M: Would you pass me the sports section, please?

W: Sure, if you give me the classified ads and local news section.

Q: What are the speakers doing?

Now you'll hear two long conversations.

Conversation One

W: Hello, Cooper. How are you?

M: Fine! And yourself?

W: Can't complain. Did you have time to look at my proposal?

M: No, not really. Can we go over it now?

W: Sure. I've been trying to come up with some new production and advertising strategies. First of all, if we want to stay competitive, we need to modernize our factory. New equipment should have been installed long ago.

M: How much will that cost?

W: We have several options ranging from one hundred thousand dollars all the way up to half a million.

M: OK. We'll have to discuss these costs with finance.

W: We should also consider human resources. I've been talking to personnel as well as our staff at the factory.

M: And what's the picture?

W: We'll probably have to hire a couple of engineers to help us modernize the factory.

M: What about advertising?

W: Marketing has some interesting ideas for television commercials.

M: TV? Isn't that a bit too expensive for us? What's wrong with advertising in the papers, as usual?

W: Quite frankly, it's just not enough anymore. We need to be more aggressive in order to keep ahead of our competitors.

M: Will we be able to afford all this?

W: I'll look into it, but I think higher costs will be justified. These investments will result in higher profits for our company.

M: We'll have to look at the figures more closely. Have finance draw up a budget for these investments.

W: All right. I'll see to it.

Questions 9 to 12 are based on the conversation you have just heard.

    9. What is the conversation mainly about?

    10. What does the woman say about the equipment of their factory?

    11. What does the woman suggest about human resources?

    12. Why does the woman suggest advertising on TV?

Conversation Two

W: Sir, you've been using the online catalogue for quite a while. Is there anything I can do to help you?

M: Well, I've got to write a paper about Hollywood in the 30s and 40s, and I'm really struggling. There are hundreds of books, and I just don't know where to begin.

W: Your topic sounds pretty big. Why don't you narrow it down to something like... uh... the history of the studios during that time?

M: You know, I was thinking about doing that, but more than 30 books came up when I typed in "movie studios".

W: You could cut that down even further by listing the specific years you want. Try adding "1930s" or "1940s" or maybe "Golden Age".

M: "Golden Age" is a good idea. Let me type that in... Hey, look, just 6 books this time. That's a lot better.

W: Oh... another thing you might consider... have you tried looking for any magazine or newspaper articles?

M: No, I've only been searching for books.

W: Well, you can look up magazine articles in the *Reader's Guide to Periodical Literature*. And we do have the *Los Angeles Times* available over there. You might go through their indexes to see if there's anything you want.

M: Okay. I think I'll get started with these books and then I'll go over the magazines.

W: If you need any help, I'll be over at the Reference Desk.

M: Great, thanks a lot.

Questions 13 to 15 are based on the conversation you have just heard.

13. What is the man doing?

14. What does the librarian think of the topic the man is working on?

15. Where can the man find the relevant magazine articles?

Section B

Directions: In this section, you will hear 3 short passages. At the end of each passage, you will hear some questions. Both the passages and the questions will be spoken only once. After you hear a question, you must choose the best answer from the four choices marked A, B, C and D.

Passage One

Design of all the new tools and implements is based on careful experiments with electronic instruments. First, a human "guinea pig" is tested using a regular tool. Measurements are taken of the amount of work done, and the buildup of heat in the body. Twisted joints and stretched muscles can not perform as well, it has been found, as joints and muscles in their normal positions. The same person is then tested again, using a tool designed according to the suggestions made by Dr. Tichauer. All these tests have shown the great improvement of the new designs over the old.

One of the electronic instruments used by Dr. Tichauer, the myograph, makes visible through electrical signals the work done by human muscle.

Another machine measures any dangerous features of tools, thus proving information upon which to base a new design. One conclusion of tests made with this machine is that a tripod stepladder is more stable and safer to use than one with four legs.

This work has attracted the attention of efficiency experts and time-and-motion study engineers, but its value goes far beyond that. Dr. Tichauer's first thought is for the health of the tool user. With the repeated use of the same tool all day long on production lines and in other jobs, even light manual work can put a heavy stress on one small area of the body. In time, such stress can cause a disabling disease.

Furthermore, muscle fatigue is a serious safety hazard.

Efficiency is the by-product of comfort, Dr. Tichauer believes, and his new designs for traditional tools have proved his point.

Questions 16 to 18 are based on the passage you have just heard.

16. What are involved in the design of a new tool according to the passage?

17. From the passage we know that joints and muscles perform best when _____.

18. Dr. Tichauer started his experiments initially to _____.

Passage Two

More and more, the operations of our businesses, governments, and financial institutions are controlled by information that exists only inside computer memories. Anyone clever enough to modify this information for his own purposes can reap big reward. Even worse, a number of people who have done this and been caught at it have managed to get away without punishment.

It's easy for computer crimes to go undetected if no one checks up on what the computer is doing. But even if the crime is detected, the criminal may walk away not only unpunished but with a glowing recommendation from his former employers.

Of course, we have no statistics on crimes that go undetected. But it's disturbing to note how many of the crimes we do know about were detected by accident, not by systematic inspections or other security procedures. The computer criminals who have been caught may have been the victims of uncommonly bad luck.

Unlike other lawbreakers, who must leave the country, commit suicide, or go to jail, computer criminals sometimes escape punishment, demanding not only that they not be charged but that they be given good recommendations and perhaps other benefits. All too often, their demands have been met.

Why? Because company executives are afraid of the bad publicity that would result if the public found out that their computer had been misused. They hesitate at the thought of a criminal boasting in open court of how he juggled（诈骗）the most confidential（保密）records right under the noses of the company's executives, accountants, and security staff. And so another computer criminal departs with just the recommendations he needs to.

147

Questions 19 to 22 are based on the passage you have just heard.

19. It is implied in the third paragraph that _____.

20. Which of the following statements is true according to the passage?

21. What may happen to computer criminals once they are caught?

22. What is the passage mainly about?

Passage Three

What kind of car will we be driving by the year 2010? Rather different from the type we know today. With the next decade bringing greater change than the past 50 years, the people who will be designing the models of tomorrow believe that environmental problems may well accelerate the pace of the car's development. The vision is that of a machine with 3 wheels instead of 4, electrically-powered, environmentally clean and able to drive itself along intelligent roads as well as equipped with built-in power supplies. Future cars will pick up the fuel during long journeys from a power source built into the road or stored in small quantities for traveling in the city. Instead of today's seating arrangement two in front, two or three behind, all facing forward the 2010 car will have an interior with adults and children in a family circle. This view of future car is based on a much more sophisticated road system. Cars will be automatically controlled by a computer. All the driver will have to do is say where to go and the computer will do the rest. It will become impossible for cars to crash into one another. The technology already exists for the car to become a true automobile.

Questions 23 to 25 are based on the passage you have just heard.

23. What is the designer's vision of the cars of tomorrow?

24. What else does the passage tell us about the future car?

25. What is the only thing that the driver of the future car has to do?

Section C

Directions: In this section, you will hear a passage three times. When the passage is read for the first time, you should listen carefully for its general idea. When the passage is read for the second time, you are required to fill in the blanks numbered from 26 to 33 with the exact words you have just heard. For blanks numbered from 34 to 36 you are required to fill in the missing information. For these blanks, you can either use the exact words you have just

heard or write down the main points in your own words. Finally, when the passage is read for the third time, you should check what you have written.

Russia is the largest economic power that is not a member of the World Trade Organization. But that may change. Last Friday, the European Union said it would support Russia's (26) effort to become a WTO member.

Representatives of the European Union met with Russian (27) officials in Moscow. They signed a trade agreement that took six years to (28) negotiate.

Russia called the trade agreement (29) balanced. It agreed to slowly increase fuel prices within the country. It also agreed to permit (30) competition in its communications industry and to remove some barriers to trade.

In (31) exchange for European support to join the WTO, Russian President Putin said that Russia would speed up the (32) process to approve the Kyoto Protocol, an international (33) environmental agreement to reduce the production of harmful industrial gases. (34) These "greenhouse gases" trap heat in the atmosphere and are blamed for changing the world's climate.

Russia had signed the Kyoto Protocol, but has not yet approved it. The agreement takes effect when it has been approved by nations that produce at least 55 percent of the world's greenhouse gases. (35) But currently, nations producing only 44 percent have approved the Protocol. Russia produces about 17 percent of the world's greenhouse gases. The United States, the world's biggest producer, withdrew from the Kyoto Protocol after President Bush took office in 2001. So, Russia's approval is required to put the Kyoto Protocol into effect.

(36) To join the WTO, a country must reach trade agreements with major trading countries that are also WTO members. Russia must still reach agreements with China, Japan, South Korea and the United States.

Unit 8

Section A

Directions: In this section, you will hear 8 short conversations and 2 long conversations. At the end of each conversation, one or more questions will be asked about what was said. Both the conversations and the questions will be spoken only once. After each question there will be a pause. During the pause, you must read the four choices marked A, B, C and D, and decide which is the best answer.

1. M: How much are these jackets?

   W: They are on sale today, sir. Twenty-five dollars each or two for forty dollars.

   Q: How much does one jacket cost?

2. W: Shall we have dinner in that French restaurant?

   M: I can't eat a thing. I feel too bad. My stomach aches.

   Q: What do you think the woman will do?

3. M: Tina's husband is friendly and easy-going.

   W: Yes, just the exact opposite to her brother.

   Q: What is Tina's brother like?

4. W: Last night, we went to Peter's house to listen to music.

   M: I heard that he has more than 300 jazz records. Is that right?

   Q: What do we learn from the conversation?

5. M: I need six stamps and I'd like to send these two books by air mail.

   W: Here are your stamps, but you have to go to the next window for the books.

   Q: Where does the conversation most probably take place?

6. W: Jim, would you mind driving me to my school?

   M: Sure, why not?

   Q: How does Jim respond to the woman?

7. M: Did you see Mary in the business office?

   W: Yes, she was applying for a student loan.

   Q: What was Mary doing?

8. W: When is the movie to start?

M: Don't worry. It doesn't start until 12:30. We've still got 30 minutes.

Q: What's the time now?

Now you will hear two long conversations.

Conversation One

M: Hi, Mary, welcome back. How's your trip to the States?

W: Very busy. I had a lot of meetings. So, of course, I didn't have much time to see New York.

M: What a pity! Actually I have a trip there myself next week.

W: Do you? Then take my advice. Do the well-being in the air program. It really works.

M: Oh, I read about that in a magazine. You say it works?

W: Yes. I did the program on the flight to the States. And when I arrived in New York, I didn't have any problem. No jet lag at all. On the way back I didn't do it, and I felt terrible.

M: You are joking.

W: Not at all. It really made a lot of difference.

M: Hmm... So, what did you do?

W: Well, I didn't drink any alcohol or coffee and I didn't eat any meat or rich food. I drink a lot of water and fruit juice and I eat the meals on the well-being menu. They are lighter. They have fish, vegetables and noodles, for example. And I did some of the exercises in the program.

M: Exercises? On a plane?

W: Yes. I didn't do many, of course. There isn't much space on the plane.

M: How many passengers did the exercises?

W: Not many.

M: And how much champagne did they drink?

W: A lot. It was more popular than mineral water.

M: So, basically it's a choice. Mineral water and exercises or champagne and jet lag.

W: That's right. It's a difficult choice.

Questions 9 to 12 are based on the conversation you have just heard.

9. Why did the woman go to New York?

10. What does the woman say about the well-being in the air program?

11. What did the woman do to follow the well-being menu?

12. What does the woman say about other passengers?

Conversation Two

W: Morning. Can I help you?

M: Well, I'm not really sure. I'm just looking.

W: I see. Well, there's plenty to look at again this year. I'm sure you'd have to walk miles to see each stand.

M: That's true.

W: Would you like a coffee? Come and sit down for a minute. No obligation.

M: Well, that's very kind of you. But...

W: No, please, is this the first year you've been to the fair, Mr...?

M: Yes. Smith. Jack Smith.

W: My name's Ann White. Are you looking for anything in particular or are you just interested in computers in general?

M: Well, actually, I have some specific jobs in mind. I own a small company. We've grown quite dramatically over the past 12 months and we really need some technological help to enable us to keep on top of everything.

W: What's your line of business, Mr. Smith?

M: We are a training consultancy.

W: I see. And what do you need to keep on top?

M: The first thing is correspondence. We have a lot of standard letters and forms. So I suppose we need some kind of word processor.

W: Right. Well, that's no problem. But it may be possible for you to get a system that does a lot of other things in addition to word processing. What might suit you is the MR5000. That's over there. It's IBM compatible.

M: What about the price?

W: Well, the MR5000 costs 1,050 pounds. Software comes free with the hardware.

M: Well, I'll think about it. Thank you.

W: Here's my card. Please feel free to contact me.

Questions 13 to 15 are based on the conversation you have just heard.

13. Where did the conversation most probably take place?

14. What is the conversation mainly about?

15. What is the man's line of business?

Section B

Directions: In this section, you will hear 3 short passages. At the end of each passage, you will hear some questions. Both the passages and the questions will be spoken only once. After you hear a question, you must choose the best answer from the four choices marked A, B, C and D.

Passage One

Florida International University has opened what it says the first computer art museum in the United States. You don't have to visit the university to see the art. You just need a computer linked to a telephone. You call the telephone number of a university computer and connect your own computer to it. All of the art is stored in the school computer. It is computer art, created electronically by artist on their own computers. In only a few minutes, your computer can receive and copy all the pictures and drawings.

Robert Shostak is the director of the new computer museum. He says he started the museum because computer artists had no place to show their work and he just wanted to help them to some extent. A computer artist could only record his pictures electronically and send the records, or floppy discs, to others to see on their computers. He could also put his pictures on paper. But to print good pictures on paper, the computer artist needs an expensive laser printer.

Questions 16 to 18 are based on the passage you have just heard.

16. If you want to see the art in the computer museum, what should you do?

17. According to the passage, why did Robert Shostak start the museum?

18. What can a laser printer do?

Passage Two

Men and Women in the United States who want to become doctors usually attend four years of college or university; next they study for four years in a medical school. After that they work in hospitals as medical residents or doctors in training. Some people study and work for as many as 13 years before they begin their lives as doctors.

During their university years, people who want to become doctors study science intensively. They must study biology, chemistry and other sciences. If they do not, they may have to return to college for more education in science before trying to enter medical school.

There are 125 medical schools in the United States. It is difficult to gain entrance to them. Those who do the best in their studies have a greater chance of entering medical school. Each student also must pass a national examination to enter a medical school. Those who get top score have the best chance of being accepted. Most people who want to study medicine seek to enter a number of medical schools. This increases their chances of being accepted by one. In 1998, almost 47,000 people competed for about 17,000 openings in medical schools.

Questions 19 to 21 are based on the passage you have just heard.

19. How many years does a student have to study before beginning his life as a doctor?

20. Which subject do the students who want to become doctors need not to study?

21. Which of the following statements is NOT true about the entrance to the medical schools?

Passage Three

The Coast Guard does what its name says: It guards the coasts of the United States. During a war, the Coast Guard becomes part of the United States Navy, and helps to protect against enemy attacks. In times of peace, however, the Coast Guard is part of the United States Department of Transportation. It has responsibility for many different duties. The Coast Guard can be found at many large lakes in America, as well as in coastal waters. It enforces laws controlling navigation, shipping, immigration, and fishing. It enforces other laws that affect the thousands of privately-owned boats in the United States. Coast Guard planes, boats and helicopters search for missing boats and rescue people in dangerous situations. Last year, Coast Guardsmen saved the lives of almost 7,000 people. The Coast Guard does scientific research on the ocean. It also uses ice-breaking boats to clear ice from rivers or lakes, so boats can travel safely. One of the Coast Guard's most important duties now is helping to keep illegal drugs out of the United States. Coast Guard boats, armed with guns, use radios and radar to find boats that may be carrying drugs. They stop the boats suspected of carrying drugs and search them. They seize the drugs and arrest the people on the boats. Last year, Coast

Guardsmen seized more than 800,000 kilograms of marijuana and cocaine. And they arrested more than 700 persons trying to bring illegal drugs into the United States. This kind of action is exciting. Most of the time, however, Coast Guardsmen say they see nothing more exciting than the ocean.

Questions 22 to 25 are based on the passage you have just heard.

22. What does Coast Guard mean?
23. Which of the following statements is NOT the duty of the U. S. Coast Guard?
24. How many lives have Coast Guardsmen saved last year?
25. What does the speaker indicate about the lives of the Coast Guardsmen for most of the time?

Section C

Directions: In this section, you will hear a passage three times. When the passage is read for the first time, you should listen carefully for its general idea. When the passage is read for the second time, you are required to fill in the blanks numbered from 26 to 33 with the exact words you have just heard. For blanks numbered from 34 to 36 you are required to fill in the missing information. For these blanks, you can either use the exact words you have just heard or write down the main points in your own words. Finally, when the passage is read for the third time, you should check what you have written.

Very high waves are destructive when they (26) strike the land. Fortunately, this (27) seldom happens. One reason is that out at sea, waves moving in one direction almost always run into waves moving in a (28) different direction. The two (29) sets of waves tend to cancel each other out. Another reason is that water is (30) shallower near the shore. As a wave gets closer to land, the shallow (31) bottom helps reduce its (32) strength.

But the power of waves striking the (33) shore can still be very great. During a winter gale, waves sometimes strike the shore with the force of 6,000 pounds for each square foot. That means a wave, 25 feet high and 500 feet along its face, (34) may strike the shore with a force of 75 million pounds.

Yet the waves, (35) no matter how big or how violent, affect only the surface of the sea. During the most raging storms, (36) the water a hundred fathoms (600 feet) beneath the surface is just as calm as on the day without a breath of wind.

Unit 9

Section A

Directions: In this section, you will hear 8 short conversations and 2 long conversations. At the end of each conversation, one or more questions will be asked about what was said. Both the conversations and the questions will be spoken only once. After each question there will be a pause. During the pause, you must read the four choices marked A, B, C and D, and decide which is the best answer.

1. M: I'm very sad. I made a 65 on the driving test, so I couldn't get my license. What did Jason get?

   W: I heard he made the highest score out of all of us.

   Q: What can we know about Jason?

2. M: I hope you can understand my reasons for deciding to leave this company. I do need to get a more challenging job.

   W: But, I have to remind you that we have spent a lot of time and money on your career here.

   Q: Which adjective can be used to describe the woman's reaction?

3. M: Was that the assignment given by Professor Brown? I don't think you have much trouble doing that experiment.

   W: No, but I didn't realize it would take me most of the day.

   Q: What does the woman say about the experiment?

4. W: The tuition will go up again next term. My parents can't pay my room and board this year. I have to take a part-time job now.

   M: It's not easy to find a good job on the campus. I have a friend in Labor Service Office. Perhaps he can do something for you.

   Q: Why does the woman have to take a part-time job?

5. M: Well, we need some temporary labor in our packing department just for a short time.

   W: I will put an ad in the newspaper this afternoon. I think there will be many applicants.

   Q: What are they talking about?

6. W: The weather report says there will be sunshine tomorrow.

   M: Good. The wheat is ready to cut. I hope it can stay bright and sunny for a few more days so that we can complete the harvest.

   Q: What is the man's probable occupation?

7. W: Professor Milton caught some students cheating on the final exam and failed them right away.

   M: Serves them right. I don't sympathize with anyone trying to pass the test that way.

   Q: What is the man's attitude toward the professor's action?

8. M: Since the topics of our term papers are similar, why don't we sit down and share some of our sources after we've each been to the library?

   W: Great idea! Should we meet at the snack bar next Wednesday at this time?

   Q: What will they do next Wednesday?

Now you will hear two long conversations.

Conversation One

W: Good morning. Can I help you?

M: Oh, good morning. Yes, please. I'd like to have some information about nice places around here because I'm going to spend the morning in this city and I don't know exactly where I could go.

W: Well, you could go to the open-air market. It's not far from the hotel and they have fresh fruits and vegetables. They also sell potteries and hand-made leather goods. I think you'd enjoy it.

M: Oh, that's a good idea. Could you tell me where it is?

W: Yes. If you leave the hotel and make a right turn and follow a winding road, you will go over a bridge onto East Island. And it's right there.

M: Oh, that sounds good. Thank you.

W: Yeah. There are also some tourist shops and cafes not far from the hotel if you are interested in buying souvenirs.

M: Oh no, I'm not so keen on that. Don't you have something special which I should see?

W: Yes, well, there's the castle. If you leave the hotel and make a left turn and go over the bridge you will go up a hill and there it is. You can climb to the top and have a very beautiful view of the city.

M: Oh, that sounds interesting. I'd love to go there. Is it far from here or. . . ?

W: No, no, it's not far at all. And there's also a very nice restaurant. It's called the Overlook and it's not far from the hotel. If you make a left turn when you leave the hotel, it's right there, and it overlooks the falls.

M: Oh, that's great. Thank you very much. That's very kind of you.

W: You're welcome. I hope you enjoy your morning here.

Questions 9 to 12 are based on the conversation you have just heard.

    9. Where are the two speakers?

    10. Which of the following is NOT suggested visiting according to the conversation?

    11. Why does the woman recommend the castle?

    12. Where will the man probably go?

Conversation Two

W: Good morning, sir. Can I help you?

M: Yes, well, I'm only looking really for something not too expensive, you know— well, not more than about £ 8,000.

W: I see. Well, did you have any particular make in mind?

M: Well, to be quite honest, I'm not very familiar with the cars. You see until now I've been more of a motorbike man, but with a baby on the way it's no longer convenient.

W: Quite right, sir. Well, you've come at a very good time as all the new spring models have just appeared. If you'd like to come over here, I'll show you.

M: Thank you. That's a rather good-looking car, that pale blue one, over there.

W: Ah, yes sir, that's the new sky-blue Fiesta—it's only just arrived and it's a very nice little car—not expensive either.

M: It certainly looks very attractive. What does it do at top speed?

W: That model, sir, about 170.

M: Hmm, not bad, I suppose, of course I'm used to much higher speeds on a motorbike.

W: Well, there is a slight difference if I may say so, sir! How about the ice-white Sierra from Dorman? That's an excellent car and it reaches 200. It's of excellent value for the price and there's a world of difference between that and the Fiesta.

M: Yes, well, it's very attractive, but...

W: It's under £ 8,000, sir. It's about £ 7,800.

M: Yes, well, it's a bit more than I can afford. Do you arrange payment by monthly installments?

W: Certainly, sir. No problem. Now if you would come over to the desk, I'll get the form...

M: Er... yes...

Questions 13 to 15 are based on the conversation you have just heard.

13. Why does the man want to buy a car?

14. Why does the woman recommend Sierra?

15. Can the man buy the car? Why?

Section B

Directions: In this section, you will hear 3 short passages. At the end of each passage, you will hear some questions. Both the passages and the questions will be spoken only once. After you hear a question, you must choose the best answer from the four choices marked A, B, C and D.

Passage One

Vitamins are special chemicals that are found in foods. Although only small amounts of vitamins are needed by the human body for good health, each vitamin is extremcly important. At the beginning of the twentieth century, scientists discovered that some diseases could be caused by the absence of certain kinds of food in a person's diet. The special chemicals in these foods were called vitamins.

Vitamin A is important for the health of eyes, skin, teeth, and bones. This vitamin is found in foods such as carrots, spinach, liver, and butter. Only small amounts of vitamin A are needed by the body as large amounts can be harmful.

There are several different kinds of vitamin B and together they are often called the vitamin B complex. Vitamin B_1 helps a person feel well, and this vitamin is found in foods such as pork, peas, beans, liver, and some cereals. Vitamin B_2 helps the eyes and skin stay healthy, and is found in milk, eggs, liver, lettuce, and meat without fat. Vitamin B_6 helps the body use food better. It is present in fish, meat without fat, liver, and some cereals. Vitamin B_{12} helps build healthy red blood, and it is found in liver,

159

eggs, milk, and meat.

Vitamin C is another important vitamin. It keeps bones, teeth, and blood vessels strong and healthy. Some people also believe that it helps prevent colds and flu. Vitamin C is found in fresh fruits such as oranges, lemons, and grapefruits, and in vegetables such as tomatoes and cabbage.

Vitamin D helps build strong bones and for this reason it is especially important for growing children. Not many foods contain vitamin D, so it is sometimes added to milk. Sunshine also helps the body make its own vitamin D. Although the body needs vitamin D, very large amounts of it can be harmful.

Questions 16 to 18 are based on the passage you have just heard.

16. For what is vitamin A important?

17. Which of the following statements is true according to the passage?

18. What is especially important for growing children?

Passage Two

The world's population continues to grow. It reached about 6 billion by the end of the last century and will reach 11 billion in a future 75 years. Experts have long been concerned about such a growth. Where will we find the food, water, jobs, houses, schools and health care for all these people?

A major new study shows that the situation may be changing. A large rapid drop in the world's birth rate has taken place during the past 10 years. Families generally are smaller now than they were a few years ago. It is happening in both developing and industrial nations.

Researchers said they found a number of reasons for this. More men and women are waiting longer to get married and are using birth control devices and methods to prevent or delay pregnancy. More women are going to school or working at jobs away from home instead of having children. And more governments, especially in developing nations, now support family planning programs to reduce population growth.

China is one of the nations that have made great progress in reducing its population growth. China has already cut its rate of population growth by about one half since 1970. Each Chinese family is now urged to have no more than one child. And the hope is to reach a zero population growth with the total number of births equaling the total number of deaths by the year 2010.

Several nations in Europe already have fewer births than deaths. Experts said that these nations could face a serious shortage of workers in the future. And the persons who are working could face much higher taxes to help support the growing number of retired people.

Questions 19 to 21 are based on the passage you have just heard.

19. What's the new change of population?
20. There are some reasons for the change. Which of the following is NOT mentioned in the passage?
21. Why do people working in Europe probably have to pay much higher taxes?

Passage Three

George Washington is one of the most famous citizens of the United States. He is remembered as the "Father of His County". For nearly twenty years, he guided his nation.

Washington was born in Westmoreland County, Virginia, on February 22, 1732. It is difficult to know much about Washington's early education. He only had seven or eight years of school in his whole life. He severed in the army during the American Revolution. In fact, he was a lieutenant general, the highest rank in the army at that time. In 1759, he married Martha Curtis. They had several children.

Washington was elected president of the United States in 1787. He was reelected to a second term in 1792. Many people wanted him to continue as president after his second term, but Washington refused.

Washington helped to shape the beginning of the United States in three important ways. First, he commanded the Continental Army that won independence from Great Britain in the Revolutionary War. Second, he served as president of the convention that wrote the United States Constitution. Third, he was the first man elected president of the United States.

No other American has been honored more than Washington. The nation's capital, Washington D. C. , was named for him. The state of Washington is the only state that was named after a president. Many counties, towns, streets, bridges, lakes, parks and schools have his name today. Washington' portrait appears on postage stamps, on the one-dollar bill, and on the quarter. His birthday is also a federal holiday.

The people of his day loved Washington very much. His army officers wanted to make him king, but he didn't let them. From the time of the Revolutionary War, his birthday has been celebrated throughout the country. Today we continue to remember this famous United States citizen.

Questions 22 to 25 are based on the passage you have just heard.

22. When did Washington serve in the army?

23. For how many terms did Washington serve as president of the United States?

24. Which of the following statements is true according to the passage?

25. Washington has been honored greatly. Which of the following statements is NOT mentioned in the passage?

Section C

Directions: In this section, you will hear a passage three times. When the passage is read for the first time, you should listen carefully for its general idea. When the passage is read for the second time, you are required to fill in the blanks numbered from 26 to 33 with the exact words you have just heard. For blanks numbered from 34 to 36 you are required to fill in the missing information. For these blanks, you can either use the exact words you have just heard or write down the main points in your own words. Finally, when the passage is read for the third time, you should check what you have written.

The United States leads all industrial nations in the (26) proportion of its young men and women who receive higher education. Why is this? What (27) motivates a middle-income family with two children to take (28) loans for up to $ 120,000 so that their son and daughter can (29) attend private universities for four years? Why would both parents in a low-income family cost of $ 4,000? Why should a woman in her forties quit her job and use her savings to (30) enroll for the college education she didn't receive when she was younger?

Americans place a high personal value on higher education. This is an (31) attitude that goes back to the country's oldest political traditions. People in the United States have always believed that education is necessary for maintaining a (32) democratic government. They believe that it prepares the individual for informed, (33) intelligent, political participation, including voting.

(34) Before World War II, a high school education seemed adequate for satisfying most people's needs, but the post-war period produced dozens of new questions for

Americans. How should atomic power be used? Should scientists be allowed to experiment in splitting genes? Should money be spent on sending astronauts into space—or should it be used for aid to another nation? (35) Americans rarely express a direct vote on such complex matters. But the representatives they elect do decide such issues. (36) In recent years, as a result, many Americans have begun to regard a college education as necessary to become an informed American voter.

Unit 10

Section A

Directions: In this section, you will hear 8 short conversations and 2 long conversations. At the end of each conversation, one or more questions will be asked about what was said. Both the conversations and the questions will be spoken only once. After each question there will be a pause. During the pause, you must read the four choices marked A, B, C and D, and decide which is the best answer.

1. W: Mr. Jones, your student, Bill, shows great enthusiasm for music instruments.

    M: I only wish he showed half as much for his English lessons.

    Q: What do we learn from the conversation about Bill?

2. M: You look like you are freezing to death. Why don't you put this on?

    W: Thank you, it was so warm at noon. I didn't expect the weather to change so quickly.

    Q: What do we learn from the conversation?

3. M: I'll have the steak, French Fries, and let's see, chocolate ice-cream for dissert.

    W: Oh, you know these things will ruin your health, too much fat and sugar. How about ordering some vegetables and fruit instead?

    Q: Where does the conversation most probably take place?

4. M: I suppose we take a taxi.

    W: Not unless you're feeling very rich. A taxi would cost about 2. 50 $. The coach is no slower and much cheaper.

    Q: What does the woman mean?

5. M: Guess what! I've decided to take two weeks off from work and to Paris this summer.

    W: Paris! I thought you were on a tight budget these days.

    Q: What does the woman imply?

6. W: This spring weather is perfect for playing tennis.

    M: Unfortunately, the only time I get to enjoy it is when I'm walking to class or to the library.

Q: What does the man imply?

7. M: I ran into our friend Mark yesterday on the street and he said he hadn't
heard from you for two months.

W: Yes, I know. But I've never been too busy to phone him.

Q: What can be inferred from the conversation?

8. M: Could you tell me the timetable of the school bus?

W: Well, the bus leaves here for the campus every two hours from 7: 00 a. m. .
But on Saturdays it starts half an hour later.

Q: When does the second bus leave on Saturdays?

Now you will hear two long conversations.

Conversation One

W: Hey, Tom! I haven't seen you for ages. How have you been?

M: Oh, I'm doing okay, but school has been really busy these days, and I haven't had
time to relax.

W: By the way, what's your major anyway?

M: Hotel management.

W: Well, what do you want to do once you graduate?

M: Uh... I haven't decided for sure, but I think I'd like to work for a hotel or travel
agency in this area. How about you?

W: Well, when I first started college, I wanted to major in French, but I realized I
might have a hard time finding a job using the language, so I changed my major to
computer science. With the right skills, landing a job in the computer industry
shouldn't be as difficult.

M: So, do you have a part-time job to support yourself through school?

W: Well, fortunately, I received a four-year academic scholarship that pays for all of
my tuition and books.

M: Wow. That's great!

W: Yeah. How about you? Are you working your way through school?

M: Yeah. I work three times a week at a restaurant near campus.

W: Oh. What do you do there?

M: I'm a cook.

W: How do you like your job?

M: It's OK. The other workers are friendly, and the pay isn't bad.

Questions 9 to 12 are based on the conversation you have just heard.

    9. What does the man want to do after he graduates?

    10. What is the woman majoring in?

    11. How does the woman pay for college?

    12. Where does the man work part-time?

Conversation Two

W: May I help you?

M: Yes. I would like to apply for one of these security guard positions you advertised in the local paper.

W: Good. May I ask you a few questions first? Have you ever worked as a security guard before?

M: Yes. At Chaffer's Plaza in San Francisco and at the Regency Hotel here in town.

W: How many years of experience have you had as a security guard? Have you had experience monitoring alarm systems?

M: I have had over four years of experience as a security guard. And I monitored several types of alarm systems in my previous job.

W: Very good. You seem to meet our minimum qualifications. Do you have any questions?

M: Yes. What are the wages and the hours?

W: The wages start at 8 dollars and 75 cents per hour. We have three shifts available, morning, evening and late night.

M: Good. I was hoping to get an evening job since I go to school in the morning.

W: Well, you can write on your application that you prefer the evening shift.

M: What do I need to do now?

W: Complete this application form and bring it back to me. Then I will schedule you for another interview.

Questions 13 to 15 are based on the conversation you have just heard.

    13. What does the woman want to know?

    14. Why does the man want to work at night?

    15. What does the woman ask the man to do before another interview?

Section B

Directions: In this section, you will hear 3 short passages. At the end of each passage, you will hear some questions. Both the passages and the questions will be spoken only once. After you hear a question, you must choose the best answer from the four choices marked A, B, C and D.

Passage One

Birds spend so much time smoothing, cleaning and arranging their feathers that it's not surprising this behavior, called preening, is associated with pride and vanity. But stop a minute and think about what feathers do for a bird. Besides allowing it to fly, feathers keep the bird warm in the winter and cool in the summer. They shed water in the rain, and they are used to communicate with other birds of the same species. A bird with dirty feathers will not live long.

Birds use their beaks to clean and straighten their feathers and to spread oil over them. They get the oil from their skin. The oil helps keep the feathers waterproof and flexible.

Birds also like to take baths to keep clean, and they don't always take them in water. Chickens, for instance, like nothing better than to scratch up some dust with their feet and then lie down and flap the dust all over their bodies. This probably helps get rid of parasites on their skin. A quick shake then sends the dust flying from their feathers, leaving them clean and comfortable.

Questions 16 to 18 are based on the passage you have just heard.

16. Why is cleaning feathers very important to birds?

17. Which of the following is the function of the oil from a bird's skin?

18. Which of the following is the best title for the passage?

Passage Two

Sara and Brown met ten years after graduating from college and they both related their stories to one another.

Sara's most embarrassing experience happened when she had just finished college. She had just started teaching at a high school in Denver. One morning her alarm clock didn't go off, for she had forgotten to set it. She woke up at 8:00, and school started at

8:30. Quickly she washed, dressed, put on some make-up, jumped in her car, and drove to school. When she got there, classes had already started. She didn't go to the office or the teacher's room but went straight into her first period class. After two or three minutes the students started laughing, and she couldn't understand why. Suddenly she looked down and understood. She had put on one black shoe and one brown shoe!

Brown's most embarrassing experience happened two years ago. He and his wife had driven into New York. The streets were very crowded and they were holding hands. Suddenly his wife saw a dress that she liked in a shop window and stopped. Mr. Brown started looking at some radios in the next window. After a minute or two, he reached for his wife's hand. There was a loud scream, and a woman slapped his face. He hadn't taken his wife's hand—he had taken the hand of a complete stranger.

Questions 19 to 21 are based on the passage you have just heard.

  19. Why didn't Sara's clock go off that morning?

  20. What made Sara embarrassed?

  21. What can be inferred from the two stories?

Passage Three

  A community theatre is an important part of almost every city or town in the United States. There are over 2,000 community theatres in the United States today, about 4.5 million people work or perform in these theatres for an audience of more than 50 million people annually. These theatres are amateur organizations and are different from professional companies. A community theatre may have its own building or perform in a school or church hall. The actors and actresses do not receive money for their work in the community theatre. They have other jobs to support themselves instead. Small communities can't support a full time theatre. They cannot pay actors, directors or stage workers, so the theatre participants work for free. One purpose of community theatre is to provide an opportunity for creative work. Many people join in community theatres because they want to perform or to be creative. Several people in a community theatre group were asked why they join. Each one said he or she needed to be creative. "In the play, I can create something." One woman said, "My whole life is occupied by husband and family. I need something more than that." Another purpose of community theatre is to educate and improve the community. Theatre is an art that also introduced new ideas to the audience.

Questions 22 to 25 are based on the passage you have just heard.

22. How many people contribute to community theatres in the United States?

23. How are community theatres different from professional companies?

24. What opportunity does the community theatre provide to the people in a community?

25. Which of the following is the best title for the passage?

Section C

Directions: In this section, you will hear a passage three times. When the passage is read for the first time, you should listen carefully for its general idea. When the passage is read for the second time, you are required to fill in the blanks numbered from 26 to 33 with the exact words you have just heard. For blanks numbered from 34 to 36 you are required to fill in the missing information. For these blanks, you can either use the exact words you have just heard or write down the main points in your own words. Finally, when the passage is read for the third time, you should check what you have written.

Children have their own rules in playing games. They seldom need a referee and rarely trouble to keep (26) scores. They don't care much about who wins or (27) loses, and it doesn't seem to worry them if the game is not finished. Yet, they like games that (28) depend a lot on luck, so that their (29) personal abilities cannot be directly (30) compared. They also enjoy games that move in stages, in which each stage, the choosing of leaders, the picking of sides or the (31) determining of which side shall start, is almost a game in itself.

Grown-ups can hardly find children's games exciting, and they often feel (32) puzzled at why there kids play such simple games again and again. However, it is found that a child plays games for very important (33) reasons. He can be a good player without having to think whether he is a popular person, and (34) he can find himself being a useful partner to someone of whom he is ordinarily afraid. He becomes a leader when it comes to his turn. He can be confident, too, in particular games, that (35) it is his place to give order, to pretend to be dead, to throw a ball actually at someone, or to kiss someone he had caught.

It appears to us that when children play a game they imagine a situation under their control. Everyone knows the rules, and more importantly, everyone plays according to the rules. (36) Those rules may be childish, but they make sure that every child has a chance to win.

Unit 11

Section A

Directions: In this section, you will hear 8 short conversations and 2 long conversations. At the end of each conversation, one or more questions will be asked about what was said. Both the conversations and the questions will be spoken only once. After each question there will be a pause. During the pause, you must read the four choices marked A, B, C and D, and decide which is the best answer.

1. M: Do you want the same cut as the last time?

   W: The same on top, but I'd like it a bit longer over the ears and in the back.

   Q: Where does this conversation probably take place?

2. W: Would you like to see those pants in another color? They also be in brown and in gray.

   M: Actually, the gray is fine, but I'd prefer something in wool.

   Q: What will the man probably do next?

3. M: I'm so confused about my notes from Professor Johnson's lectures.

   W: How about reviewing them now over a cup of coffee?

   Q: What does the woman suggest they do about the notes?

4. M: Mary, what are you doing with that budget report?

   W: I keep adding and reading the numbers, but they just don't balance.

   Q: What's the probable profession of Mary?

5. W: If Professor Thomson is willing to give us a three-day extension to finish the project, maybe she'll give us a few more days.

   M: Let's not push our luck, Mary! OK?

   Q: What does the man mean?

6. M: I wonder why Mary quit the job at the public relations firm. She hadn't been there that long, and the pay wasn't bad.

   W: Well, she's very creative. I imagine she felt her talents were being wasted there.

   Q: Why did Mary probably leave her job?

171

7. W: May I have this prescription filled here? I have a terrible headache.

M: Yes, but you'll have a 15-minute wait.

Q: Where did this conversation most probably take place?

8. M: Look at this note from the landlord.

W: What? We can't afford another twenty dollars a month.

Q: What are the two speakers talking about?

Now you will hear two long conversations.

Conversation One

M: Is that a map? Are you going sailing or something?

W: I wish. It's a hurricane-tracking chart. It's a map of tropical ocean areas southeast of the U. S. . It follows the development of tropical storms, even hurricanes. They develop and move around the Atlantic in Caribbean and here on Florida coast. We often get hit a lot by those in July or August, at least wind or rain.

M: Do you think that a storm is on the way?

W: Too early to tell, but we need to be prepared. The radio mentioned possible evacuation routes.

M: Really? It's that serious?

W: You'd better believe it. Late summer is hurricane season. The television updates locations and speeds every hour.

M: What did they say is out there now?

W: A couple of tropical depressions, two storms and two hurricanes.

M: What's the difference?

W: Wind velocity. A depression is least serious actually, and a hurricane is the most serious.

M: How serious is the wind in hurricanes?

W: They have sustained wind of 74 miles per hour and up.

M: What are the names of the hurricanes? David, Arlene, Francisco, and Gina.

W: You know weather forecasters give the hurricanes the names of people to make storms easy to identify.

M: I wonder what the status of the storm is now.

W: You shall turn on the television, and it has the best coverage. There is an update coming up in five minutes.

Questions 9 to 12 are based on the conversation you have just heard.

 9. What is the conversation mainly about?

 10. What can we learn about a depression, a storm and a hurricane?

 11. Why are hurricanes named after people?

 12. What are the man and the woman going to do next?

Conversation Two

M: Hi, Janet. You are so lucky to be done with your final exams and term paper.

W: I still have 2 more final exams to take.

M: Really?

W: Yeah. What are you doing this summer? Anything special?

M: Well, actually yes. My parents always like taking my sister and me to different places in the United States, you know, places with historical significance.

W: I guess they wanted to reinforce the stuff you learned in school about history.

M: Maybe. And so even though we are older now, they still do it once in a while.

W: Oh, so where are you going this summer?

M: Well, this summer it's finally going to be Gettysburg.

W: Finally? You mean they never took you yet? I mean Gettysburg. It's probably the most famous Civil War site in the country, and it's only a couple of hours away. I think that would be one of the first places that they've taken you to. I have been there a couple of times.

M: We were planning about time to travel several places 10 years ago, but something happened. I cannot remember what.

W: Something changed your plans?

M: Yeah, don't ask me what it was, but we ended up not going anywhere that year, I hope that doesn't happen again this year.

Questions 13 to 15 are based on the conversation you have just heard.

 13. What are the students mainly discussing?

 14. What does the woman find surprising about the man?

 15. What is the man unable to remember?

Section B

Directions: In this section, you will hear 3 short passages. At the end of each passage, you will hear some questions. Both the passages and the questions will be spoken only once. After you hear a question, you must choose the best answer from the four choices marked A, B, C and D.

Passage One

When Midori was two years old, she often climbed onto the piano bench and reached for the violin that belonged to her mother, a 38-year-old professional musician. "Please don't touch, Midori," her mother scolded.

But Midori persisted, she longed to handle the graceful instrument that made beautiful sounds. Finally, on her third birthday, Midori was handed a package: a tiny violin, about half the normal size.

Almost from the moment Midori was born, her mother knew she was sensitive to music. For several years mother and daughter practised together day after day. Failure often led to tears, but she never stopped learning. She persisted until the problem was overcome.

One day, Johnston, an American musician, heard Midori playing the violin. He couldn't believe she was just eight years old. "She must make a tape and I will take it to the United States," the musician said.

A famous American violin teacher heard the tape. He, too, couldn't believe his ears. The playing was absolutely astonishing. He immediately accepted her as a pupil and recommended her for a full scholarship. In 1982, Midori and her mother moved to New York City, leaving behind a comfortable life in Japan.

Questions 16 to 18 are based on the passage you have just heard.

16. What was Midori's mother?
17. What did Midori receive as a present for her third birthday?
18. Why did Midori move to the United States?

Passage Two

Telephone books in the United States have white, blue and yellow pages. The white pages list people with phones by last name. The blue pages contain numbers of city services, government agencies, and public schools. Businesses and professional services are listed in a special section—the yellow pages.

To make a long-distance call, you need an area code. Each area in the U. S. has an area code. The area covered by an area code may be small or large. For example, New York City has one area code, but so does the whole state of Oregon. If you want to know the area code of a place, you can look it up in the area code map which is printed in the front of the white pages.

There are a lot of public telephones in the U. S.. They have their own numbers. If you are making a long-distance call on public telephone and run out of money, give the number on your phone to the person you're talking to. Then hang up, and he can call you back. If you make a long-distance call and get a wrong number, call the operator and explain what happened. This means that you can make the call again to the right number without having to pay more money.

Questions 19 to 21 are based on the passage you have just heard.

19. Where can you find the telephone number of a city council in the telephone book?
20. Where can you find an area code map of the U. S. ?
21. What are you advised to do when you get a wrong number in making a long-distance call?

Passage Three

Federal Express is a private airline service which expands the Postal Service in the United States. It is the only U. S. airline specializing in the transportation of small packages—35 kilos or less.

Federal Express links 130 major U. S. cities and 10,000 surrounding communities. An urgent package picked up in one part of the country this afternoon can be delivered to any other part of the country tomorrow morning. All of the Federal Express jets fly into the International Airport at Memphis, Tennessee, because it is located in the center of the United States.

The sorting facility of Federal Express is called "The Hub". Every night from about 12 midnight to 3 a. m. , the packages are gathered and sorted into shipments for specific destinations. The main laborforce is comprised of students working part time.

Since Federal Express started business in 1971, it has flown millions of air kilometers without fail. In the space of one hour, 39 jets will take off to destinations all across the United States.

Questions 22 to 25 are based on the passage you have just heard.

22. How many major U. S. cities does Federal Express link?

23. What makes the Federal Express so unique in the U. S. airline service business?

24. Why do all of the Federal Express jets fly into the International Airport at Memphis, Tennessee?

25. Who comprises the main laborforce of Federal Express?

Section C

Directions: In this section, you will hear a passage three times. When the passage is read for the first time, you should listen carefully for its general idea. When the passage is read for the second time, you are required to fill in the blanks numbered from 26 to 33 with the exact words you have just heard. For blanks numbered from 34 to 36 you are required to fill in the missing information. For these blanks, you can either use the exact words you have just heard or write down the main points in your own words. Finally, when the passage is read for the third time, you should check what you have written.

Cyber Café (网吧) computer centers are found in many cities around the world. Now, a few American high schools are (26) opening these centers. All students can use the Cyber Café but school officials say it (27) especially helps students who have no computer or cannot use the Internet at home.

The officials say thirteen percent of the students at the school are from poor families. Many students have (28) arrived in the United States from other countries only recently. Students in the school's (29) program for learning English speak twenty-three other languages. The idea for a Cyber Café began three years ago. At that time, officials were planning to (30) restore the school building. Parents interested in technology (31) proposed a Cyber Café. They wanted this center even though schools in the area had suffered (32) budget cuts. The community wanted to help. It wanted all students to have the best chances to learn.

Officials in the area (33) supported the idea. (34) So did parents, teachers, former students, and business community and some organizations. Over two years, the foundation collected more than 170,000 dollars. (35) Students use the Internet to complete research, writing homework and required papers on the computers. In addition, they can send and receive electronic mail. (36) <u>That is especially helpful for many students who have family members in other nations.</u> The Cyber Café also serves a social purpose. Visitors can stop by for a drink of coffee, tea, or hot chocolate.

Unit 12

Section A

Directions: In this section, you will hear 8 short conversations and 2 long conversations. At the end of each conversation, one or more questions will be asked about what was said. Both the conversations and questions will be spoken only once. After each question there will be a pause. During the pause, you must read the four choices marked A, B, C and D, and decide which is the best answer.

1. W: It's always hard to get this car into first gear, and now something seems wrong with the brake.

   M: If you leave it with me, I'll fix it for you this afternoon.

   Q: What's the man's probable occupation?

2. W: I wish Mike would improve his writing. His spelling and grammar are always so messed up.

   M: You are right. Not to mention his composition skills.

   Q: What can we learn from the conversation?

3. M: Only a few people showed up in the election, so the other candidate won the victory.

   W: What a shame. Our people need to take part in it if they want a bigger voice in the city council.

   Q: What does the woman mean?

4. W: Is everything ready? The meeting is supposed to start at 7:30.

   M: I have five minutes to clean the table. Afterwards we'll have five more minutes to arrange the chairs before the meeting begins.

   Q: What time is it now?

5. M: Excuse me. Could you tell me where I can find a book on American history?

   W: Well, you can start by looking at the card catalogue under A.

   Q: Where does this conversation take place?

6. M: I heard that you are really busy at work since you got the promotion.

   W: I can't complain. At least I don't have to work this evening. So we can go out.

  Q: What will the man do this evening?

7. M: You'll love this place. It has two bedrooms, a big kitchen and a wonderful view.

  W: Yes, it certainly has a fine view and plenty of space, but I have a sleeping problem and it's too near the freeway.

  Q: Where does this conversation most probably take place?

8. W: I got a bad start in the last race. It was hard to catch up with others then.

  M: We'll work on your start mainly. The most important thing is concentration before a race starts.

  Q: What is the probable relationship between the two people?

Now you will hear two long conversations.

Conversation One

M: How are your new next-door neighbors, Linda?

W: They seem nice enough, but they have a son who is driving me crazy.

M: What do you mean?

W: He comes home very late every night and makes a lot of noise after he turns his car off. Then at that time the kids are wide awake.

M: Oh, no. Have you tried talking to them?

W: We haven't even really met them yet, except to say a quick hello. I hate to get off on the wrong foot and I feel stupid complaining. It's not as though he's blasting stereo all night.

M: You said yourself it is driving you crazy.

W: Well, you know how early I have to be here at the office. I just have not got enough sleep and neither have the kids. They are so irritable when I get home in the afternoon.

M: Maybe you could go over sometimes with a little gift. Then you could ask about their children, and they will be sure to ask about yours.

W: Yes, and then what?

M: And then you could mention that the hardest thing at this stage is getting your kids to go to sleep at night.

W: And keeping them asleep.

M: That's the idea and you should do it soon. The longer you wait, the harder it will be to do it politely.

Questions 9 to 12 are based on the conversation you have just heard.

9. What bothers the woman?

10. Why is Linda unwilling to talk about the problem with her neighbor?

11. What does Linda's friend suggest?

12. Which of the following statements is NOT true?

Conversation Two

M: Well, I know that it is smaller than you wanted, but it is one of the nicest apartments in the building.

W: Does it have three bedrooms?

M: No. There are two. The master bedroom is quite spacious though. Maybe you could let the children share the larger room, and you and your husband could use the smaller one.

W: I suppose that I could do that.

M: A three-bedroom apartment will be difficult to find.

W: Yes, I know. I have been looking for one over a week. The few three-bedroom apartments that I have found are either extremely expensive or the owner won't allow children as tenants.

M: Well, the owner allows two children in this apartment complex.

W: Aren't you the owner?

M: No, I am the manager. I live here, too, on the first floor of this building.

W: Oh. That's nice. Then if anything gets broken. . .

M: Just leave a note on my door.

W: You said that the rent would be $ 350 a month. Does that include any utilities?

M: Yes. It includes gas. Your furnace and stove are gas, so, as you can imagine, your other utilities, electricity and water, are quite inexpensive.

W: This sounds better and better. But before I sign a lease I would like my husband to see it.

M: Why not come here this evening?

W: How late are you open? He doesn't get off work until five.

M: Come by at six. I will still be in the office. I am sure that you are eager to move from the hotel, and if we get the paper work out of the way tonight, you can move in tomorrow.

W: Oh, that would be wonderful.

Questions 13 to 15 are based on the conversation you have just heard.

13. Who is the man in this conversation?

14. Where is the woman living now?

15. Why didn't the woman sign a lease?

Section B

Direction: In this section, you will hear 3 short passages. At the end of each passage, you will hear some questions. Both the passages and the questions will be spoken only once. After you hear a question, you must choose the best answer from the four choices marked A, B, C and D.

Passage One

Over one million earthquakes occur every year, but most of these are too small to notice. An earthquake often happens on land or under water. A major quake may last for only a minute, but in that time it can kill thousands of people and destroy complete towns and villages.

In the early hours of the morning of 18th April, 1906, people in San Francisco were suddenly thrown to the ground as one of history's most famous natural disasters struck, and the buildings around them collapsed. At the time damage caused by the earthquake was estimated at around $ 7 million with fire damage at $ 140 million. The quake measured 7.8 on the Richter scale.

On 1st September, 1923, three massive 8.3 magnitude shocks hit the cities of Tokyo and Yokohama. Only 1% of Tokyo's buildings were severely damaged, but massive fires broke out and swept across the wood and paper houses in the city. Of the 140,000 people who died in the disaster, the vast majority were victims of the fire. Over 200,000 buildings were burned down, leaving more than half a million people homeless. September 1st is now named Disaster Prevention Day in Japan and earthquake drills are held in preparation for the inevitable next big quake, during which volunteers are shown how to put out fires and use essential equipment.

Questions 16 to 18 are based on the passage you have just heard.

16. Which of the following statements is NOT true about earthquakes?

17. What is the estimated fire damage of the 1906 earthquake in San Francisco?

18. What is the purpose of Disaster Prevention Day in Japan?

Passage Two

Weather has a powerful effect on people. It influences health, intelligence, and feelings. In August, it is very hot and wet in the southern part of the United States. Southerners have many heart attacks or other kinds of health problems during this month. In the Northeast and the Middle West, it is very hot at some times and very cold at other times. Many people in these states have heart attacks after the weather changes in February or March.

Weather can influence intelligence. For example, in a 1938 study by scientists, the IQ scores of undergraduate college students were very high during a hurricane, but after the storm, their scores were 10% below average. Hurricanes can increase intelligence. Very hot weather, on the other hand, can lower it. Students in the United States often do badly in exams in the hot months of the year (July and August).

Weather also has a strong influence on people's feelings. Winter may be a hard time for thin people; they usually feel cold during these months. They might feel depressed during cold weather. In hot summer weather, on the other hand, fat people may feel unhappy. At about 65 degree Fahrenheit people become stronger.

Low air pressure relaxes people. It increases sexual feeling. It also increases forgetfulness; people leave more packages and umbrellas on buses and in stores on low-pressure days—merely because it is a "perfect weather" for work and health. People feel best at a temperature of about 64°F with 65% humidity.

Are you feeling sick, sad, tired, forgetful, or very intelligent today? The weather may be the cause.

Questions 19 to 21 are based on the passage you have just heard.

19. When may heart attacks be more likely to happen in the southern part of the U. S. ?

20. Which of the following can increase intelligence?

21. What is the "perfect weather"?

Passage Three

Today I'll be talking about the invention of the camera and photography. The camera is often thought to be modern invention, but as early as 1727, a German physicist discovered that light darkens silver salt, a chemical compound. Using a camera, a big box with a small hole to let the light in, he made temporary images on the salt. Silver salt is still the base of film today. Then a French scientist made the first permanent picture by using a special piece of metal sensitized with silver salt. A photograph he made in 1826 still exists. The painter, le Guelle, improved on the process by placing the common salt, the kind we eat, on the metal. This was 1839, the official date of the beginning of photography. But the problem was the printing of the photographs, and it wasn't until other scientists developed the kind of paper we now use that good printing was possible and photography became truly modern. In the 1860's Matthew Brady was able to take his famous picture of the American Civil War, thus making portrait very popular. In the 20th century, Joe Jessman of the U. S. simplified film developing and Doctor Edward Land invented the so-called "instant" camera with self-developing film. If we say that photography came into existence in 1839, it follows that has taken more than 100 years for the camera to reach its present condition of technical refinement.

Questions 22 to 25 are based on the passage you have just heard.

22. What discovery was the basis of photography?

23. How was the first permanent picture made?

24. According to the speaker, why is Matthew Brady remembered today?

25. What did Doctor Edward Land invent?

Section C

Directions: In this section, you will hear a passage three times. When the passage is read for the first time, you should listen carefully for its general idea. When the passage is read for the second time, you are required to fill in the blanks numbered from 26 to 33 with the exact words you have just heard. For blanks numbered from 34 to 36 you are required to fill in the missing information. For these blanks, you can either use the exact words you have just heard or write down the main points in your own words. Finally, when the

passage is read for the third time, you should check what you have written.

Most of us grow up taking certain things for granted. We tend to assume that experts and (26) religious leaders will tell us the truth. We tend to believe that things (27) advertised on television or in news papers can't be bad for us.

However, (28) encouragement of critical thinking in students is one of the goals of most colleges and universities. Few professors (29) require students to share the professor's own (30) beliefs. In general, professors are more (31) concerned that students learn to question and critically (32) examine the arguements of others. This does not mean that professors insist that you change your beliefs, either. It does mean, however, professors will usually ask you to support the views you (33) express in class or in your wiring.

(34) If your arguments are not logical, professors personally point out the false reasoning in your arguements. Most professors want you to recognize the premises of your argument, to examine whether you really accept them, and understand whether or not you draw logical conclusions. (35) Put it this way: professors don't tell you what to think, they try to teach you how to think.

On the other hand, if you intend to disagree with your professors in class, you should be prepared to offer a strong argument in support of your ideas. (36) Arguing just for the sake of arguing usually does not promote a critical examination of ideas. Many professors interpret it as rudeness.

Unit 13

Section A

Directions：In this section, you will hear 8 short conversations and 2 long conversations. At the end of each conversation, one or more questions will be asked about what was said. Both the conversations and questions will be spoken only once. After each question there will be a pause. During the pause, you must read the four choices marked A, B, C and D, and decide which is the best answer.

1. W：Your room is a mess！Your books and pens are all over the floor and your quilt and sheet are not in order. You ought to try to be neater. Tidy them up now.

   M：OK. But when I've finished, can we go on a picnic?

   Q：Who are these two speakers?

2. W：With the company in such financial difficulties, I wonder what will happen to the president.

   M：Haven't you heard? The board of directors has asked for his resignation.

   Q：What happened to the president of the company?

3. M：Tickets for the art museum are three dollars for adults and children's tickets are half price.

   W：I see. I'd like two adults'and three children's tickets, please.

   Q：How much would the woman pay for the tickets altogether?

4. W：What a bad day. I was late for work again. My car broke down on the way, and now it's in the repair shop.

   M：Maybe you should consider trading it for a new one.

   Q：What does the man suggest that the woman do?

5. M：What kind of dress are you looking for?

   W：Since it's getting warmer this time of the year, I want something lightweight. What do you think would be the best?

   Q：What are these people talking about?

6. M：Hey！Where did you find that journal? I need it for my research, too.

   W：Right here. But don't worry, I'll take it out on my card for both of us.

Q: Where is this conversation probably taking place?

7. M: Monica, I'm very excited! I just got my scholarship approved by the university council.

W: That's fantastic! I didn't apply this year, because my grades weren't good enough.

Q: Why is the man excited?

8. W: Can you help me? I haven't done this before.

M: It's easy. All you do is to put the worm on the hook, loosen the line, and case it.

Q: What is the man showing the woman how to do?

Now you will hear two long conversations.

Conversation One

M: I'm not sure if I can find work this summer. There aren't many jobs out there for inexperienced workers, and I can't just sit around all day.

W: Say, have you heard about house-sitting? Mark is going to house-sit for Professor Green's family this summer when they travel to Europe. They'll be away for four weeks and don't want to leave the house empty.

M: What exactly is house-sitting? I've never heard of it.

W: It seems like baby-sitting, but you're watching a house instead of kids.

M: It sounds good. So all I do all day is sit around their house?

W: It's not so simple. Part of Mark's responsibilities includes walking their dog and tending their garden. When Bill house-sat last spring breaks, he had to clean their swimming pool.

M: I'll take any job that pays! How do I sigh up?

W: There are a few notices posted in the student lounge.

M: So I just call them and tell them that I want the job?

W: Not exactly. Mark and Bill had an interview with the homeowners. In addition, they submitted two references.

M: It seems quite complicated.

W: Well, the homeowners need to feel that you're trustworthy. They want the kind of person who will do the job and not throw wild parties or move lots of friends in while they're away.

M: I suppose if that happens, they won't pay you.

W: Most of the time, they'll pay you anyway, just because the homeowners don't want to fuss about it. But if they filed a complaint, the house-sitter would never be hired again.

M: Hmm. I think I'll have a try.

Questions 9 to 12 are based on the conversation you have just heard.

9. What is the man's plan for the summer?

10. What is house-sitting?

11. What do homeowners do to determine whether or not an applicant is trustworthy?

12. What is the relationship between the two speakers?

Conversation Two

M: Excuse me, can you help me please? I've lost my watch.

W: Where do you think you lost it?

M: Well, I think I must have left it in the gentlemen's toilet.

W: Do you know what time?

M: Well, it was only about a quarter of an hour ago. I think I took it off to wash my hands and I left it on the window edge just in front of the wash basin. And I went back to my room and I realized I'd lost my watch, so I went back to the gentlemen's toilet again to see if it was there, and it disappeared. I wondered if maybe one of the cleaners had picked it up.

W: Did you ask the attendant if he'd seen it?

M: Er, the attendant wasn't there at the time actually. I didn't see anyone else there.

W: Right, can you give me some details please?

M: Well, it's an ordinary sort of watch, you know, not one of those fancy digital things.

W: Can you describe your watch?

M: It's a wind-up watch. Erm, it's got the date on it. Well, you know, a date indicator and a second hand and it's got a, a brown leather strap on it as well.

W: Right. And what color is it?

M: It's a silver color.

W: OK. Well, leave it with me and I'll check with the attendant.

Questions 13 to 15 are based on the conversation you have just heard.

    13. Where does the conversation most probably take place?

    14. When and where does the man think he lost his watch?

    15. Which of the following statements is NOT true about the watch?

Section B

Direction: In this section, you will hear 3 short passages. At the end of each passage, you will hear some questions. Both the passages and the questions will be spoken only once. After you hear a question, you must choose the best answer from the four choices marked A, B, C and D.

Passage One

    In the next few decades people are going to travel very differently from the way they do today. Everyone is going to drive electrically powered cars. So in a few years people won't worry about running out of gas.

    Some of large automobile companies are really moving ahead with this new technology. F & C Motors, a major auto company, for example, is holding a press conference next week. At the press conference the company will present its new, electronically operated models.

    Transportation in the future won't be limited to the ground. Many people predict that traffic will quickly move to the sky. In the coming years, instead of radio reports about road conditions and highway traffic, news reports will talk about traffic jams in the sky.

    But the sky isn't the limit. In the future, you'll probably even be able to take a trip to the moon, Instead of listening to regular airplane announcements; you'll hear someone say, "The spacecraft to the moon leaves in ten minutes. Please check your equipment. And remember, no more than ten ounces of carry-on baggage are allowed."

Questions 16 to 18 are based on the passage you have just heard.

    16. What will be used to power cars in the next few decades?

    17. What will future news reports focus on when talking about transportation?

    18. What is the special requirement for passengers traveling to the moon?

Passage Two

    The first English dictionary, called *An Alphabetical Table of Hard Words*, was published in 1604. The dictionary actually gave only about 3,000 difficult words, each followed by one word definition. The author, Robert Cawdrey, made no attempt to include everyday words in his dictionary. No one, he reasoned, would ever have to look up a word in a dictionary if he already knew the meaning of the word. During the 1600's more dictionaries were published.

Each followed Cawdrey's lead and presented a few thousand hard words. Around 1700 one dictionary maker, John, Kersey, did define easy words as well as hard ones. But until the 1750's all dictionaries were rather simple and not very valuable.

A man named Dr. Samuel Johnson changed all this. In 1755 Dr. Johnson produced the first modern dictionary. He included in his dictionary all important words, both easy and hard, and he gave good meanings. He also gave good sentences to show how each word was actually used in speech and writing. By the end of the 1700's most dictionary makers had followed Johnson's lead. Dictionaries were getting better and better.

The 1800's saw the greatest improvement in the quality of dictionaries. In England scholars planned and prepared the Oxford English Dictionary, a twenty-volume work. One of the most interesting features of the *Oxford English Dictionary* is its word histories. It traced the history of each word from its earliest recorded use up to the time of the printing of the dictionary.

Questions 19 to 21 are based on the passage you have just heard.

19. When was the first English dictionary published?
20. Who produced the first modern dictionary?
21. What was one of the most interesting features of the *Oxford English Dictionary*?

Passage Three

The human nose has given many interesting expressions to the language of the world. Of course, this is not surprising. Without nose, we could not breathe nor smell. It is a part of the face that gives a person special character. It is said that a large nose shows a great man—courageous, courteous, manly, and intellectual.

A famous woman poet wished that she had two noses to smell a rose! Blaise Pascal, a French philosopher, made an interesting comment about Cleopatra's nose. If it had been shorter, he said, it would have changed the whole face of the world!

Historically, man's nose has had a principal role in his imagination. Man has referred to the nose in many ways to express his emotions. Expressions concerning the nose refer to human weakness: anger, pride, jealousy and revenge.

In English there are a number of phrases about the nose. For example, to hold up one's nose expresses a basic human feeling—pride. People can hold up their noses at people, things, and places.

The phrase, to be led around by the nose, shows man's weakness. A person who is led around by the nose lets other people control him. On the other hand, a person who follows his nose lets his instinct guide him.

For the human emotion of rejection, the phrase to have one's nose put out of joint is very descriptive. The expression applies to persons who have been turned aside because of a rival. Their pride is hurt and they feel rejected. This expression is not new. It was used by Erasmus in 1542.

This is only a sampling of expressions in English dealing with the nose. There are a number of others. However, it should be as plain as the nose on your face that the nose is more than an organ for breathing and smelling!

Questions 22 to 25 are based on the passage you have just heard.

22. What does "hold up one's nose" mean?

23. What does "A person who follows his nose" mean?

24. Who can be described as "a man to have his nose put out of joint"?

25. What is the main idea of the passage?

Section C

Directions: In this section, you will hear a passage three times. When the passage is read for the first time, you should listen carefully for its general idea. When the passage is read for the second time, you are required to fill in the blanks numbered from 26 to 33 with the exact words you have just heard. For blanks numbered from 34 to 36 you are required to fill in the missing information. For these blanks, you can either use the exact words you have just heard or write down the main points in your own words. Finally, when the passage is read for the third time, you should check what you have written.

Nancy Jessie's sleeping difficulties began on (26) <u>vacation</u> a few summers ago. She (27) <u>blamed</u> the noisy motel room, but her sleeping did not improve at home. Instead of her usual six to seven hours a night, the 37-year-old teacher slept just three or four hours. "I'd toss and turn for hours, then get up and pace," she says.

Nancy tried going to bed earlier, but the (28) <u>slightest</u> noise, even her husband's (29) <u>breathing</u>, disturbed her. She drank a glass of wine at bedtime and fell asleep immediately, but was (30) <u>awaked</u> two hours later. Her doctor (31) <u>prescribed</u> a sleeping pill for two weeks. When she stopped taking the pills, though, she slept worse than ever.

Most of us have the (32) <u>occasional</u> short period of troubled sleep and then return to normal a few nights later. However, for one in six people insomnia is a (33) <u>continual</u> problem.

Now the Johns Hopkins's Sleep Disorders Center in Baltimore (34) <u>has developed a nine-step treatment to help</u> insomniacs cure themselves. It is based on the idea that by deliberately reducing time in bed and by modifying your waking activities (35) <u>you will be able to sleep more soundly.</u>

Psychologist Richard Alien, co-director of the Johns Hopkins Center, considers insomnia a 24-hour disorder. Thus, his treatment, which draws on research done by Arthur Spielman of the Sleep Disorders Center of the City College of New York, (36) <u>includes advice on daytime as well as bedtime behavior.</u>

第六部分　听力历年全真试题录音原稿

2008 年 6 月英语四级全真试题听力材料

Part Ⅲ　　　　　　　**Listening Comprehension**　　　　（35 minutes）

Section A

Directions：In this section，you will hear 8 short conversations and 2 long conversations. At the end of each conversation，one or more questions will be asked about what was said. Both the conversations and the questions will be spoken only once. After each question there will be a pause. During the pause，you must read the four choices marked A，B，C and D，and decide which is the best answer. Then mark the corresponding letter on Answer Sheet 2 with a single line through the centre.

11. M：Today's a bad day for me！I fell off a step and twisted my ankle.

    W：Don't worry. Usually ankle injuries heal quickly if you stop regular activities for a while.

    Q：What does the woman suggest the man do?

12. W：May I see your ticket，please？I think you're sitting in my seat.

    M：Oh，you're right！My seat is in the balcony. I'm terribly sorry！

    Q：Where does the conversation most probably take place?

13. W：Did you hear Jay Smith died in his sleep last night?

    M：Yes，it's very sad. Please let everybody know that whoever wants to attend the funeral.

    Q：What are the speakers talking about?

14. M：Have you taken Prof. Yang's exam before？I'm kind of nervous.

W: Yes. Just concentrate on the important ideas she's talked about in the class and ignore the details.

Q: How does the woman suggest the man prepare for Prof. Yang's exam?

15. W: I'm so sorry, sir. And you'll let me pay to have your jacket cleaned, won't you?

   M: That's all right. It could happen to anyone. And I'm sure that coffee doesn't leave lasting marks on clothing.

   Q: What can we infer from the conversation?

16. W: Have you seen the movie *The Departed*? The plot was so complicated that I really got lost.

   M: Yeah, I felt the same. But after I saw it a second time, I could put all the pieces together.

   Q: How did the two speakers feel about the movie?

17. M: I'm really surprised you got an A on the test. You didn't seem to have done a lot of reading.

   W: Now you know why I never missed a lecture.

   Q: What contributes to the woman's high score?

18. W: Have you heard about a new digital television system? It lets people get about 500 channels.

   M: Yeah. But I doubt that they have anything different from what we watch now.

   Q: What does the man mean?

Long Conversations:

Conversation One

W: Gosh! Have you seen this, Richard?

M: Seeing what?

W: In the paper, it says there is a man going around pretending he is from the electricity board. He's been calling at people's homes, saying he's come to check that all their appliances are safe. Then he gets around them to make him a cup of tea. While they are out of their room, he steals their money, handbag, and other things.

M: But you know, Jane. It is partly their own fault; you should never let anyone like that in unless you are expecting them.

W: It's all very well to say that, but someone comes to the door and says electricity or gas, and you automatically think they are OK. Especially if they flash a card to you.

M: Does this man have an ID then?

W: Yes, that's just it. It seems he used to work for the electricity board at one time. According to the paper, the police are warning people, especially pensioners not to meet anyone unless they have an appointment. It's a bit sad. One old lady told them she'd just been to the post office to draw her pension when he called, she said he must have followed her home. He stole the whole lot.

M: But what does he look like? Surely they must have a description.

W: Oh yes, they have. Let's see. In his 30s, tall, bushy dark hair, a slight northern accent, sounds a bit like you actually.

Questions 19 to 22 are based on the conversation you have just heard.

19. What does the woman want the man to read in the newspaper?

20. How did the man mention in the newspaper try to win further trust from the victims?

21. What is the warning from the police?

22. What does the woman speaker tell us about the old lady?

Conversation Two

M: Ms. Jones, could you tell me more about your fist job with hotel marketing concepts?

W: Yes, certainly. I was a marketing consultant, responsible for marketing ten UK hotels. They were all luxury hotels in the leisure sector, all of a very high standard.

M: Which market were you responsible for?

W: For Europe and Japan.

M: I see from your resume that you speak Japanese. Have you ever been to Japan?

W: Yes, I have. I spent a month in Japan in 2006. I met all the key people in the tourist industry, the big tour operators and the tourist organizations. As I speak Japanese, I had a very big advantage.

M: Yes, of course. Have you had any contact with Japanese in your present job?

W: Yes, I've had a lot. The truth is I've become very popular with the Japanese, both for holidays and for business conferences. In fact, the market for all types of luxury holidays for the Japanese has increased a lot recently.

M: Really? I am interested to hear more about that, but first tell me, have you ever traveled on a luxury train? The Orient Express, for example?

W: No, I haven't, but I have traveled on the Glacier Express to Switzerland and I traveled across China by train about 8 years ago. I love train travel. That's why I am very interested in this job.

Questions 23 to 25 are based on the conversation you have just heard.

23. What did the woman do in her first job?

24. What gives the woman an advantage during her business trip in Japan?

25. Why is the woman applying for the new job?

Section B

Directions: In this section, you will hear 3 short passages. At the end of each passage, you will hear some questions. Both the passages and the questions will be spoken only once. After you hear a question, you must choose the best answer from the four choices marked A, B, C and D. Then mark the corresponding letter on Answer Sheet 2 with a single line through the centre.

Passage One

Time! I think a lot about time. And not just because it's the name of the news organization I work for. Like most working people, I find time or the lack of it, are never ending frustration and an unwinnable battle. My everyday is a race against the clock that I never ever seem to win. This is hardly a lonesome complaint. According to the families and work institutes, national study of the changing workforce, 55% of employees say they don't have enough time for themselves, 63% don't have enough time for their spouses or partners, and 67% don't have enough time for their children. It's also not a new complaint. I bet our ancestors returned home from hunting wild animals and gathering nuts and complained about how little time they had to paint the pour battle scenes on their cave walls. The difference is that the boss of animal-hunting and the head of nut-gathering probably told them to "shut up" or "no survival for you". Today's workers are still demanding control of their time. The difference is:

Today's bosses are listening. I've been reading a report issued today called "When Work Works", produced jointly by three organizations. They set out to find and award the employers who employ the most creative and most effective ways to give their workers flexibility. I found this report worth reading and suggest every boss should read it for ideas.

Questions 26 to 28 are based on the passage you have just heard.

26. What is the speaker complaining about?

27. What does the speaker say about our ancestors?

28. Why does the speaker suggest all bosses read the report by the three organizations?

Passage Two

Loving a child is a circular business. "The more you give, the more you get, the more you want to give." Penelope Leach once said. What she said proves to be true of my blended family. I was born in 1931. As the youngest of six children, I learned to share my parents' love. Raising six children during the difficult times of the Great Depression took its toll on my parents' relationship and resulted in their divorce when I was 18 years old. Daddy never had very close relationships with his children and drifted even farther away from us after the divorce. Several years later, a wonderful woman came into his life, and they were married. She had two sons, one of them is still at home. Under her influence, we became a "blended family" and a good relationship developed between the two families. She always treated us as if we were her own children.

It was because of our other mother—Daddy's second wife—that he became closer to his own children. They shared over twenty-five years together before our father passed away. At the time of his death, the question came up of my mother—Daddy's first wife—attending his funeral.

I will never forget the unconditional love shown by my stepmother when I asked her if she would object to mother attending Daddy's funeral. Without giving it a second thought, she immediately replied, "Of course not, Honey—she's the mother of my children."

Questions 29 to 31 are based on the passage you have just heard.

29. According to the speaker, what contributed to her parents' divorce?

30. What brought the father closer to his own children?

31. What message does the speaker want to convey in this talk?

Passage Three

In February last year, my wife lost her job. Just as suddenly, the owner of the greenhouse where I worked as manager died of heart attack. His family announced that they were going to close the business because no one in the family wanted to run it. Things looked pretty gloomy, my wife and I read the want ads each day.

Then one morning, as I was hanging out the "going out of business" sign at the greenhouse, the door opened, and in walked a customer. She was an office manager whose company had just moved into the new office park on the edge of town. She was looking for pots and plants to place in the reception areas in the offices. "I don't know anything about plants," she said, "I'm sure in a few weeks they'll all be dead."

Why was I helping her select her purchases? My mind was racing. Perhaps as many as a dozen firms have recently opened offices in the new office park, and there were several hundred more acres with construction under way. That afternoon, I drove out to the office park. By 6 o'clock that evening, I had signed contracts with seven companies to rent plants from me and pay me a fee to maintain them. Within a week, I had worked out an agreement to lease the greenhouse from the owner's family. Business is now increasing rapidly. And one day, we hope to be the proud owner of the greenhouse.

Questions 32 to 35 are based on the passage you have just heard.

32. What do we learn about the greenhouse?

33. What was the speaker doing when the customer walked in one morning?

34. What did the speaker think of when serving the office manager?

35. What was the speaker's hope for the future?

Section C

Directions: In this section, you will hear a passage three times. When the passage is read for the first time, you should listen carefully for its general idea. When the passage is read for the second time, you are required to fill in the blanks numbered from 36 to 43 with the exact words you have just heard. For blanks numbered from 44 to 46 you are required to fill in the missing information. For these blanks, you can either use the exact words you have just heard or write

down the main points in your own words. Finally, when the passage is read for the third time, you should check what you have written.

We are now witnessing the emergence of an advanced economy based on information and knowledge. Physical (36) labor, raw materials, and capital are no longer the key (37) ingredients in the creation of wealth. Now the (38) vital raw material in our economy is knowledge. Tomorrow's wealth depends on the development and exchange of knowledge. And (39) individuals entering the workforce offer their knowledge, not their muscles. Knowledge workers get paid for their education and their ability to learn. Knowledge workers (40) engage in mind work. They deal with symbols: words, (41) figures, and data.

What does all this mean for you? As a future knowledge worker, you can expect to be (42) generating, processing, as well as exchanging information. (43) Currently, three out of four jobs involve some form of mind work, and that number will increase sharply in the future. Management and employees alike (44) will be making decisions in such areas as product development, quality control, and customer satisfaction.

In the new world of work, you can look forward to being in constant training (45) to acquire new skills that will help you keep up with improved technologies and procedures. You can also expect to be taking greater control of your career. Gone are the nine-to-five jobs, lifetime security, predictable promotions, and even the conventional workplace, as you are familiar with. (46) Don't expect the companies will provide you with a clearly defined career path. And don't wait for someone to "empower" you. You have to empower yourself.

2007 年 12 月英语四级听力全真试题

Part III　　　　　　　　**Listening Comprehension**　　　　（35 minutes）

Section A

Directions：In this section，you will hear 8 short conversations and 2 long conversations. At the end of each conversation，one or more questions will be asked about what was said. Both the conversations and the questions will be spoken only once. After each question there will be a pause. During the pause，you must read the four choices marked A，B，C and D，and decide which is the best answer. Then mark the corresponding letter on the Answer Sheet 2 with a single line through the centre.

11. W：I ran into Sally the other day. I could hardly recognize her. Do you remember her from high school?

    M：Yeah, she was a little out of shape back then. Well, has she lost a lot of weight?

    Q：What does the man remember of Sally?

12. W：We don't seem to have a reservation for you, sir? I'm sorry.

    M：But my secretary said that she had reserved a room for me here. I phoned her from the airport this morning just before I got on board the plane.

    Q：Where does the conversation most probably take place?

13. W：What would you do if you were in my place?

    M：If Paul were my son, I'd just not worry. Now that his teacher gives him extra help and he is working hard himself, he's sure to do well in the next exam.

    Q：What's the man's suggestion to the woman?

14. M：You've had your hands full and have been overworked during the last two weeks. I think you really need to go out and get some fresh air and sunshine.

    W：You are right. That's just what I'm thinking about.

    Q：What's the woman most probably going to do?

15. W：Hello, John. How are you feeling now? I hear you've been ill.

    M：They must have confused me with my twin brother Rod. He's been sick all week, but I've never felt better in my life.

Q: What do we learn about the man?

16. M: Did you really give away all your furniture when you moved into the new house last month?

W: Just the useless pieces, as I'm planning to purchase a new set from Italy for the sitting room only.

Q: What does the woman mean?

17. M: I've brought back your *Oxford Companion to English literature*. I thought you might use it for your paper. Sorry not to have returned it earlier.

W: I was wondering where that book was.

Q: What can we infer from that conversation?

18. W: To tell the truth, Tony, it never occurs to me that you are an athlete.

M: Oh, really? Most people who meet me, including some friends of mine, don't think so either.

Q: What do we learn from the conversation?

Long Conversations:

Conversation One

M: Mary, I hope you are packed and ready to leave.

W: Yes, I'm packed, but not quite ready. I can't find my passport.

M: Your passport? That's the one thing you mustn't leave behind.

W: I know. I haven't lost it. I've packed it, but I can't remember which bag it's in.

M: Well, you have to find it at the airport. Come on, the taxi is waiting.

W: Did you say taxi? I thought we were going in your car.

M: Yes, well, I have planned to, but I'll explain later. You've got to be there in an hour.

W: The plane doesn't leave for two hours. Anyway, I'm ready to go now.

M: Well, now you are taking just one case, is that right?

W: No, there is one in the hall as well.

M: Gosh, what a lot of stuff! You are taking enough for a month instead of a week.

W: Well, you can't depend on the weather. It might be cold.

M: It's never cold in Rome. Certainly not in May. Come on, we really must go.

W: Right, we are ready. We've got the bags, I'm sure there is no need to rush.

M: There is. I asked the taxi driver to wait two minutes, not twenty.

W: Look, I'm supposed to be going away to relax. You are making me nervous.

M: Well, I want you to relax on holidays, but you can't relax yet.

W: OK, I promise not to relax, at least not until we get to the airport and I find my passport.

Questions 19 to 22 are based on the conversation you have just heard.

    19. What does the woman say about her passport?

    20. What do we know about the woman's trip?

    21. Why does the man urge the woman to hurry?

    22. Where does the conversation most probably take place?

Conversation Two

W: Oh, I'm fed up with my job.

M: Hey, there is a perfect job in the paper today. You might be interested.

W: Oh, what is it? What do they want?

M: Wait a minute. Eh, here it is. The European Space Agency is recruiting translators.

W: The European Space Agency?

M: Well, that's what it says. They need an English translator to work from French or German.

W: So they need a degree in French or German, I suppose. Well, I've got that. What's more, I have plenty of experience. What else are they asking for?

M: Just that. A university degree and three or four years of experience as a translator in a professional environment. They also say the person should have a lively and enquiring mind, effective communication skills and the ability to work individually or as a part of the team.

W: Well, if I stay at my present job much longer, I won't have any mind or skills left. By the way, what about salary? I just hope it isn't lower than what I get now.

M: It's said to be negotiable. It depends on the applicant's education and experience. In addition to basic salary, there is a list of extra benefits. Have a look yourself.

W: Hm, travel and social security plus relocation expenses are paid. Hey, this isn't bad. I really want the job.

Questions 23 to 25 are based on the conversation you have just heard.

    23. Why is the woman trying to find a new job?

24. What position is being advertised in the paper?

25. What are the key factors that determine the salary of the new position?

Section B

Directions: In this section, you will hear 3 short passages. At the end of each passage, you will hear some questions. Both the passages and the questions will be spoken only once. After you hear a question, you must choose the best answer from the four choices marked A, B, C and D. Then mark the corresponding letter on the Answer Sheet 2 with a single line through the centre.

Passage One

When couples get married, they usually plan to have children. Sometimes, however, a couple can not have a child of their own. In this case, they may decide to adopt a child. In fact, adoption is very common today. There are about 60,000 adoptions each year in the U. S. alone. Some people prefer to adopt infants, others adopt older children, some couples adopt children from their own countries, others adopt children from foreign countries. In any case, they all adopt children for the same reason—they care about children and want to give their adopted child a happy life.

Most adopted children know that they are adopted. Psychologists and child-care experts generally think this is a good idea. However, many adopted children or adoptees have very little information about their biological parents. As a matter of fact, it is often very difficult for adoptees to find out about their birth parents because the birth records of most adoptees are usually sealed. The information is secret, so no one can see it. Naturally, adopted children have different feelings about their birth parents. Many adoptees want to search for them, but others do not. The decision to search for birth parents is a difficult one to make. Most adoptees have mixed feelings about finding their biological parents. Even though adoptees do not know about their natural parents, they do know that their adopted parents want them, love them and will care for them.

Questions 26 to 29 are based on the passage you have just heard.

26. According to the speaker, why do some couples adopt children?

27. Why is it difficult for adoptees to find out about their birth parents?

28. Why do many adoptees find it hard to make the decision to search for their birth parents?

29. What can we infer from the passage?

Passage Two

Catherine Gram graduated from the University of Chicago in 1938 and got a job as a news reporter in San Francisco. Catherine's father used to be a successful investment banker. In 1933, he bought a failing newspaper, *the Washington Post*.

Then Catherine returned to Washington and got a job, editing letters in her father's newspaper. She married Philip Gram, who took over his father-in-law's position shortly after and became a publisher of *the Washington Post*. But for many years, her husband suffered from mental illness and he killed himself in 1963. After her husband's death, Catherine operated the newspaper. In the 1970s, the newspaper became famous around the world and Catherine was also recognized as an important leader in newspaper publishing. She was the first woman to head a major American publishing company, the Washington Post Company. In a few years, she successfully expanded the company to include newspaper, magazine, broadcast and cable companies.

She died of head injuries after a fall when she was 84. More than 3 thousand people attended her funeral, including many government and business leaders. Her friends said she would be remembered as a woman who had an important influence on events in the United States and the world. Catherine once wrote, "The world without newspapers would not be the same kind of world." After her death, the employees of *the Washington Post* wrote, "The world without Catherine would not be the same at all."

Questions 30 to 32 are based on the passage you have just heard.

30. What do we learn from the passage about Catherine's father?
31. What does the speaker tell us about Catherine Gram?
32. What does the comment by employees of *the Washington Post* suggest?

Passage Three

Obtaining good health insurance is a real necessity while you are studying overseas. It protects you from minor and major medical expenses that can wipe out not only your savings but your dreams of an education abroad. There are often two different types of health insurance you can consider buying, international travel insurance and student insurance in the country where you will be going.

An international travel insurance policy is usually purchased in your home country before you go abroad. It generally covers a wide variety of medical services and you are often given a list of doctors in the area where you will travel who may even speak your native language. The drawback might be that you may not get your money back immediately. In other words, you may have to pay all your medical expenses and then later submit your receipt to the insurance company.

On the other hand, getting student heath insurance in the country where you will study might allow you to only pay a certain percentage of the medical cost at the time of the service and thus you don't have to have sufficient cash to pay the entire bill at once. Whatever you decide, obtaining some form of health insurance is something you should consider before you go overseas. You shouldn't wait until you are sick with a major medical bills to pay off.

Questions 33 to 35 are based on the passage you have just heard.

33. Why does the speaker advice overseas students to buy health insurance?

34. What is the drawback of students buying international travel insurance?

35. What does the speaker say about students getting health insurance in the country where they will study?

Section C

Directions: In this section, you will hear a passage three times. When the passage is read for the first time, you should listen carefully for its general idea. When the passage is read for the second time, you are required to fill in the blanks numbered from 36 to 43 with the exact words you have just heard. For blanks numbered from 44 to 46 you are required to fill in the missing information. For these blanks, you can either use the exact words you have just heard or write down the main points in your own words. Finally, when the passage is read for the third time, you should check what you have written.

More and more of the world's population are living in towns or cities. The speed at which cities are growing in the less developed countries is (36) <u>alarming</u>. Between 1920 and 1960, big cities in developed countries (37) <u>increased</u> two and a half times in size, but in other parts of the world the growth was eight times their size.

The (38) <u>sheer</u> size of growth is bad enough, but there are now also very (39) <u>disturbing</u> signs of trouble in the (40) <u>comparison</u> of percentages of people living in towns and percentages of people working in industry. During the 19th century, cities grew as a result of the growth of industry. In Europe, the (41) <u>proportion</u> of people living in cities was always smaller than that of the (42) <u>workforce</u> working in factories. Now, however, the (43) <u>reverse</u> is almost always true in the newly industrialized world. (44) <u>The percentage of people living in cities is much higher than the percentage</u> <u>working in industry.</u> Without a base of people working in industry, these cities cannot pay for their growth. (45) <u>There is not enough money to build adequate houses for the</u> <u>people that live there, let alone the new arrivals.</u> There has been little opportunity to build water supplies or other facilities. (46) <u>So the figures for the growth of towns and</u> <u>cities represent proportional growth of unemployment and underemployment,</u> a growth in the number of hopeless and despairing parents and starving children.

2007 年 6 月英语四级听力全真试题

Part III   **Listening Comprehension**   **(35 minutes)**

Section A

Directions: In this section, you will hear 8 short conversations and 2 long conversations. At the end of each conversation, one or more questions will be asked about what was said. Both the conversations and the questions will be spoken only once. After each question there will be a pause. During the pause, you must read the four choices marked A, B, C and D, and decide which is the best answer. Then mark the corresponding letter on the Answer Sheet 2 with a single line through the centre.

11. W: Did you watch the 7 o'clock program on channel 2 yesterday evening? I was about to watch it when someone came to see me.

    M: Yeah! It reported some major breakthrough in cancer research. People over 40 would find a program worth watching.

    Q: What do we learn from the conversation about the TV program?

12. W: I won a first prize in the National Writing Contest and I got this camera as an award.

    M: It's a good camera! You can take it when you travel. I had no idea you were a marvelous writer.

    Q: What do we learn from the conversation?

13. M: I wish I hadn't thrown away that reading list!

    W: I thought you might regret it. That's why I picked it up from the waste paper basket and left it on the desk.

    Q: What do we learn from the conversation?

14. W: Are you still teaching at the junior high school?

    M: Not since June. My brother and I opened a restaurant as soon as he got out of the army.

    Q: What do we learn about the man from the conversation?

15. M: Hi, Susan! Have you finished reading the book Professor Johnson recommended?

    W: Oh, I haven't read it through the way I read a novel. I just read a few chapters which interested me.

Q: What does the woman mean?

16. M: Jane missed the class again, didn't she? I wonder why.

W: Well, I knew she had been absent all week. So I called her this morning to see if she was sick. It turned out that her husband was badly injured in a car accident.

Q: What does the woman say about Jane?

17. W: I'm sure the Smiths' new house is somewhere on the street, but I don't know exactly where it is.

M: But I'm told it's two blocks from their old home.

Q: What do we learn from the conversation?

18. W: I've been waiting here almost half an hour! How come it took you so long?

M: Sorry, honey! I had to drive two blocks before I spotted a place to park the car.

Q: What do we learn from the conversation?

Long Conversations:

Conversation One

M: Hello, I have a reservation for tonight.

W: Your name, please.

M: Nelson, Charles Nelson.

W: OK, Mr. Nelson. That's a room for five and...

M: But excuse me, you mean a room for five pounds? I didn't know the special was so good.

W: No, no..., according to our records, a room for 5 guests was booked under your name.

M: No, no—hold on. You must have two guests under the name.

W: OK, let me check this again. Oh, here we are.

M: Yeah?

W: Charles Nelson, a room for one for the 19th...

M: Wait, wait. It's for tonight, not tomorrow night.

W: Em..., I don't think we have any rooms for tonight. There's a conference going on in town and—er, let's see... yeah, no rooms.

M: Oh, come on! You must have something, anything!

W: Well, let... let me check my computer here... Ah!

M: What?

W: There has been a cancellation for this evening. A honeymoon suite is now available.

M: Great, I'll take it.

W: But, I'll have to charge you 150 pounds for the night.

M: What? I should get a discount for the inconvenience!

W: Well, the best I can give you is a 10% discount plus a ticket for a free continent breakfast.

M: Hey, isn't the breakfast free anyway?

W: Well, only on weekends.

M: I want to talk to the manager.

W: Wait, wait, wait... Mr. Nelson, I think I can give you an additional 15% discount...

Questions 19 to 22 are based on the conversation you have just heard.

19. What's the man's problem?

20. Why did the hotel clerk say they didn't have any rooms for that night?

21. What did the clerk say about the breakfast in the hotel?

22. What did the man imply he would do at the end of the conversation?

Conversation Two

M: Sarah, you work in the Admissions Office, don't you?

W: Yes, I am... I've been here ten years as Assistant Director.

M: Really? What does that involve?

W: Well, I'm in charge of all the admissions of postgraduate students in the university.

M: Only postgraduates?

W: Yes, postgraduates only. I have nothing at all to do with undergraduates.

M: Do you find that you get a particular... sort of... different national groups? I mean, do you get large numbers from Latin America or...

W: Yes. Well, of all the students enrolled last year, nearly half were from overseas. They were from African countries, the Far East, the Middle East, and Latin America.

M：Em. But have you been doing just that for the last 10 years, or, have you done other things?

W：Well, I've been doing the same job. Er, before that, I was secretary of the medical school at Birmingham, and further back, I worked in the local government.

M：Oh, I see.

W：So I've done different types of things.

M：Yes, indeed. How do you imagine your job might develop in the future? Can you imagine shifting into a different kind of responsibility or doing something...

W：Oh, yeah, from October 1st I'll be doing an entirely different job. There's going to be more committee work. I mean, more policy work, and less dealing with students, unfortunately... I'll miss my contact with students.

Questions 23 to 25 are based on the conversation you have just heard.

23. What is the woman's present position?

24. What do we learn about the postgraduates enrolled last year in the woman's university?

25. What will the woman's new job be like?

Section B

Directions：In this section, you will hear 3 short passages. At the end of each passage, you will hear some questions. Both the passages and the questions will be spoken only once. After you hear a question, you must choose the best answer from the four choices marked A, B, C and D. Then mark the corresponding letter on the Answer Sheet 2 with a single line through the centre.

Passage One

My mother was born in a small town in northern Italy. She was three when her parents immigrated to America in 1926. They lived in Chicago where my grandfather worked making ice-cream. Mama thrived in the urban environment. At 16, she graduated first in her high school class, went on to secretarial school and finally worked as an executive secretary for a railroad company. She was beautiful too. When a local photographer used her pictures in his monthly window display, she felt pleased. Her favorite portrait showed her sitting by Lake Michigan, her hair wind-blown, her gaze reaching towards the horizon.

My parents were married in 1944. Dad was a quiet and intelligent man. He was 17 when he left Italy. Soon after, a hit-and-run accident left him with a permanent limp. Dad worked hard selling candy to Chicago office workers on their break. He had little formal schooling. His English was self-taught. Yet he eventually built a small successful whole sale candy business. Dad was generous and handsome. Mama was devoted to him. After she married, my mother quit her job and gave herself to her family.

In 1950, with three small children, Dad moved the family to a farm 40 miles from Chicago. He worked on a farm and commuted to the city to run his business. Mama said good-bye to her parents and friends, and traded her busy city neighborhood for a more isolated life. But she never complained.

Questions 26 to 28 are based on the passage you have just heard.

    26. What does the speaker tell us about his mother's early childhood?

    27. What do we learn about the speaker's father?

    28. What does the speaker say about his mother?

Passage Two

During a 1995 roof collapse, a firefighter named Donald Herbert was left brain damaged. For 10 years, he was unable to speak. Then one Saturday morning, he did something that shocked his family and doctors—he started speaking. "I want to talk to my wife," Donald Herbert said out of the blue. Staff members of the nursing home where he has lived for more than 7 years, ruled to get Linda Herbert on the telephone. "It was the first of many conversations the 44-year-old patient had with his family and friends during the 14 hour stretch. " Herbert's uncle Simon Manka said. "How long have I been away?" Herbert asked. "We told him almost 10 years. " The uncle said. He thought it was only three months.

Herbert was fighting a house fire Dec. 29, 1995, when the roof collapsed, burying him underneath. After going without air for several minutes, Herbert was unconscious for two and a half months and has undergone therapy ever since.

News accounts in the days and years after his injury, described Herbert as blind and with little if any memory. A video shows him receiving physical therapy but apparently unable to communicate and with little awareness of his surroundings. Manka declined to discuss his nephew's current condition or whether the apparent progress was continuing. "The family was seeking privacy while doctors evaluated Herbert," he said. As word of Herbert's progress spread, visitors streamed into the nursing home. "He is resting comfortably," the uncle told them.

Questions 29 to 32 are based on the passage you have just heard.

29. What happened to Herbert 10 years ago?
30. What surprised Donald Herbert's family and doctors one Saturday?
31. How long did Herbert remain unconscious?
32. How did Herbert's family react to the public attention?

Passage Three

Almost all states in America have a state fair. They last for one, two or three weeks. The Indiana state fair is one of the largest and oldest state fairs in the United States. It is held every summer.

It started in 1852. Its goals were to educate, share ideas and present Indiana's best products. The cost of a single ticket to enter the fair was 20 cents. During the early 1930s, officials of the fair ruled that people could attend by paying something other than money. For example, farmers brought a bag of grain in exchange for a ticket.

With the passage of time, the fair has grown and changed a lot. But it is still one of the Indiana's celebrated events. People from all over Indiana and from many other states attend the fair.

They can do many things at the fair. They can watch the judging of the priced cows, pigs and other animals. They can see sheep getting their wool cut and they learn how that wool is made into clothing. They can watch cows giving birth. In fact, people can learn about animals they would never see except at the fair. The fair provides a chance for the farming community to show its skills and fun products. For example, visitors might see the world's largest apple, or the tall sunflower plant.

Today, children and adults at the fair can play new computer games, or attend more traditional games of skill. They can watch performances put on by famous entertainers. Experts say such fairs are important, because people need to remember that they are connected to the earth and its products, and they depend on animals for many things.

Questions 33 to 35 are based on the passage you have just heard.

33. What were the main goals of the Indiana's state fair when it started?

34. How did some farmers gain entrance to the fair in the early 1930s?

35. Why are state fairs important events in America?

Section C

Directions: In this section, you will hear a passage three times. When the passage is read for the first time, you should listen carefully for its general idea. When the passage is read for the second time, you are required to fill in the blanks numbered from 36 to 43 with the exact words you have just heard. For blanks numbered from 44 to 46 you are required to fill in the missing information. For these blanks, you can either use the exact words you have just heard or write down the main points in your own words. Finally, when the passage is read for the third time, you should check what you have written.

Students' pressure sometimes comes from their parents. Most parents are well (36) meaning, but some of them aren't very helpful with the problems their sons and daughters have in (37) adjusting to college. And a few of them seem to go out of their way to add to their children's difficulties. For one thing, parents are often not (38) aware of the kinds of problems their children face. They don't realize that the (39) competition is keener, that the required (40) standards of work are higher, and that their children may not be prepared for the change. (41) Accustomed to seeing A's and B's on the high school report cards, they may be upset when their children's first (42) semester college grades are below that level. At their kindest, they may gently (43) inquire why John or Mary isn't doing better, whether he or she is trying as hard as he or she should, and so on. (44) At their worst, they may threaten to take their children out of college, or cut off funds. Sometimes parents regard their children as extensions of themselves, and (45) think it only right and natural that they determine what their children do with their lives. In their involvement and identification with their children, they forget that everyone is different, and that each person must develop in his or her own way. They forget that their children, (46) who are now young adults, must be the ones responsible for what they do and what they are.

2006 年 12 月英语四级听力全真试题

Part Ⅲ   Listening Comprehension   (35 minutes)

Section A

Directions: In this section, you will hear 8 short conversations and 2 long conversations. At the end of each conversation, one or more questions will be asked about what was said. Both the conversations and the questions will be spoken only once. After each question there will be a pause. During the pause, you must read the four choices marked A, B, C and D, and decide which is the best answer. Then mark the corresponding letter on the Answer Sheet 2 with a single line through the centre.

11. M: Christmas is around the corner. And I'm looking for a gift for my girlfriend. Any suggestions?

    W: Well, you have to tell me something about your girlfriend first. Also, what's your budget?

    Q: What does the woman want the man to do?

12. M: What would you like for dessert? I think I'll have apple pie and ice-cream.

    W: The chocolate cake looks great, but I have to watch my weight. You go ahead and get yours.

    Q: What will the woman most probably do?

13. W: Having visited so many countries, you must be able to speak several different languages.

    M: I wish I could. But Japanese and, of course English are the only languages I can speak.

    Q: What do we learn from the conversation?

14. M: Professor Smith asked me to go to his office after class. So it's impossible for me to make it to the bar at ten.

    W: Then it seems that we'll have to meet an hour later at the library.

    Q: What will the man do first after class?

15. M: It's already 11 now. Do you mean I ought to wait until Mr. Bloom comes back from class?

W: Not really. You can just leave a note. I'll give it to her later.

Q: What does the woman mean?

16. M: How is John now? Is he feeling any better?

W: Not yet. It still seems impossible to make him smile. Talking to him is really difficult and he gets upset easily over little things.

Q: What do we learn about John from the conversation?

17. M: Do we have to get the opera tickets in advance?

W: Certainly. Tickets at the door are usually sold at a higher price.

Q: What does the woman imply?

18. M: The taxi driver must have been speeding.

W: Well, not really. He crashed into the tree because he was trying not to hit a box that had fallen off the truck ahead of him.

Q: What do we learn about the taxi driver?

Long Conversations:

Conversation One

W: Hey, Bob, guess what? I'm going to visit Quebec next summer. I'm invited to go to a friend's wedding. But while I'm there, I'd also like to do some sightseeing.

M: That's nice, Shelly. But do you mean the province of Quebec or Quebec City?

W: I mean the province. My friend's wedding is in Montreal, so I'm going there first. I'll stay there for five days. Is Montreal the capital city of the province?

M: Well, Many people think so because it's the biggest city, but it's not the capital. Quebec City is, but Montreal is great. The Saint Royal River runs right through the middle of the city. It's beautiful in summer.

W: Wow, and do you think I can get by in English? My French is OK, but not that good. I know most people there speak French, but can I also use English?

M: Well, people speak both French and English there, but you'll hear French most of the time. And all the street signs are in French. In fact, Montreal is the third largest French-speaking city in the world. So you'd better practise your French before you go.

W: Good advice. What about Quebec City? I'll visit a friend from college who lives there now. What's it like?

M: It's a beautiful city, very old. Many old buildings have been nicely restored. Some of them were built in the 17th or 18th centuries. You'll love there.

W: Fantastic. I can't wait to go.

Questions 19 to 21 are based on the conversation you have just heard.

19. What's the woman's main purpose of visiting Quebec?

20. What does the man advise the woman to do before the trip?

21. What does the man say about the Quebec City?

Conversation Two

M: Hi, Miss Rowling, how old were you when you started to write? And what was your first book?

W: I wrote my first Finnish story when I was about six. It was about a small animal, a rabbit I mean. And I've been writing ever since.

M: Why did you choose to be an author?

W: If someone asked me how to achieve happiness. Step one would be finding out what you love doing most. Step two would be finding someone to pay you to do this. I consider myself very lucky indeed to be able to support myself by writing.

M: Do you have any plans to write books for adults?

W: My first two novels were for adults. I suppose I might write another one. But I never really imagine a target audience when I'm writing. The ideas come first, so it really depends on the ideas that grasp me next.

M: Where did the ideas for the *Harry Potter* books come from?

W: I've no ideas where the ideas came from. and I hope I'll never find out. It would spoil my excitement if it turned out I just have a funny little wrinkle on the surface of my brain, which makes me think about the invisible train platforms.

M: How do you come up with the names of your characters?

W: I invented some of them, but I also collected strange names. I've gotten them from ancient saints, maps, dictionaries, plants, war memoirs and people I've met.

M: Oh, you are really resourceful.

Questions 22 to 25 are based on the conversation you have just heard.

22. What do we learn from the conversation about Miss Rowling's first book?

23. Why does Miss Rowling consider herself very lucky?

24. What dictates Miss Rowling's writing?

25. According to Miss Rowling, where did she get the ideas for the *Harry Porter*

books?

Section B

Directions: In this section, you will hear 3 short passages. At the end of each passage, you will hear some questions. Both the passages and the questions will be spoken only once. After you hear a question, you must choose the best answer from the four choices marked A, B, C and D. Then mark the corresponding letter on the Answer Sheet 2 with a single line through the centre.

Passage One

Reducing the amount of sleep students get at night has a direct impact on their performance at school during the day. According to classroom teachers, elementary and middle school students who stay up late exhibit more learning and attention problems. This has been shown by Brown Medical School and Bradley Hospital Research. In the study, teachers were not told the amount of sleep students received when completing weekly performance reports, yet they rated the students who had received eight hours or less as having the most trouble recalling all the material, learning new lessons and completing high-quality work. Teachers also reported that these students had more difficulty paying attention. The experiment is the first to ask teachers to report on the effects of sleep deficiency in children. "Just staying up late cause increased academic difficulty and attention problems for otherwise healthy, well-functioning kids", said Garharn Forlone, the study's lead author. "So the results provide professionals and parents with a clear message: When a child is having learning and attention problems, the issue of sleep has to be taken into consideration." "If we don't ask about sleep and try to improve sleep patterns in kids' struggling academically, then we aren't doing our job", Forlone said. For parents, he said, the message is simple, "getting kids to bed on time is as important as getting them to school on time".

Questions 26 to 28 are based on the passage you have just heard.

26. What were teachers told to do in the experiment?
27. According to the experiment, what problem can insufficient sleep cause in students?
28. What message did the researcher intend to convey to parents?

Passage Two

Patricia Pania never wanted to be a public figure. All she wanted to be was a mother and homemaker. But her life was turned upside down when a motorist, distracted by his cell phone, ran a stop sign and crashed into the side of her car. The impact killed her 2-year-old daughter. Four months later, Pania reluctantly but courageously decided to try to educate the public and fight for laws to ban drivers from using cell phones while a car is moving. She wanted to save other children from what happened to her daughter. In her first speech, Pania got off to a shaky start. She was visibly trembling and her voice was soft and uncertain. But as she got into her speech, a dramatic transformation took place. She stopped shaking and spoke with a strong voice. For the rest of her talk, she was a forceful and compelling speaker. She wanted everyone in the audience to know what she knew without having to learn it from a personal tragedy. Many in the audience were moved to tears and to action. In subsequent presentations, Pania gained reputation as a highly effective speaker. Her appearance on a talk show was broadcast three times transmitting her message to over 40 million people. Her campaign increased public awareness of the problem, and prompted over 300 cities and several states to consider restrictions on cell phone use.

Questions 29 to 32 are based on the passage you have just heard.

29. What was the significant change in Patricia Pania's life?

30. What had led to Pania's personal tragedy?

31. How did Pania feel when she began her first speech?

32. What could be expected as a result of Pania's efforts?

Passage Three

Many people catch a cold in the spring time or fall. It makes us wonder if scientists can send a man to the moon. Why can't they find a cure for the common cold? The answer is easy. There're actually hundreds of kinds of cold viruses out there. You never know which one you will get, so there isn't a cure for each one. When a virus attacks your body, your body works hard to get rid of it. Blood rushes to your nose and causes a blockade in it. You feel terrible because you can't breathe well, but your body is actually eating the virus. Your temperature rises and you get a fever, but the heat of your body is killing the virus. You also have a running nose to stop the virus from getting into your cells. You may feel miserable, but actually your wonderful body is doing everything it can kill the cold. Different people have different remedies for colds. In the United States and some other countries, for example, people might eat chicken soup to feel better. Some people take hot bath and drink warm liquids. Other people take medicines to relieve various symptoms of colds. There was one interesting thing to note. Some scientists say taking medicines when you have a cold is actually bad for you. The virus stays in your longer because your body doesn't develop a way to fight it and kill it.

Questions 33 to 35 are based on the passage you have just heard.

33. According to the passage, why haven't the scientists found a cure for the common cold?

34. What does the speaker say about the symptoms of the common cold?

35. What do some scientists say about taking medicines for the common cold according to the passage?

Section C

Directions: In this section, you will hear a passage three times. When the passage is read for the first time, you should listen carefully for its general idea. When the passage is read for the second time, you are required to fill in the blanks numbered from 36 to 43 with the exact words you have just heard. For blanks numbered from 44 to 46 you are required to fill in the missing information. For these blanks, you can either use the exact words you have just heard or write down the main points in your own words. Finally, when the passage is read for the third time, you should check what you have written.

You probably have noticed that people express similar ideas in different ways depending on the situation they are in. This is very (36) natural. All languages have two general levels of (37) usage: a formal level and an informal level. English is no (38) exception. The difference in the two levels is the situation in which you use a (39) particular level. Formal language is the kind of language you find in textbooks, (40) reference books and in business letters. You would also use formal English in compositions and (41) essays that you write in school. Informal language is used in conversation with (42) colleagues, family members and friends, and when we write (43) personal notes or letters to close friends.

Formal language is different from informal language in several ways. First, formal language tends to be more polite. (44) What we may find interesting is that it usually takes more words to be polite. For example, I might say to a friend or a family member "Close the door, please", (45) but to a stranger, I probably would say "Would you mind closing the door?" Another difference between formal and informal language is some of the vocabulary. (46) There are bound to be some words and phrases that belong to formal language and others that are informal. Let's say that I really like soccer. If I am talking to my friend, I might say "I am just crazy about soccer", but if I were talking to my boss, I would probably say "I really enjoy soccer".

2006 年 6 月英语四级听力全真试题

Part I   Listening Comprehension   (20 minutes)

Section A

Directions: In this section, you will hear 10 short conversations. At the end of each conversation, a question will be asked about what was said. Both the conversations and the questions will be spoken only once. After each question there will be a pause. During the pause, you must read the four choices marked A, B, C and D, and decide which is the best answer. Then mark the corresponding letter on the Answer Sheet with a single line through the center.

1. M: I think the hostess really went out of her way to make the party a success.

   W: Yes, the food and drinks were great, but if only we had known a few of other guests.

   Q: What did the two speakers say about the party?

2. M: Can you stop by the post office and get me some envelopes and 39 cents' stamps?

   W: Well, I am not going to stop by the post office, but I can buy you some at the bookstore after I see the dentist on Market Street.

   Q: Where will the woman go first?

3. M: How do you like the new physician who replaced Dr. Andrews?

   W: He may not seem as agreeable or as thorough as Dr. Andrews, but at least he doesn't keep patients waiting for hours.

   Q: What can we infer from the woman's answer?

4. W: Tom must be in a bad mood today. He hasn't said half a dozen words all afternoon.

   M: Oh, really? That's not like Tom we know.

   Q: What does the man imply?

5. W: Do you have the seminar schedule with you? I'd like to find out the topic for Friday.

   M: I gave it to my friend, but there should be copies available in the library. I can pick one up for you.

   Q: What does the man promise to do?

6. W: I wonder if you could sell me the psychology textbooks. You took the course last semester, didn't you?

   M: As a matter of fact, I already sold them back to the school bookstore.

   Q: What do we learn from the conversation?

7. W: Here is this week's schedule, Tony. On Monday, there is the board meeting. Your speech to the lion's club is on Tuesday afternoon. Then on Wednesday you have an appointment with your lawyer and...

   M: Wait, you mean the business conference on Tuesday is cancelled?

   Q: What will the man do this Tuesday?

8. M: Can you believe it? Jessie told her boss he was wrong to have fired his marketing director.

   W: Yeah, but you know Jessie. If she has something in mind, everyone will know about it.

   Q: What does the woman mean?

9. M: We've got three women researchers in our group: Mary, Betty and Helen. Do you know them?

   W: Sure. Mary is active and sociable. Betty is the most talkative woman I've ever met. But guess what? Helen's just the opposite.

   Q: What do we learn from the woman's remark about Helen?

10. W: Jimmy said that he was going to marry a rich French businesswoman.

    M: Don't be so sure. He once told me that he had bought a big house. Yet he's still sharing an apartment with Mark.

    Q: What does the man imply?

Section B

Directions: In this section, you will hear 3 short passages. At the end of each passage, you will hear some questions. Both the passages and the questions will be spoken only once. After you hear a question, you must choose the best answer from the four choices marked A, B, C and D. Then mark the corresponding letter on the Answer Sheet with a single line through the centre.

Passage One

Unless you have visited the southern United States, you probably have never heard of Kudzu. Kudzu, as any farmer in the south will sadly tell you, is a super-powered weed. It is a strong climbing plant. Once it gets started, Kudzu is almost impossible to stop. It climbs to the tops of the tallest trees. It can cover large buildings. Whole barns and farm houses have been known to disappear from view. Wherever it grows, its thick twisting stems are extremely hard to remove. Kudzu was once thought to be a helpful plant. Originally found in Asia, it was brought to America to help protect the land from being swallowed by the sea. It was planted where its tough roots which grow up to five feet long could help hold back the soil. But the plant soon spread to places where it wasn't wanted. Farmers now have to fight to keep it from killing other plants. In a way, Kudzu is a sign of labor shortage in the South. Where there is no one to work the fields, Kudzu soon takes over. The northern United States faces no threat from Kudzu. Harsh winters kill it off. The plant loves the warmth of the South, but the South surely doesn't love it. If someone could invent some use for Kudzu and remove it from southern farmland, his or her fortune would be assured.

Questions 11 to 13 are based on the passage you have just heard.

    11. What do we learn about "Kudzu" from the passage?

    12. What will happen if the fields are neglected in the southern United States?

    13. Why isn't Kudzu a threat to the northern United States?

Passage Two

    The word "university" comes from the Latin word "universitas", meaning "the whole". Later, in Latin legal language, "universitas" meant a society or corporation. In the Middle Ages, the word meant "an association of teachers and scholars". The origins of universities can be traced back to the 12th to 14th centuries. In the early 12th century, long before universities were organized in the modern sense, students gathered together for higher studies at certain centers of learning. The earliest centers in the Europe were at Bolonia in Italy, founded in 1088. Other early centers were set up in France, the Czech Republic, Austria and Germany from 1150 to 1386. The first universities in Britain were Oxford and Cambridge. They were established in 1185 and 1209 respectively. The famous London University was founded in 1836. This was followed by the foundation of several universities such as Manchester and Birmingham, which developed from provincial colleges. It was in the 1960's that the largest expansion of higher education took place in Britain. This expansion took 3 basic forms: existing universities were enlarged, new universities were developed from existing colleges and completely new universities were set up. In Britain, finance for universities comes from three source: The first, and the largest source, is grants from the government, the second source is fees paid by students and the third one is private donations. All the British universities except one receive some government funding. The exception is Buckingham, which is Britain's only independent university.

Questions 14 to 16 are based on the passage you have just heard.

    14. What did the word "universitas" mean in the Middle Ages?

    15. Why was the 1960s so significant for British Higher Education?

    16. What is the main financial source for British universities?

Passage Three

One of the biggest problems in developing countries is hunger. An organization called Heifer International is working to improve the situation. The organization sends farm animals to families and communities around the world. An American farmer Dan West developed the idea for Heifer International in the 1930s. Mr. West was working in Spain where he discovered a need for cows. Many families were starving because of the Civil War in that country. So Mr. West asked his friends in the Unites States to send some cows. The first Heifer animals were sent in 1944. Since that time more than 4 million people in 115 countries have had better lives because of Heifer animals. To receive a Heifer animal, families must first explain their needs and goals. They must also make a plan which will allow them to become self-supporting. Local experts usually provide training. The organization says that animals must have food, water, shelter, health care and the ability to reproduce. Without them, the animals will not remain healthy and productive. Heifer International also believes that families must pass on some of their success to others in need. This belief guarantees that each person who takes part in the program also becomes a giver. Every family that receives a Heifer animal must agree to give that animal's first female baby to other people in need. Families must also agree to pass on the skills and training they receive from Heifer International. This concept helps communities become self-supporting.

Questions 17 to 20 are based on the passage you have just heard.

    17. What does the speaker tell us about Mr. West?

223

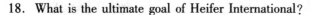
18. What is the ultimate goal of Heifer International?
19. What are families required to do after they receive support from Heifer International?
20. What is the major achievement of Heifer International?

2005 年 12 月英语四级听力全真试题

Part Ⅰ　　　　　　　　**Listening Comprehension**　　　　　（**20 minutes**）

Section A

Directions：In this section, you will hear 10 short conversations. At the end of each conversation, a question will be asked about what was said. Both the conversations and the questions will be spoken only once. After each question there will be a pause. During the pause, you must read the four choices marked A, B, C and D, and decide which is the best answer. Then mark the corresponding letter on the Answer Sheet with a single line through the center.

1. W：Carol told us on the phone not to worry about her. Her left leg doesn't hurt as much as it did yesterday.

   M：She'd better have it examined by a doctor anyway. And I will call her about it this evening.

   Q：What does the man think Carol should do?

2. M：There is a non-stop train for Washington and it leaves at 2:30.

   W：It's faster than the 2 o'clock train. Besides, we can have something to eat before getting on the train.

   Q：What do we learn from the conversation?

3. M：Hi, Melissa, how's your project going? Have you thought about going to graduate school? Perhaps you can get into Harvard.

   W：Everything is coming along really well. I have been thinking about graduate school. But I'll talk to my tutor Dr. Garcia first and see what she thinks.

   Q：What do you learn about the woman from the conversation?

4. W：Did you attend Alice's presentation last night? It was the first time for her to give a speech to a large audience.

   M：How she could be so calm in front of so many people is really beyond me!

   Q：What do we learn from the conversation?

5. W：You've been doing weather reports for nearly 30 years. Has the weather got any worse in all these years?

   M：Well, not necessarily worse. But we are seeing more swings.

   Q：What does the man say about the weather?

225

6. M: Excuse me, I am looking for the textbook by a Professor Jordon for the marketing course.

W: I am afraid it's out of stock. You'll have to order it. And it will take the publisher 3 weeks to send it to us.

Q: Where did this conversation most probably take place?

7. M: I am going to New York next week, but the hotel I booked is really expensive.

W: Why book a hotel? My brother has 2 spare rooms in his apartment.

Q: What does the woman mean?

8. W: In my opinion, watching the news on TV is a good way to learn English. What do you think?

M: It would be better if you could check the same information in English newspapers afterwards.

Q: What does the man say about learning English?

9. M: I hear a newly-invented drug can make people tell the truth and it may prove useful in questioning terrorists. Isn't it incredible?

W: Simple solutions to complex problems rarely succeed. As far as I know, no such drugs are ever known to work.

Q: What does the woman think of the new drug?

10. M: You know the electronics company is coming to our campus to recruit graduate students next week.

W: Really? What day? I'd like to talk to them and hand in my resume.

Q: What does the woman want to do?

Section B

Directions: In this section, you will hear 3 short passages. At the end of each passage, you will hear some questions. Both the passages and the questions will be spoken only once. After you hear a question, you must choose the best answer from the four Choices marked A, B, C and D. Then mark the corresponding letter on the Answer sheet with a single line through the center.

Passage One

A new study reports the common drug aspirin greatly reduces life threatening problems after an operation to replace blocked blood vessels to the heart. More than 800,000 people around the world have this heart surgery each year. The doctors who carried out the study say giving aspirin to patients soon after the operation could save thousands of lives. People usually take aspirin to control pain and reduce high body temperature. Doctors also advise some people to take aspirin to help prevent heart attacks. About 10-15 percent of these heart operations end in death or damage to the heart or other organs. The new study shows that even a small amount of aspirin reduced such threats. The doctors said the chance of death for patients who took aspirin would fall by 67%. They claimed this was true if the aspirin was given within 48 hours of the operation. The doctors believe aspirin helps heart surgery patients because it can prevent blood from thickening and blood vessels from being blocked. However, the doctors warned that people who have stomach bleeding or other bad reactions from aspirin should not take it after heart surgery.

Questions 11 to 13 are based on the passage you have just heard.

11. What is the finding of the new study of aspirin?

12. In what way can aspirin help heart surgery patients according to the doctors?

13. What warning did the doctors give about the use of aspirin?

Passage Two

Were you the first or the last child in your family? Or were you a middle or an only child? Some people think it matters where you were born in your family. But there are different ideas about what birth order means. Some people say that oldest children are smart and strong-willed. They are very likely to be successful. The reason for this is simple. Parents have a lot of time to their first child, they give him or her a lot of attention. So this child is very likely to do well. An only child will succeed for the same reason. What happens to the other children in the family? Middle children don't get so much attention, so they don't feel that important. If a family has many children, the middle one sometimes gets lost in the crowd. The youngest child, though, often gets special treatment. He or she is the baby. Often this child grows up to be funny and charming. Do you believe these ideas of birth order too? A recent study saw things quite differently. The study found that first children believed in family rules. They didn't take many chances in their lives. They usually followed orders. Rules didn't mean as much to later children in the family. They went out and followed their own ideas. They took chances and they often did better in life.

Questions 14 to 16 are based on the passage you have just heard.

14. According to common belief, in what way are the first child and the only child alike?

15. What do people usually say about middle children?

16. What do we learn about later children in a family from a recent study of birth order?

Passage Three

When my interest shifted from space to the sea, I never expected it would cause such confusion among my friends, yet I can understand their feelings. As I have been writing and talking about space flight for the best part of 20 years, a sudden switch of interest to the depth of the sea does seem peculiar. To explain, I'd like to share my reasons behind this unusual change of mind. The first excuse I give is an economic one. Underwater exploration is so much cheaper than space flight. The first round-trip ticket to the moon is going to cost at least 10 billion dollars if you include research and development. By the end of this century, the cost will be down to a few million. On the other hand, the diving suit and a set of basic tools needed for skin-diving can be bought for 20 dollars. My second argument is more philosophical. The ocean, surprisingly enough, has many things in common with space. In their different ways, both sea and space are equally hostile. If we wish to survive in either for any length of time, we need to have mechanical aids. The diving suit helped the design of the space suit. The feelings and the emotions of a man beneath the sea will be much like those of a man beyond the atmosphere.

Questions 17 to 20 are based on the passage you have just heard.

17. How did the speaker's friends respond to his change of interest?

18. What is one of the reasons for the speaker to switch his interest to underwater exploration?

19. In what way does the speaker think diving is similar to space travel?

20. What is the speaker's purpose in giving this talk?

2005 年 6 月英语四级听力全真试题

Part I　　　　　　　　Listening Comprehension　　　　　（20 minutes）

Section A

Directions: In this section, you will hear 10 short conversations. At the end of each conversation, a question will be asked about what was said. Both the conversations and the questions will be spoken only once. After each question there will be a pause. During the pause, you must read the four choices marked A, B, C and D, and decide which is the best answer. Then mark the corresponding letter on the Answer Sheet with a single line through the center.

1. W: Simon, oh, well, could you return the tools I lend you for building the bookshelf last month?

   M: Oh, I hate to tell you this, but it seems that I can't find them.

   Q: What do we learn from the conversation?

2. W: I found an expensive diamond ring in the restroom this morning.

   M: If I were you, I would turn it in to the security office. It is behind the administration building.

   Q: What does the man suggest the woman do?

3. W: I am going to Martha's house. I have a paper to complete. And I need to use her computer.

   M: Why not buy one yourself? Think how much time you could save.

   Q: What does the man suggest the woman do?

4. W: Daddy, I have decided to give up science and go to business school.

   M: Well, it is your choice as long as pay your own way, but I should warn you that not everyone with a business degree will make a successful manager.

   Q: What do we learn from the conversation?

5. W: I just read in the newspaper that *Lord of the Rings* is this year's greatest hit. Why don't we go and see it at the Grand Cinema?

   M: Don't you think that cinema is a little out of the way?

   Q: What does the man mean?

6. W: Bob said that Seattle is a great place for conferences.

   M: He is certainly in the position to make that comment. He has been there so often.

Q: What does the man say about?

7. W: Mr. Watson, I wonder whether it's possible for me to take a vacation early next month?

M: Did you fill out a request form?

Q: What is the probable relationship between the two speakers?

8. M: Do you want to go to the lecture this weekend? I heard that the guy who is going to deliver the lecture spent a year living in the rainforest.

W: Great, I am doing a report on the rainforest. Maybe I can get some new information to add it.

Q: What does the woman mean?

9. W: Wow, I do like this campus. All big trees, green lawns, and the old buildings with tall columns. It's really beautiful.

M: It sure is. The architecture of these buildings is in the Greek style. It was popular in the 18th century here.

Q: What are the speakers talking about?

10. M: This article is nothing but advertising for housing developers. I don't think the houses for sale are half that good.

W: Come on, David. Why so negative? We are thinking of buying a home, aren't we? Just a trip to look at the place won't cost us much.

Q: What can be inferred form the conversation?

Section B

Directions: In this section, you will hear 3 short passages. At the end of each passage, you will hear some questions. Both the passages and the questions will be spoken only once. After you hear a question, you must choose the best answer from the four choices marked A, B, C and D. Then mark the corresponding letter on the Answer Sheet with a single line through the centre.

Passage One

In the next few decades, people are going to travel very differently from the way they do today. Everyone is going to drive electrically-powered cars, so in the few years, people won't worry about running out of gas. Some of the large automobile companies are really moving ahead with this new technology. F&C Motors, a major auto company, for example, is holding a press conference next week. After the press conference, the company will present its new electronically-operated models. Transportation in the future won't be limited to the ground, many people predict that traffic will quickly move to the sky. In the coming years, instead of radio reports about road conditions and highway traffic, news reports will talk about traffic jams in the sky. But the sky isn't the limit. In the future, you will probably even be able to take a trip to the moon. Instead of listening to regular airplane announcements, you will hear someone say: the spacecraft to the moon leaves in 10 minutes. Please check your equipment. And remember no more than 10 ounces of carry-on baggage are allowed.

Questions 11 to 13 are based on the passage you have just heard.

11. What will be used to power cars in the next few decades?

12. What will future news reports focus on when talking about transportation?

13. What will passengers be asked to do when they travel to the moon?

Passage Two

County fairs are a tradition in New England towns. They offer great entertainment. One popular event is the pie-eating contest. If you want to take part in the contest, it is a good idea to remember these guidelines: First, make sure your stomach is nearly empty of food. Eating a whole pie can be hard if you have just finish a meal. Next, it is helpful to like the pie you are going to eat. The cream types are a good choice. They slide down the throat more easily. Placing your hands in the right position adds to the chances of winning. There is a temptation to reach out and help the eating process. This will result in becoming disqualified. Don't just sit on your hands, if your hands are tied behind your back, you will not be tempted to make use of them.

Now you are ready to show your talent at eating pies. The object of course, is to get the bottom of the pie plate before the other people. It is usually better to start at the outside and work toward the middle. This method gives you a goal to focus on. Try not to notice what the other people near you are doing. Let the cheers from the crowd spur you on. But don't look up. All you should think about is eating that pie.

Questions 14 to 17 are based on the passage you have just heard.

14. Where is pie-eating contest usually held?

15. What should a person do before entering into the pie-eating contest?

231

16. Where is person advised to put his hands during the contest?

17. What suggestion is offered for eating up the pie quickly?

Passage Three

The period of engagement is the time between the marriage proposal and the wedding ceremony. Two people agree to marry when they decided to spend their lives together. The man usually gives the woman a diamond engagement ring. That tradition is said to have started when an Austrian man gave a diamond ring to the woman he wanted to marry. The diamond represented beauty. He placed it on the third finger of her left hand. He chose that finger because it was thought that a blood vessel in that finger went directly to the heart. Today, we know that this is not true. Yet the tradition continues.

Americans generally are engaged for a period of about one year, if they are planning a wedding ceremony and a party. During this time, friends of the bride may hold a party at which women friends and family members give the bride gifts that she will need as a wife. These could include cooking equipment or new clothing. Friends of the man who is getting married may have a bachelor party for him. This usually takes place the night before the wedding. Only man are invited to the bachelor party.

During the marriage ceremony, the bride and her would-be husband usually exchange gold rings that represent the idea that their union will continue forever. The wife often wears both the wedding ring and the engagement ring on the same finger. The husband wears his ring on the third finger on his left hand. Many people say the purpose of the engagement period is to permit enough time to plan the wedding. But the main purpose is to let enough time pass so the two people are sure that they want to marry each other: Either person may decide to break the engagement, if this happens, the woman usually returns the ring to the man. They also return any wedding gifts they have received.

Questions 18 to 20 are based on the passage you have just heard.

18. What was the diamond ring said to represent?

19. Why did the Austrian man place the diamond ring on the third finger of the left hand of his would-be wife?

20. What is the chief advantage of having the engagement period?